ROCKET SCIENCE

Emily Mayer

Copyright © 2020 Emily Mayer

All rights reserved

The characters and events portrayed in this book are fictitious. Any similarity to real persons, living or dead, is coincidental and not intended by the author.

No part of this book may be reproduced, or stored in a retrieval system, or transmitted in any form or by any means, electronic, mechanical, photocopying, recording, or otherwise, without express written permission of the publisher.

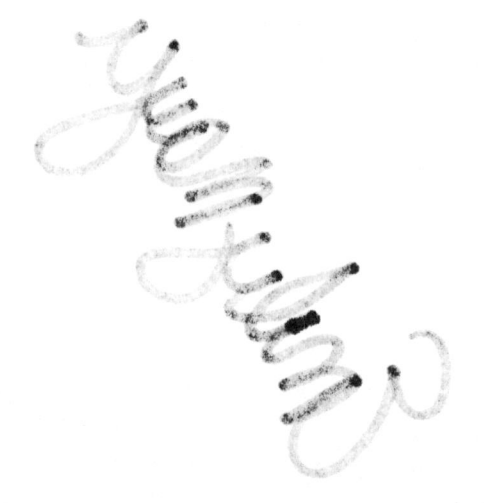

*To my sisters, Katharine and Laura.
My very first and very best friends.*

1.

Tap.
Tap.
Tap.
Tap.

I could feel my right eye starting to twitch to the rhythm of Kyle's pen. Since I couldn't reach over and knock the pen out of his hands, I pressed two fingers into the muscles above my eye hoping to make the twitching stop.

The chat icon on the tablet in front of me bounced, alerting me to an incoming message. I snuck glances around the conference table to confirm that everyone was focused on their own tablets, not me or our fearless team leader droning on about budgets, and clicked the message.

Janie: Dude, it's hella cool that you can move one eyebrow like that. You look like the Grinch right now. Only less green obvi.

I shot a look across the table at Janie, who attempted to wiggle an eyebrow at me. Janie was my work bestie, and let me tell you, the competition for that coveted spot was pretty stiff. It was between her and Carl, the guy from IT who told everyone way too much information about absolutely everything. He always hooked me up with the newest tech, though, which counted as friendship in my book. Janie was an accountant at Spatium so we weren't usually working together, but a twist of fate otherwise known as maternity leave had placed Janie on the same project I was working on.

Spatium was developing a powerful launch vehicle which would be capable of transporting large quantiles of cargo and human beings long distances, and would be fully reusable upon reentry. The ultimate goal was taking people to Mars, but we had a contract with NASA's Commercial Crew Program that was slated to begin next year. That translated into a big budget requiring an accountant to keep costs in line with projections: Enter Janie.

I was one of the aerospace engineers working on the project. Our project leader insisted on holding weekly status conferences even though everyone on this project talked to each other pretty much daily, which meant no one needed an update so no one paid attention during the meetings. Once every few months, the CEO or some other very important person would show up from the corporate floor, and then we would all pretend like these meetings were super-informative. Today was not one of those days.

Me: I'm not controlling it! I will buy you cookies from Lola's for a month if you knock the pen out of Kyle's hand.

Janie: Don't tempt me, Lennon. You know I love those cookies more than life. More than this job. What is space compared to cookies, amiright?

Me: Lola's does have the best oatmeal raisin cookies.

My stomach made a loud rumble that I was pretty sure could be heard from space. I looked up in horror, pressing a hand to my abdomen as if that would silence the beast that had taken up residence in there. Thankfully, everyone was too busy not paying attention to take notice of a weird noise. It helped that our team leader, Dr. Schramm, was a notorious throat-clearer.

Me: Why does he make these meetings right before lunch?

Janie: I don't know. Why do you like oatmeal raisin cookies? The world is just filled with unsolvable mysteries, Lennon. Embrace it. Btdubs, I totally heard your stomach.

Me: Great. Do you think Theo heard?

Theo was the love of my life. We were meant to be together. He just didn't know it yet. To date, we had exchanged around 572,916 words. It sounds impressive, I know. But considering the average person speaks between 125 to 150 words per minute and the average employed adult in the United States works approximately 1,811.16 hours per year and I had been working with Theo for a little over two years, I was not making much progress toward our impending nuptials.

Janie: Aww, babycakes, you could fall out of your chair and Theo wouldn't notice. He's too busy chatting up his GIRLFRIEND to notice what's happening in here.

And then there was that. Theo's girlfriend, Sam, was a chemical engineer specializing in polymers. In a sad twist of fate, I was actually responsible for bringing them together. I have never been the best at social situations, so at a company mixer we were all forced to attend, I completely panicked when Theo started talking to me. Scrambling for something to say, I pointed out Sam and proceeded to list all the things they had in common. What I lacked in social skills, I made up for in sales. Since then, Janie had made it her personal mission to remind me that Theo had a girlfriend.

Janie: They're making dinner plans to celebrate their SIX-MONTH ANNIVERSARY tonight. Basil at 7.

Dang it. I loved Basil. They had the best Italian. I glanced up to see Janie sneaking glances at Theo's tablet. She was conveniently seated next to him, well convenient for creeping purposes anyway.

Me: Who suggested Basil?

Janie: Why do you want to know that? Ugh, you want to know if Theo suggested it so you can add a shared love of Basil to your list of reasons why you are meant to be together, don't you?

Me: What? No. I just like complete data sets.

Lie. I wanted to add it to the running lists of reasons Theo and I were a perfect match. Janie snorted from across the table.

Janie: Lucky for you, this meeting is about to end.

"Okay, folks, looks like we all have a busy rest of the week—" Dr. Schramm cleared his throat and began collecting his stack of papers— "so I won't keep you."

Everyone shot out of their seats and made for the door like their sanity depended on it. Janie waited for me to catch up before joining the mob.

"Want to grab lunch?" she asked, as if she didn't already

know the answer to that question.

"Yes, definitely." My stomach let out another grumble for extra emphasis.

One of the many perks of working for Spatium was the amazing cafeteria. The company hired actual chefs who prepared entire menus every week.

My phone buzzed in my hand as we made our way on to the elevator. I pulled it out and felt a smile tug the corner of my mouth up when I saw the name.

Harrison: Did you try that protein shake I put in your refrigerator?

Harrison was my older brother. Even though he was only four years older than me at the ripe old age of thirty, he acted like he was my keeper and a sixty-year-old man.

Me: Yep. It tasted like dirty socks trying to disguise themselves as chocolate.

Three little dots let me know Harrison wasn't prepared to let the subject drop. I could almost picture him sitting in his tattoo station wearing his signature scowl while typing his response. He'd bought his tattoo shop from his mentor two years ago, and it was his baby. As far as siblings went, we couldn't have been more different. Harrison was an amazing artist whereas I couldn't even color in the lines. He'd majored in art at UCLA while interning at Bad Wolf Ink for four years. He was almost a foot taller than me and built like he lived in the gym while I was built like a bean pole that didn't get enough sunlight. Harrison always told people that I got all the brains and he got all the brawn, but he was super smart in his own right. You just had to look at the success of Bad Wolf Ink to know he was a secret smartypants.

Harrison: You need to stop skipping breakfast.

My fingers flew across the screen forming a reply, but before I could hit send, another message appeared below it.

Harrison: Your fancy coffee shit doesn't count.

I deleted my previous message, which did in fact say that I had a mocha with almond milk every morning. Almond milk was a health food as far as I was concerned. Breakfast required way too much effort in the morning. I barely managed to pull myself together quickly enough to make it to work on time after I finished hitting snooze for the eighth time. I had hitting snooze down to a science. If I hit it three times, I would have forty minutes to get ready. Every extra tap of the button decreased my preparation time by intervals of ten.

Me: Sir, yes sir.

I couldn't help smiling as I imagined Harrison rolling his eyes while reading my response. Ah, siblings—gotta love 'em.

"So," Janie said, loudly enough to be heard over the noise in the cafeteria, "have you thought anymore about the dating site I showed you?"

"Sure." I hoped my noncommittal response would be the end of the dating discussion.

I did not want to have this conversation with Janie again. She may have tended toward 'nerd' on the spectrum of behaviors, but she was beautiful and outgoing. Her dad was Korean and her mother Swedish, and the result was pretty much perfection in physical form. With long caramel-colored hair, stunning almond-shaped eyes that were the color of melted chocolate, and a complexion like porcelain, Janie never lacked for attention from the opposite sex. If she wasn't one of the nicest people I'd ever met, I would have been required to hate her on behalf of all of us physically inferior beings.

"And?" Janie prodded, placing a salad on her tray next to some yogurt.

"I'm still thinking about it," I mumbled as I made room on my own tray for a basket of French fries. I was feeling like a little comfort food. Between Theo's anniversary planning and this dating talk, I was starting to feel a defeating combination of sad and pathetic.

I followed her to the cash register, swiping my ID and shooting a weak smile at the cashier. But my reprieve was short-lived. As soon as we sat down at an empty table, Janie continued her lecture.

"I know you love complete data sets, so here are some data points about online dating." She spent the entire lunch trying to convince me online dating was an excellent idea, while I shoveled French fries into my mouth and mentally named my future cats. By the time we left the cafeteria and parted ways, I knew exactly what I needed—and it wasn't an online dating service.

2.

Dulce de leche cheesecake cradled protectively in my arms, I started walking the block and a half from the only parking spot I'd been able to find near my apartment. Our building's tiny parking lot had been "under construction" almost the entire time I'd lived in the building, so I used the daily walk to justify things like eating an entire cheesecake. I'd spent the drive home planning the perfect wallow night. Who needed a partner to share your life with when you had cheesecake and reruns of Buffy the Vampire Slayer? Not me. I barely thought about the fact that Theo was probably busy getting ready for his anniversary dinner with someone who was not me.

"Lennon!"

I turned my head to see Paige bouncing toward me, a smile stretching wide across her perfect face. I'd met Paige when I was moving into the building. She lived at the end of the hall in an apartment that was almost identical to mine. Paige was a yoga instructor and did some modeling on the side. Her blonde hair had been styled into a high ponytail that bobbed enthusiastically with each step.

I slowed down and waited for her to catch up, which didn't take long thanks to her boundless energy and long legs.

"Hey girl! Ohhh, what's that?" she said, peering down to check out the box in my arms.

"Dulce de leche cheesecake from Lola's." I hugged it a little tighter to my chest when I caught the wistful look that crossed her face at the mention of cheesecake. Paige claimed to be a vegan but was always declaring it cheat day. We all knew that wasn't how veganism worked, but no one called her out on it.

"What's the occasion?" she asked, finally tearing her gaze from the box to dig out her building keys. She unlocked the door and held it open for me.

"No occasion." I tried to sound nonchalant as I walked past her.

Paige was firmly on Team Online Dating with Janie. I regretted introducing my friends to each other. I was questioning my need to have a social circle at all.

"You just decided to eat an entire cheesecake by yourself today?" Paige's question was laced with skepticism.

I was suddenly grateful that walking up the first flight of stairs left me slightly out of breath. Climbing the two flights of stairs to our floor every day was my cardio. Catching my breath gave me the excuse I needed to order my thoughts. I didn't really feel like talking about my feelings—I felt like retreating into my apartment and eating them. But despite her inherent peppiness, Paige was relentless and would probably not leave until she knew I was okay. And I was at least socially aware enough to understand that a pastry box for one person was the universal sign for emotional distress.

"You are giving off some very sad energy right now. I can sense your aura's in serious distress. What's going on?" Paige asked, scanning me from head to toe.

I sighed. "Theo and his girlfriend were planning their six-month anniversary dinner at work."

Her large blue eyes widened in concern. I knew with one hundred percent certainty that the box in my arms was the only thing keeping Paige from throwing her arms around me. She was a firm believer in the healing power of human contact.

"Oh Lennon, I'm sorry." She squeezed my arm. "I know what we need!"

"We?" I yelled at her back. She was already halfway down

the hall.

"Yes, we! You're not wallowing all alone," Paige called over her shoulder, pushing open the door of her apartment and disappearing from sight.

I grumbled to myself as I opened my own door but left it unlocked for Paige. I smiled, thinking that somewhere Harrison's blood pressure was spiking and he couldn't figure out why. He texted me almost-nightly reminders to make sure my door was locked.

A few minutes later, Paige opened my door waving a bottle of wine.

"Ta-dah! No pity party is complete without wine. Well, any booze will do but hard liquor might actually kill you and it's Wednesday."

I wasn't much of a drinker. I had been the exact opposite of a partier in high school, and my group of friends in college weren't big drinkers. The result was a very low threshold for intoxication.

Paige went straight to the kitchen, getting glasses for wine and making herself right at home.

"I'm just going to go change," I said, ready to admit defeat. I'd be sharing my pity party—and, more than likely, my dessert.

I quickly slipped out of my bra and into my favorite oversized MIT sweater and a pair of leggings. Most of the time, I wished I was better endowed in the chest region—I was lucky to fill a B cup—but there were times I didn't hate it. I could admit that being able to free-boob it was a perk. I wandered the two feet from my room to the couch where Paige was waiting with two glasses of wine and two forks.

"I just went ahead and assumed we were past plates. Are we going with sad songs or a sad movie?" she asked, taking a sip of wine.

"I was going to watch *Buffy* reruns." I picked up a fork and took a large bite.

"That's... an interesting choice," Paige said around a forkful of cheesecake. I didn't have the heart to point out that it contained large quantities of multiple forms of dairy. I may have wanted to be pathetic alone, but I knew Paige was being the very best kind of friend—the kind who refused to let you be alone.

"Yeah, I was in the mood to watch some supernatural creatures get stabbed." I washed the cheesecake down with a drink of wine, the two forms of sweetness combining in a way I liked. "This wine is good."

"Whoa, that's dark." Paige ignored my comment about the wine and clicked on the last episode of *Buffy* I had watched. "But I can get behind some girl power, butt-kicking action."

We made it about three minutes into the episode before Paige was back with more questions.

"So, Theo and Sam are still going strong?" she asked tentatively. I nodded my response, taking another drink of wine. "How do you feel about that?"

I lifted one shoulder slightly. "Not great, obviously. I know I need to accept that Theo's probably going to marry Sam and make smart, beautiful babies, and I'll probably die alone with my cats who will inevitably eat my corpse when their food supply runs out."

Paige blinked at me a few times before throwing her arms around me. She squeezed me tightly while shaking her head.

"You're not going to die alone." She released me. "Even if you and Theo weren't meant to be together, there's still someone out there for you. You just need to stop living in a fantasy world—"

"Says the vegan eating cheesecake," I mumbled.

"—and put yourself out there," Paige finished, completely undeterred by my interruption. "Have you thought any more about the dating website Janie suggested?"

Sweet baby Patrick Stewart, why was the universe trying to kill me today? I fingered the worn hem of my sweatshirt.

"I don't think online dating would work for me. I don't do well with strangers, especially when there are expectations defined by social convention." I admitted, embarrassed. I knew the heat I felt creeping up my neck wasn't from the alcohol.

"Dating does have a lot of rules, but that doesn't mean everyone has to—or even wants to—follow them. Most of them are super stupid anyway. And the whole point of online dating is that you wouldn't be strangers by the time you meet. You can get to know each other through the magic of the internet before you meet each other face to face."

I knew her argument had merit. It was the same one Janie had made at lunch, but the idea of meeting someone from the internet in person made me feel physically anxious.

"I just don't think it's for me." I wiped my sweaty palms on my leggings. "Besides, I don't think I'm any less awkward over the internet."

"Stop it! You're not awkward! You're just shy. And anyone who deserves to be with you is going to look past your shyness and work to get to know you." Paige's voice had softened by the time she finished.

"Now you sound like my mom," I said, rolling my eyes. I figured I was allowed to be a little petulant since this was my pity party and she was technically a party crasher.

"Mama Walker knows her stuff." Paige jabbed her fork in my direction. "You're not going to meet any of the misters sitting on your couch watching old TV shows."

"Misters?" I asked through a mouthful of cake.

Yeah, you know—Mister Right, Mister Right Now, Mister Great in Bed. All the misters," she said matter-of-factly, like this was all common knowledge. "Like how Harrison is Mister Right and Jimmy is Mister Right Now. But at the rate you're going, your misters are going to have to be food delivery guys."

"Hey, I go out!" I exclaimed, suddenly feeling the need to defend myself.

"Yes, you physically leave your apartment, but you don't go out with the intention of meeting new people. If you meet new people, it's an accident."

"I go to your yoga class once a week," I pointed out.

"Yes, and you sit in the back of the room and don't mingle

before or after class," Paige responded flatly.

"Do you have to be so reasonable right now? Can't you just tell me that Theo's an idiot for not being in love with me? Or that he's going to realize Sam is actually a mutant and I'm the one he is supposed to be with?" I whined, shoveling more cheesecake into my mouth.

"Theo is—" Paige suddenly sat up straight. "Wait. OMG, Lennon! I have the best idea!"

"Oh no. Whatever it is, thank you but no thank you." I shook my head. Paige's eyes were lit up like a Christmas tree and I did not like it one bit. She was wearing the same expression she'd had right before I agreed to go with her to get a bikini wax.

"You have to promise to keep an open mind, okay?" She plowed on valiantly, not even waiting for me to respond. "Tamara got a bunch of tickets to check out a new club opening Saturday and she gave me four of them. Jimmy's coming and you should totally take one of the extra tickets."

"A club? That's your great idea? Paige, no. I can't go to a club. It's literally a loud room filled with strangers. How is that better than online dating? It's not. It's worse—so much worse."

"Because you'd be going with a group of people you know! And I'll be there to help when you get nervous." She smiled triumphantly. "We'll go shopping and get our nails done Saturday afternoon! It's perfect."

I scrambled to come up with an excuse. "There's a new Marvel movie coming out Friday. I was going to invite you—"

Paige interrupted. "Does it have a Hemsworth in it?"

"Nooo," I drawled.

"You know my rule about superhero movies. No Hemsworth, no Paige."

I decided to exercise the nuclear option. "I'll get Harrison to go on a date with you."

Paige was in love with Harrison. She'd met him when he was picking me up for dinner one night, and it was the one and only time I had ever seen Paige at a loss for words. Harrison largely ignored her presence in typical Harrison style, so her newest plan to get his attention was to book a tattoo appointment with him.

"Tempting, but no. When Harrison finally asks me out, I want it to be for real and not as a favor to his sister. I'll stick with Mr. Right Now until then—and you are going clubbing."

Who knew defeat would taste like Moscato and cheesecake?

"Fine," I relented. "I'll go with you."

Paige bounced up and down, clapping her hands.

"We're going to have so much fun. I can't wait!"

I could wait. Preferably a lifetime.

3.

Thursday seemed to come and go faster than normal. Even Friday seemed to be moving at an unnatural speed. Usually work on Friday started to drag the closer it got to quitting time, but I swear I blinked once and the day was over. Even the new data sets I was reviewing weren't enough to distract me from my looming doom. My mind didn't seem willing to focus on the equations I usually found soothing. Instead, it was busy dreaming up new ways Saturday could go wrong. I had no idea I could be so creative! Or such a pessimist.

Social interaction was not one of my strengths. It wasn't that I didn't want friends or didn't like people. I wasn't antisocial. I envied people who were at ease no matter what situation they were thrown into. I had to carefully plan any event that was even remotely outside my comfort zone, analyzing the likely outcomes of all the possible variables in any given scenario. I even came up with lists of possible conversation topics based on occupation, hobbies, general interests, and so forth.

My problem was that I had grown up being largely socially isolated. I was born with VSD—ventricular septal defect, or in less fancy words, a hole in the wall between the two lower chambers of my heart. In most babies, it's just a scary little blip for the parents; the hole is small and closes on its own as the child grows. But a lucky few like me have pretty big holes that don't close.

A few weeks after I was born, my mom noticed I was losing

weight and passing out while feeding. The doctors heard the telltale murmur in my heart during a physical when I was about six weeks old. My stubborn heart just didn't want to follow the normal path: The hole in my heart got bigger as I grew instead of smaller. When I should have been running around with other kids, I was stuck inside reading, playing video games with Harrison, or hanging out with my grandpa.

We lived in a small town more than an hour south of Los Angeles, so my mom and I had to travel to see specialists at the UCLA Children's Hospital every month. I would have missed too much normal school going back and forth to doctors, and I eventually went into mild congestive heart failure, so I was homeschooled. Alone. Harrison got to go to regular school and have all the normal experiences. I lived vicariously through him.

I spent a lot of time with my grandpa tinkering in his garage. He was probably not the best influence for an adolescent girl, but I did get my love of engineering from him. Grandpa Walker owned a repair shop that mostly fixed cars, but also the occasional toaster or microwave. After he retired, our garage became his workshop. I spent countless hours assisting him with repairs and learning about engines of all kinds. He was the one who convinced my mom to let me get a computer, and he helped me build my own PC. The internet was a game changer for a lonely kid like me, let me tell you.

When I was fifteen, I had open-heart surgery to repair the hole. It was as miserable as it sounds, but the patch job meant I could lead a normal life. The next year I enrolled in high school. I had been dreaming of going to school for years, watching wistfully as Harrison walked to the bus stop every day. He told me it was completely overrated, but I always thought he was just saying that to make me feel better about missing out on so much.

Turned out he wasn't lying. High school was no place for a shy girl whose cultural references came mainly from her sixty-year-old grandfather and public broadcasting. Even *Saved by the Bell* hadn't prepared me for walking into the cafeteria on my first day. Tardis lunch box in hand, I scanned the room looking for a friendly face. My heart pounded in my chest and my lungs didn't seem to be able to take in enough oxygen. For a second, I thought the patch had failed and I was having a heart attack. I finally worked up enough courage to ask a table of girls if I could sit with them. The ringleader looked me up and down, her gaze landing on my lunchbox, before telling me she was sorry but their table was full. I proceeded to cry in the bathroom for the rest of the period and ate lunch alone in the library for half the year.

Eventually, I made a small group of friends. We were all on the robotics team together and some of them were on my mathlete team. It was easier to make friends in college, where I was surrounded by people with the same interests as me and who were more than willing to let me join their proverbial lunch tables. But I still felt the knowledge gap between my peers and me. It wasn't uncommon for me to have mild panic attacks when I went anywhere large groups of people tended to congregate. I still preferred the predictability of numbers over the inconsistency of people.

Leaving my nerd herd behind to move to LA was difficult. I didn't relish the idea of starting all over again, but the engineering job with Spatium was literally my dream job and I wanted to be closer to my family. Plus, have you ever experienced a Massachusetts winter? No thank you. Making friends in the adult world was turning out to be just as challenging as I'd thought it would be, too, so it wasn't all that surprising that I spent a lot of Friday nights helping Harrison at Bad Wolf. Friday and Saturday night were the busiest times so Harrison never minded me helping out, and working the front desk was good practice interacting with strangers. I also genuinely liked everyone who worked here.

I pushed through the door and was greeted with the familiar scent of antiseptic, cologne, and stale cigarettes. It was a strange combination, but I loved it. Kay spun around in her seat behind the reception desk and gave me a wide smile.

"Lennon! Girl, am I glad to see you!" Kay hopped up and walked around the desk to give me a quick squeeze. "Teddy has the stomach flu so we're all covering the front desk. I'm not going to lie to you, it's been ugly. These guys are Neanderthals. It's like they've never seen a computer."

I laughed, slipping my purse off and heading around to the empty seat. "What do you need me to do?"

She leaned over and indicated a stack of mangled slips of paper and sticky notes. "This is going to shock you, but Lou messed up the scheduling software. These are all the appointments that need to be entered from today. It would also be helpful if we could see the rest of the appointments lined up for the night, so we can accommodate walk-ins."

"No problem." I smiled up at her. "I can get you guys back up and running in no time."

"You're a lifesaver. Pretty sure your brother is about to have a stroke. Or kill Lou. Could go either way," she said, tucking a strand of silver hair behind her ear.

Kay was basically the epitome of cool. Besides the fact that she was a super talented tattoo artist, her hair was dyed an amazing shade of silver and she had a tiny nose ring that made her look trendy and edgy at the same time. She wore a lot of black, which, instead of looking goth, showed off the amazing colors in the intricate tattoos that covered one of her arms. She took no nonsense from the men who worked here, or the ones who came in looking to get inked.

"Tater tot!" Lou's voice called out over the music. He slapped his hands on the desk and gave me one of his signature grins. "What's happening?"

"Not too much, just saving your life." I returned his smile with a smaller one of my own. I loved Lou. He was a gigantic goofball who had a talent for making me laugh and driving Harrison insane, which incidentally was one of the things I liked best about him.

He groaned, looking up toward the ceiling dramatically. "Lies, Lennon, all lies. Don't listen to Kay. She's just bitter I keep turning down her advances."

"In your dreams, Louis," she called out over her shoulder as she walked toward her station.

"Don't worry, Lenny Lou. I only have eyes for you." He leaned forward to place a kiss on my cheek before he was yanked back. I smiled at Harrison, who had appeared behind Lou wearing his signature scowl.

"Don't you have something better to be doing than bothering Lennon?" Harrison asked, turning that scowl from me to Lou. Lou just shrugged his shoulders, totally unfazed by the burly man shooting death rays at him.

"Nah, my next client won't be here for another twenty minutes."

Harrison grunted in response. He was definitely more of a nonverbal creature and could communicate a wide range of emotions through his grunts, frowns, and sighs.

"Did you eat dinner?" His green eyes, the mirror image of my own, turned back to me. "Something with actual nutritional value?"

I rolled my eyes at his overbearing question. It was like he still expected me to drop dead from heart failure at any moment. It was unclear how he thought I had survived six years on my own all the way across the country. I tried to remind myself not to get too frustrated with him. I knew it hadn't been easy for him to watch his little sister get sicker and sicker; he had walked away from the experience with a few nasty scars of his own.

"Yes. I had three slices of veggie pizza from Leonardo's," I answered honestly, even though I was confident veggie pizza was not the answer he was looking for.

"Veggie pizza is not nutritional," he replied, crossing his arms over his chest.

"But it had vegetables on it," I offered weakly. Lou snickered from his spot on the couch in the lobby. Harrison ignored him, his wrath solely focused on me for the moment.

The door swung open, saving me from a lecture about the

importance of the bottom half of the food pyramid. Two girls dressed in tight skirts that barely covered any of their important parts sauntered through the door, their sky-high stilettos only emphasizing how little skin their skirts covered. Both of their gazes skipped straight over me and landed on Harrison.

Objectively speaking, I understood that my brother qualified as extremely good-looking. His whole aloof, bad-boy vibe was like catnip to single women.

"Hey." One of the girls gave Harrison a ridiculous little wave, followed by a giggle. My gaze found Lou's and we shared an eyeroll. "I have an appointment with Aaron at seven. Sheri."

A look of relief washed over Harrison's face, but was quickly replaced by his customer service look—which was just a tiny little uptick at the corner of his mouth.

"Great, Sheri. Lennon will get you checked in and show you where Aaron's design books are if you still need some ideas." He gestured to me with one hand before abandoning me to the she-wolves.

I gave them a tentative smile, reminding myself to maintain eye contact while I ran through the standard check-in questions. Aaron appeared from his station, chatting with his client. I watched as the two girls got their first look at him and then turned to each other with wide eyes.

Aaron was stupid hot—as in, he was so attractive that it rendered one stupid. It had taken me three months to be able to look him in the eye *and* form coherent sentences, though I still couldn't accomplish that feat without turning red. Lou mimed swooning on the couch, fanning himself as he sprawled out on one end.

"Hey, Lennon," Aaron said, the corners of his chocolate-brown eyes crinkling. "Can you get John all checked out for me? I already went over aftercare with him."

"Sure thing," I said, briefly meeting his eyes before gazing back at the computer screen. I could feel that telltale heat creeping up my neck. "Sheri's here and all checked in."

"Awesome." He turned his gaze to Sheri and her friend. He

shook John's hand with a "Catch you later, man" and then waved the girls back. "I'll catch up with you later, Lennon."

I made a strangled noise in response—definitely not my finest moment. I recovered enough to get John all checked out and schedule his next appointment to finish the massive piece of work on his back.

The shop got pretty busy after that and between helping people and fixing the schedule, I barely had time to worry about Saturday.

I stifled a yawn as I checked out Harrison's last customer of the night. Lou and Kay were sitting on the couch eating tacos from the taco truck parked down the street.

"Why don't you take off." Harrison's question came out sounding more like a command. "We're almost done for the night and you look like you're going to fall out of your chair."

"Okay," I said around a yawn. I stood up, stretching my arms over my head.

"Are you okay to drive home?" he asked. I nodded my head in response, too afraid to open my mouth and let out another yawn. Harrison pulled me into a hug. "See you tomorrow?"

"I don't think so. I'm going to some club opening with Paige," I said, pulling out of his embrace and grabbing my purse.

The shop had descended into complete silence; even the buzzing of Aaron's tattoo gun had stopped. Lou had paused with a taco halfway to his mouth and Kay's mouth was hanging open a little.

Lou recovered first. He lowered his taco and placed a hand behind his ear like he was trying to listen. "Ex-squeeze me, but did I just hear you say that you were going to a club?" he asked, skepticism lacing his voice.

Well, *that* was the boost in confidence I needed.

"What club?" Harrison barked before I could answer Lou.

I shrugged casually, trying to act like it was no big deal. "I don't know the name. Paige's friend Tamara got tickets for the opening or something. I'm going with them."

"Who the fuck is Tamara?" Harrison asked, half-growling.

Kay literally sprang into action, jumping up from her spot and coming to stand next to me in a show of support. She shot a look at Harrison, silently warning him to back off. It would have been humorous, watching tiny Kay stand up to my hulk of a brother, if I hadn't been getting increasingly annoyed.

"That's great, Lennon! You'll have to text me all the good details after." She wiggled her eyebrows at me. "And send me a picture of your outfit!"

"I will," I said, fidgeting with my purse strap and trying to avoid the glare Harrison was aiming our way.

Kay gave me a quick hug, pausing close to my ear so no one else could hear her hushed words. "You can call me if you get nervous."

I smiled gratefully at her.

"I'll call you tomorrow." I tossed the words over my shoulder in the general direction of Harrison, who was still standing with his arms crossed and a scowl firmly in place. "Love you."

I was a firm believer in always telling people you loved them, even when they were making it hard to remember why. It was probably a leftover from being the sick kid whose heart was slowly failing.

The short drive back to my apartment helped smooth over the raw edges of my anger. Everyone's surprise was fair. I didn't go to clubs—ever. Kay and Lou had invited me out for drinks on multiple occasions and I had only taken them up on the offer once, because they'd said that particular bar had the best chicken wings. I spent most of the night standing by the bar like a gangly gargoyle, protecting my plate of wings.

I went directly to bed when I got home, slipping into my favorite 'Snuggle this Muggle' sleep shirt before diving deep under my covers. I sighed, wishing I could hide here forever. My hand found its way to the tight line of raised skin between my breasts, and I traced it up and down. The scar was a permanent reminder that I could be brave, *had* been brave.

If I had survived open-heart surgery, I could survive a club opening.

4.

I managed to ignore the first series of thuds echoing through my small apartment. Whoever was pounding on my door could come back at a reasonable hour. The second round of pounding was harder to ignore, especially when it was followed by a familiar voice threatening to let himself in.

"I'm coming!" I called, sticking my arm out from the warm cocoon of blankets to swipe for my phone. It was 10 a.m. I groaned, pulling back the covers and rubbing my eyes. Why for the love of protons did my brother have to be such an early riser?

I made the short trip to the door and swung it open prepared to give him a piece of my mind, but the words died in my throat when I saw a box of Brecken Donuts cradled in one arm and a drink carrier in his other hand.

"Whatever it is, I forgive you," I said, reaching for the box of donuts. I set them down on counter and peeled back the lid. All my favorites. These were clearly apology donuts.

"Kay said I was an ass last night." Harrison swiped a donut out of the box and moved to sit on the couch. Classic Harrison apology, but I wasn't going to hold a grudge when there were baked goods involved. He was kind of an idiot, but he meant well.

"Since when do you listen to Kay?" I asked, sitting down next to him.

"It's not gonna become a habit," he assured me.

We settled into a comfortable silence, both absorbed in our donuts. I flipped on the morning news program I knew he liked even though I would have preferred cartoons. I watched as his hand started tapping a rhythm on his leg, a nervous trait we shared.

"So," he began. "You're going to a club opening tonight?"

"Yep," I answered, not giving him an inch. I was fully prepared to make him work for it.

"With Paige and Tamara?" he prodded.

"Yes, and I think Tamara is bringing people too, so it's a group thing."

"How do you know this Tamara?"

I sighed, trying to stem the rising frustration. I was too old for this type of interrogation and it was too early for my patience to be awake.

"Paige met Tamara at a photo shoot. Now Tamara takes some of Paige's yoga classes. She's not necessarily my favorite, but she's fine."

"You actually want to do this? Go to a club?" His voice was brimming with skepticism.

I shrugged. "Not really. But I think it's a good idea. It would be good for me to try new things and meet some new people. You're always telling me to step outside my comfort zone more."

I counted the tics of Harrison's jaw. *One. Two. Three.* He rubbed a hand over his face. "You're right," he conceded.

I almost choked on my coffee at his admission.

"Could you repeat that?" He shot me a withering look. "Please. It can be my birthday present."

"You should be getting out and meeting people. A club just doesn't seem like your scene," he said, clearly still not sold on the idea. To be fair, I was also not sold on the idea.

I nodded. "I might hate it, but I can always leave. Plus, I trust Paige."

"That makes one of us," Harrison grumbled.

The ding of my phone alerting me to a text message saved

Harrison from a recitation of all Paige's virtues.

Paige: Class ran a little long today and it took me forever to roll up the mats, sorry! I'm on my way now though!

Me: No worries. Just an FYI, Harrison is here.

Paige: WHAT?! Ugh, I'm gross right now. I'm going to pull myself together real quick.

I rolled my eyes at the phone. I didn't think Paige even possessed the ability to sweat. I took one of her classes every week and I had yet to witness even a tiny bead of sweat form on her perfect skin. I, on the other hand, usually looked like I had run four marathons through the desert by the time class was over. And we weren't even doing hot yoga!

"Paige is on her way over," I warned Harrison in case he wanted to escape—but also out of genuine concern that he might try to lecture her too.

"Okay." He settled further into the couch, taking a drink of his coffee.

"We're going shopping for tonight," I added.

The arm Harrison had tossed across the back of the couch moved to tug my hair gently, then pinched the skin between my ear and neck.

"Ouch!" I protested, knocking his hand away. "What was that for?"

"Just making sure you weren't abducted by aliens and this is a Lennon decoy." His wandering arm wrapped me into a quick side hug. "I'm proud of you, kid."

A soft knock on the door interrupted the moment, which was probably for the best. I could feel the tears starting to collect. I popped up and swung the door open to a glowing Paige.

"Hi!" she said, her eyes darting past me to track Harrison's progress through my apartment. She smoothed one hand nervously over her sleek ponytail.

"Hey, Paige," Harrison greeted her, coming to a stop by me.

"Oh, um… hey. It's… um… good to see all of y—er… to see you." Her cheeks were tinted a light pink by the time she was done stumbling through her response. I fought a cringe.

"Yeah, you too. You ladies have fun tonight. But not too much," he amended, leaning down to give me a quick kiss on the head. "We still on for tomorrow?"

"Yep. I'll see you then."

"Paige." He inclined his head in passing.

"Uh-huh," she squeaked, watching him walk down the hall.

"Wow, Paige, you're one smooth operator," I said, a little pleased to see her being the awkward one for a change.

Paige groaned. "I'm such an idiot."

"Don't feel too bad. Harrison tends to have that effect on the opposite sex. And actually, I have seen a few men—" But I didn't get a chance to finish that thought.

"That is not actually as helpful as you think," she interrupted, walking to the box of donuts and picking up a classic chocolate iced.

I chewed on my lip, trying to decide if it would be unkind to point out that donuts had dairy in them.

Paige must have been able to read my expression. "I know they have dairy in them. This is an emotional support donut so it doesn't count," she said through a mouthful of donut.

I nodded my head like her vegan rules made sense. "Definitely. Do you want some coffee?"

She dusted the crumbs off her hands. "Nope. Yoga gets my blood flowing plenty, and your brother—"

"Please don't finish that sentence." It was my turn to interrupt. I had zero interest in hearing what Harrison did to her.

"Fine. Let's see if you have anything in your closet to work with before we hit the stores." She walked to my bedroom like she owned the place and started riffling through hangers. "Wow, that's... this is a lot of white and grey. I mean I know that's what I usually see you in, but I guess I always imagined you had a secret, untouched section of your closet dedicated to color."

It was true. My work wardrobe consisted of mainly white blouses and grey skirts or pants. If she dug a little further, she would find some black pants and skirts for when I felt like switching things up.

"I know. I'm not good with clothes or mornings. I don't really understand how to mix colors and patterns," I told Paige honestly. I really did want to be more like the fashionable business professionals I saw filling LA's streets. It's not like I thought fashion was stupid or beneath me, or that I was too much of an intellectual to worry about trivial things like style. I just didn't understand how it all worked. When you combined that with how much I hated waking up early, a neutral-toned wardrobe made the most sense.

Paige turned to look at me, her hand still clutching a hanger. "Okay, that'll be our next shopping trip. Do you own anything that is not work clothes or leggings?"

"No. Oh wait! I have some jeans."

"Fine, we'll just start from scratch. You should wear a strapless bra," Paige suggested, waving a hand toward my chest.

"Why?" I asked, covering my chest with my arms protectively.

"Just in case we find something you can't wear a regular bra with. It makes it easier to try things on," she said, returning another white blouse to its spot in my closet.

"I don't own a strapless bra. They're uncomfortable."

"Throw some clothes on." Paige sighed. "We have a long afternoon ahead of us."

Somehow, I didn't think Paige was going to let me get away with reading a comic book in the food court while she picked everything out for me, Mama Walker style. Did malls even have food courts anymore? How would I survive this trip without a soft pretzel?

5.

Two hours later, I looked down at my Chucks, wondering when they had become medieval torture devices. Spoiler alert: There was no food court. Paige had chosen a trendy outdoor shopping area that was just endless streets filled with boutiques. Not a single soft pretzel in sight.

Paige was bringing new meaning to the phrase "shop 'til you drop." But despite how badly my feet hurt, I was actually having a pretty good time. As it turned out, I loved manicures. I kept sneaking glances at my red nails and smiling, strangely mesmerized by the way they looked doing routine things like holding a fork or signing a receipt. Even trying on clothes had been fun. Paige helped me pick out some new clothes that were both appropriate for work and really cute. She had suggested I try dresses so I wouldn't have to worry about mixing and matching early in the morning. I suggested she become my personal shopper.

I blamed the "Three Alarm Fire" shade of red coating my nails for the bold dress we'd picked out for the evening—a dress that was sitting in a bag next to our table at the vegan Indian restaurant Paige wanted to try. My curry tasted like wet grass covered in cumin, but I wasn't going to complain after she had been so patient and helpful. It's a rare friend who will show you how to tape your boobs into a dress and keep a mostly straight face.

"Oh wow, this cauliflower coconut curry is interesting!"

Paige exclaimed, pushing rice around with her fork.

"Interesting good or interesting bad?" I asked, thinking it would be impossible for something the exact shade of vomit to be good.

She scrunched up her nose. "I don't know. I can't decide. Anyway, we should head back soon and start getting ready."

I pulled out my phone to check the time.

"It's only five thirty," I pointed out. It only took me fifteen minutes to blow my hair dry and another five minutes tops for eyeliner and mascara. Most of my work was already done, since my entire outfit was in a bag at my feet.

"Yeah, that gives us less than two hours to get ready, so we're already cutting it close." She smiled up at the waitress who appeared to refill our glasses. "We'll take our checks whenever you get a chance, please."

It took us a good ten minutes to try to fit all our bags into the trunk of my little hatchback, then I hijacked our trip to a place I knew that served vegan and regular hamburgers. It was well after six by the time we made it back to our apartments. Paige instructed me to shower, blow dry my hair, and then head over to her place to finish getting ready. I spent extra time shaving all of my legs—and other places that didn't really seem necessary if I wasn't going to be in a swimsuit. Then I put on my favorite lavender lotion and blew my hair dry. I slipped on a pair of leggings and a button-up shirt, as instructed, and headed to Paige's apartment. I knocked, and she called for me to come in. Harrison would have to add her to his security lecture world tour.

I loved Paige's apartment. She managed to make the small space open and inviting in a way that made you want to sit down on her couch and stay a while. It was bright and cheerful, just like its tenant.

Paige breezed out of her bathroom wrapped in a light pink robe with a glass of wine in her hand. She reached for my bags and replaced them with the glass of wine.

"I am so excited for tonight! We never go out together. Well, I mean we go to dinner or a movie but this is our first time going *out* out," she said, looking genuinely excited.

Her enthusiasm must have been contagious, because I found myself smiling back.

"I'm excited too," I answered surprised to find it was true. "But I think the wine was a good idea."

"I thought you might need some liquid courage, even though you are totally going to kill in that dress. I literally cannot wait to see you when we're done." She grabbed my free hand and pulled me to her bathroom. She motioned for me to sit on the toilet, then freed my hair from the claw keeping it pinned to my head. Pop songs I wasn't familiar with played from a speaker on her dresser, making me feel like this was one of those moments I had dreamed about having in high school. Getting ready to go to football games on Friday night or preparing for a school dance. I swallowed around a lump in my throat.

"Thanks for doing this, Paige. I know it probably sounds dumb, but I always wanted to do things like this." My hand moved absently to rub the scar lining my chest.

Paige wrapped her arms around my shoulders in a half-hug, careful to keep the curling iron away from my face. I'd told Paige about my heart defect a little after we met. I had felt the need to explain both why Harrison was so insanely overprotective and why I was such a social disaster.

"Anytime you want to hit the town, Lennon, you know who to call. I'm having so much fun using you as my human doll." She smiled at me in the mirror.

Forty minutes later, I didn't recognize the person looking back at me.

"Holy spaceballs, Paige, I don't even look like myself." I ran my hands down the smooth waves in my hair. It was shining and curled to perfection. I thought I might honestly be in shock. Paige had given my eyes a natural smoky look that wasn't too dark and made them look super green. Even my cheekbones looked more defined. The bright red lipstick that matched my nails was my favorite part. It made me feel bold.

"Go put your dress on!" She shoved me lightly out of the bedroom. "I want to see the whole look."

I pulled the dress out of its bag and laid it on the bed next to the black clutch that I loved. I slid off my leggings and top and stepped into the dress. I had felt so good about it back in the store, but now I was suddenly nervous about all the skin it showed. Thin black straps supported a tight bodice that gave me some serious cleavage, way more than I was used to displaying. The dress was covered in gold sequins with intricate lines of black sequins that made it look like I actually had curves. I tried to tug the material further down my thighs.

"Turn around, let me see," Paige called from the bathroom.

I slid my feet into the nude heels and turned to face her. I had to stop myself from chewing on my lip while her critical gaze swept over me.

"Lennon, you look absolutely amazing!"

"Really? You don't think this is too short?" I tried again to pull the dress down. I didn't think that much skin above my knee had ever been shown in public. I was pretty sure I had bathing suits that covered more.

"Uh, I don't think that dress is short enough. You have a killer body," she said, waving a tube of lipstick in my direction.

I snorted. "Yeah, if you're into the whole thirteen-year-old boy look."

"Hey, some of us would kill to be able to eat like you do and not gain weight. I have seen you eat an entire large pizza and wash it down with an order of breadsticks."

It was my turn to roll my eyes.

"Oh puh-lease, you are perfect. Seriously," I said, watching her pull on a blush-colored dress that hugged her body like it had been made just for her. She tossed her blonde hair over her shoulder.

"I don't know about that, but I do love the way my butt looks in this dress." She gave her butt a little wiggle.

I laughed. "Jimmy's going to love that dress for sure."

"He better. Now get over here. We need some selfies to document this occasion." She motioned me over. I smiled into the phone, which Paige held at a weird angle that she assured me was very flattering. The secret to taking a good selfie was all about the angle, she told me as she snapped away.

"Eat your heart out, Theo," she said, sending our pictures out to the interwebs.

When she said his name, I realized I hadn't even thought of him all day.

6.

Harrison: Don't let anyone buy you a drink.
Harrison: And don't leave your drink alone.
Harrison: You know what, just don't drink anything.
Me: I thought accepting a drink was a signal to a potential partner that you're interested?
Lou: Oh shit short stack, your brosef just lost it.
Harrison: Lennon, I swear to God...

I tucked my phone back into my purse as our ride pulled up to the curb. People were already swarming outside the doors. I noticed my hands were shaking a little as I followed Paige out of the car.

"You ready?" Paige asked, slipping her arm through mine.

I took a deep breath and nodded. I tried to force a smile to my lips as we approached the door. Paige showed the bouncers her phone with our tickets on them. The bouncers held the doors open for us and I felt like I was stepping into a new world.

The lights were just bulbs suspended from the ceiling, casting a dim light over the whole space. A bar made of some dark material stood to one side of the club, directly across from a small elevated platform where a DJ was hard at work mixing music. To the right of the bar, farthest from the stage, were mazes of alcoves filled with black velvet couches in all different shapes. Closer to the stage was an open area where people were standing or dancing to the music. Paige pulled us toward one of the alcoves nestled into a corner near the stage. I saw Tamara and Jimmy seated around a small table. The seats around the table were broken into segments big enough to fit two people.

Tamara rose when she saw Paige and gave her a kiss on the cheek.

"Paige, you look gorgeous as always," she said, then turned toward me. "Wow, Lennon, I didn't recognize you. You look good."

My 'thank you' sounded more like a question than a statement. Somehow Tamara had made her compliment sound more like a small dig at my usual appearance. Paige took the spot next to Jimmy, and Tamara returned to her seat next to a man who hadn't bothered to glance up from his phone. I was impressed with how quiet it was in the alcove—it created a sense of privacy, but still let you see most of the club's interior.

"Lennon, you remember Lia right? And this is her boyfriend, Craig," Paige said, gesturing at the couple occupying one of the seats.

"Hi, it's nice seeing you again Lia." I gave a shy wave and fought to make eye contact. I fidgeted with the hem of my dress trying to cover the vast swaths of leg that had appeared when I sat down.

"Your dress is amazing, Lennon," Lia said, giving me a warm smile. "You ladies need drinks."

"Brett, baby, will you get us a bottle of that champagne I like so much?" Tamara cooed, leaning into the man who still had not looked up from his phone.

"Sure, babe," Brett said, rising and heading toward the bar.

"We're celebrating tonight. Brett's character on *All Our Days* was going to die in a tragic car accident but the writers decided he was going to survive and have a secret baby!" Tamara informed us.

"Wow, that's great, Tam." Paige sounded genuinely happy for Brett's survival and impending fatherhood. "Definitely calls for champagne."

Brett reappeared without champagne and I was left wondering what I was supposed to do with my hands. I was the only one not wrapped around a significant other and it was starting to feel like a seventh-wheel situation. I silently reminded myself that Paige had invited me because she wanted me to be here. I took a deep breath and tried to catch the thread of conversation around our table.

A waiter showed up with a tray of glasses and bottle of champagne in a bucket of ice. He popped the cork and poured us each a glass before disappearing back into the crowd.

"All right everyone, let's do a cheers picture," Tamara instructed, holding her glass out toward the center of the table while the other held her phone. "Wait, should we wait for Sebastian, Paige?"

"No, that's okay. He texted earlier saying he would be a little late," Paige said, moving her glass toward the table. I followed their lead and waited patiently for Tamara to finish taking her pictures, just happy to have something to do.

She looked at her screen and then announced we needed a redo. "Lennon, can you take your glasses off for this one? They're ruining the flow of the picture," she asked with a hint of annoyance in her voice.

"Oh, uh, sure, sorry about that." I reached up and slipped my glasses off.

The scene in front of me blurred slightly, but not before I caught Paige and Lia shooting disapproving looks at Tamara. She snapped a picture and then thanked me for being such a peach.

I smiled and returned my glasses to their perch on my nose. My glasses were the one thing I had refused to compromise on tonight. They were like my security blanket and I needed their comfort for this. I took a drink of champagne, loving the way the bubbles felt in my mouth. The buzz from the bottle of wine Paige and I had split earlier was wearing off at the same rate as my confidence.

I fought the urge to retreat inside myself and start reciting equations—that always calmed me down. Instead, I tried to remember what I knew about the people sitting at the table so I could come up with questions to ask them. Tamara was a model Paige had met on one of her modeling gigs, and she took some of Paige's yoga classes now. Paige had met Lia through Tamara. Lia was a makeup artist and had a popular blog where she reviewed beauty products and gave tutorials. Craig was a total mystery—clearly the strong silent type.

"I think Sebastian is here," Lia said, pointing with her champagne flute to where the crowd was parting.

"Yep, that's him. Be right back." Paige popped up and headed in the direction of the door. I had no idea who this Sebastian character was, but I was pretty sure Paige hadn't mentioned him at all.

"Who is Sebastian?" I directed my question at Lia, since she was the one who had pointed him out and she was friendlier than Tamara.

"You don't know who he is?" Lia's eyes widened in disbelief. "Sebastian Kincaid?"

I followed her gaze to where Paige had pushed through the crowd to reach the man causing the commotion. His lips tugged to the side when he saw her approaching him.

It was possible that the right words to describe him didn't exist. He was tall and lean, and everything about his movements screamed power and confidence. His dark jeans hugged powerful thighs and his T-shirt stretched tightly over muscles that made me a little light-headed. Even from this distance, I could see the tattoos covering both arms. His hair was so dark it almost looked black, and was rumpled in that just-rolled-out-of-bed way. Light stubble covered a square jaw that I previously believed existed only in magazines and my fantasies, and his cheekbones looked like they had been chiseled out of marble.

I watched, mesmerized, as he placed a hand on Paige's lower back and walked toward our table. The closer he got the more I felt myself fidgeting in my seat.

"Hey guys, this is Sebastian. From my yoga class." As Paige introduced him, she moved forward enough to allow his hand to drop away from her back.

Brett tore his gaze away from his phone for only the second time, and stood to offer Sebastian his hand. "Brett. I'm a big fan."

I noted the small hesitation before Sebastian grasped his outstretched hand. "Nice to meet you, mate."

My eyebrows rose in surprise at his British accent. It was deep and crisp and not at all what I was expecting. Craig popped up and greeted Sebastian enthusiastically, also making sure to declare that he was a big fan. I filed that information away for later.

Any other time, I would have been curious about the reaction of the two men in the group, who had been largely silent until the arrival of Sebastian. But right now my nerves were winning out over any curiosity I had about the scene unfolding in front of me, and I forced myself to pay attention to the man whose presence seemed to take up the entire space. He triaged the scene, his eyes darting over the small group clustered around the table. I followed their track. I saw the moment his gaze hit the empty spot next to Jimmy, then swept the rest of the table. His small smile faltered as it landed on the other empty spot—beside me—and his eyes bounced back to Paige. He looked slightly unsure, mirroring a little of the uncertainty I was feeling.

"You remember Tamara and Lia from yoga," Paige added brightly, slipping back into her spot next to Jimmy. "And this is my friend Lennon. She lives down the hall from me."
No. No. No. No. *No.* I tried to swallow the rising panic. This was a set-up. Sebastian had clearly come to the same conclusion, and his careful smile had slipped to something that looked wary and slightly feral. His gaze traveled over me and I felt a blush spreading through me like a wildfire. Instinctively, I adjusted my glasses and glanced around for the nearest exit before turning my eyes back to him. I gave him what I hoped was a smile, but felt more like a grimace.

"It's nice to meet you, Sebastian." I scooted farther across the seat to make room for him, clinging to my champagne flute like it was a life raft. "You have a British accent."

I closed my eyes, letting the full stupidity of that comment sink in. I felt a dip in the seat and then a distinctly masculine smell invaded my space. I opened my eyes and trained them on his knees.

"You're very observant," he said, his voice too flat for me to determine if that was an insult or joke, or something else I wasn't socially competent enough to understand. Either way, my hands had started to sweat and my heart was beating erratically in my chest.

"Lennon is an aerospace engineer for Spatium," Paige pointed out, as if that explained my oh-so-observant comment.

I shot her a pleading look. I didn't want to do this. I wanted to step out of my comfort zone, not demolish it with a wrecking ball. Paige just gave me an encouraging smile. I looked away and focused on the muscle twitching in Sebastian's jaw instead. There are forty-three muscles in the human face, but the exact number of muscles used to smile or frown is unknown. I resisted the urge to rub the tiny portion of scar peeking out from my cleavage.

"Sebastian plays for the Novas," Paige prompted, as if that would solve everything for me.

I scrunched my nose in confusion.

"The Novas? I don't know what that is." The words slipped past my lips before I could think better of it. Everyone in the group reacted like I had just committed the very worst of the seven deadly sins; Brett actually gasped. Realizing my error, I did my best to retract my question while focusing on one corner of the table.

"I mean, unless you're talking about supernovas, as in the explosion of a star. It's actually a common misconception that supernovas only occur at the end of a star's life cycle. They can also occur when one star in a binary system steals too much matter from its companion star. The excess mass results in an explosion. I know a lot about those types of supernovas, but obviously, you can't really play for a cosmic supernova," I added helpfully, finally lifting my eyes away from the table to survey the group.

My face turned the color of a boiled lobster as I took in the shocked expressions of the people around me. They were all looking at me like I was from some distant galaxy where supernovas were actually visible simultaneous to the event. Even Paige looked a little dazed by my minilecture. It took her several long blinks before she laughed a little too enthusiastically.

"And that's why I always make sure Lennon is on my team for trivia night!"

Fact: Paige and I had never once played any type of trivia, let alone on a team. Additional fact: I am very good at trivia games, but not so good at lying. I looked at Paige, trying to determine if I should provide more information about our fake trivia team. She widened her eyes and gave an almost imperceptible shake of her head like she could read my mind.

Craig looked at me and spoke very slowly, like I was a small child on the verge of a tantrum. "The Novas are LA's professional soccer team." He emphasized professional. "He's the captain of the team. Led Manchester United to two championships before coming here. He's kind of a big deal."

I nodded my head and slid my gaze toward the big deal sitting next to me. Sebastian Kincaid, leader of soccer teams on two continents, was looking at me like I had sprouted two more heads since he'd sat down.

He scrubbed his face with both large, perfectly formed hands. I could almost imagine the rough sound his hands would make traveling over the light dusting of hair. A loud sigh startled me, abruptly dragging me back to the real world. That sigh was like a shot straight to my chest, an actual ache forming just under my ribs. I felt myself deflating like a balloon with a hole in it. I looked down, blinking back tears.

We sat in uncomfortable silence for a beat before Brett and Craig began monopolizing Sebastian's attention. Lia and Tamara managed to interject a comment here or there, and Paige kept trying in vain to turn his attention back to me. I felt like the companion star in a binary system whose mass was being stolen by the other star, just waiting to have my existence stamped out completely.

7.

It had been fifteen minutes since Sebastian had excused himself to get a drink. Exactly nine hundred seconds. The first five or so minutes had passed in reasonably mild awkwardness; Paige gave me a pep talk and everyone else pretended I didn't exist. Lia gave me a sympathetic smile but didn't seem to know what to say. Ten minutes in, I realized Sebastian had ditched our group: There was no way such a "big deal" would have to wait ten minutes to be served a drink. The last five minutes passed with excruciating awkwardness—at least for me. Then the questions started about what could be taking Sebastian so long.

I caught a whispered exchange between Lia and Tamara followed by Lia darting a furtive glance behind her. My eyes followed hers to the bar. Sebastian was chatting up a pretty blonde who was leaning into him, stroking his arm with her free hand. He took a sip of beer before leaning in even closer to speak into her ear. She shoved his chest and laughed. As if that display wasn't enough, two more women joined the blonde, seeming equally unaware of the rules governing personal space.

In what I can only assume was an unconscious self-preservation effort, my brain started to wander. I thought about how the bubbles in champagne were just chemical reactions aided by the tiny fibers left behind on the glass by towels or dust. I glanced over to where Sebastian was standing and saw that one of the hands I'd been admiring earlier had found a home on the hip of yet another new addition to the group. What did you call a group of beautiful women who seemed to orbit around the gravitational pull of an equally beautiful man? A harem was a close fit, but not quite right. A group of geese was a gaggle. My mind kept wanting to settle on a murder, commonly used in reference to a group of crows and also the best way to describe how I was feeling at the moment.

While I could logically explain the phenomenon of bubbles in a glass of champagne, I was unable to come up with any sort of reasonable explanation for the discomfort I was experiencing as I watched Sebastian with those women. I tried to convince myself that what I felt was simply the sting of being passed over for someone—or someones—deemed more desirable, combined with the fact that there were people present to witness the slight. Or maybe it was my frustration over being the socially awkward one in a group of people who seemed to so easily manage human interactions.

But none of the explanations I came up with rang true.

I pushed up out of my seat just as the lips of the original blonde groupie made contact with Sebastian's neck.

"I'm just going to the bathroom," I said, hitching my thumb over my shoulder toward the only hallway visible. I didn't care if it led to a secret dungeon, as long as it took me away from here.

"I'll go with you." Paige started to stand, a concerned frown tugging down her mouth.

"No, no. I'll be right back. You have fun. Drink some more champagne." I barely finished my sentence before turning and walking away. I released the breath I had been holding once I was sure Paige hadn't followed me, then put my head down and started weaving through people.

I didn't look up until I was safely through the door labeled with a sparkly silver L. The bathroom was occupied by only a few girls reapplying lipstick, so I had no problem finding an empty stall to hide—er... pee in.

The cold plastic on my butt might have been the saddest

feeling I had ever experienced. I covered my hands with my face and tried to pull myself together, aware that there was definitely a point of no return when it came to crying. There was a threshold, and once you reached it there was no way to stop the tears—a threshold I was getting dangerously close to in this stall. I tried some of the deep breathing techniques I'd learned in yoga in an attempt to re-center my aura or something. It didn't escape my notice that there was an alarming correlation between me putting myself out there and me ending up crying in a public bathroom. I let out one more watery sigh before exiting the safety of my stall.

The person staring back at me in the brightly lit mirrors above the sink made me a little nauseated. What was I even doing? I hated, *hated*, the version of Lennon I saw looking back at me. This person had given other people the power to determine her self-worth and looked heartbroken that she had somehow been found lacking. I promised myself a long time ago that I would never give anyone else that power, and for the most part, I had kept that vow.

I straightened my spine. Okay, objectively this night was a failure. A huge dumpster fire of a disaster. But it wasn't the worst thing to ever happen to me. Not by a long shot. These people didn't like me, but so what? I had friends who really knew me and thought I was great. I might only have a handful, but the ones I did have were amazing. I had my dream job, and I was good at it. I knew my own worth.

Sebastian Kincaid might be a god among men on the soccer field (and, okay, everywhere he went because he also looked like a god), but I helped build rocket ships! And satellites! If he thought I wasn't even worth trying to get to know, it was his loss. I was just fine before I knew he existed, and I would be just fine after. While he was definitely the most attractive man I had met in real life, physical attributes were never the most important part of a person. It had just made the sting of his obvious dismissal of me as a potential new friend or more even worse, that's all it was. There were other fish in the sea.

Less shiny, physically spectacular fish but still—lots and lots of fish who wouldn't mind meeting a less-than-socially-gifted fish who knew about things like exploding stars and the finer points of propulsion system design.

Decision made, I finished drying my hands and pulled my phone out of my purse to order a ride before leaving the restroom. Against my will, my eyes traced the line of the bar searching for Sebastian. Apparently I was still a glutton for punishment despite the conversation with myself in the bathroom. When I couldn't find him at the bar, I reminded myself that, regardless of whether he was back at our table or had left with one of the beautiful women surrounding him earlier, I was not interested in getting to know him.

Lia was the first one to see me return, and she gave me a sympathetic smile which I returned as I made my way around the seats to Paige. Sebastian had returned to the group with a very pretty woman who was wrapped around him like a boa constrictor trying to crush lunch.

Paige hopped out of her seat and grabbed my arm to drag me a little distance from the group, making me teeter unsteadily on my heels.

"I am going to kill him, Lennon," Paige growled. The death glares she was shooting over my shoulder would have made Harrison proud. "I'm so sorry. I swear he's not usually such an asshole. He comes to my yoga classes to help with an old injury, and I swear to you, he's the nicest guy. This is a total Jekyll and Hyde situation."

I shrugged my shoulders. "It's no big deal. I'm sure he's just having a bad day. Anyway, I don't think my insides appreciated that Indian food, so I'm going to head home." I mentally high-fived myself for how steady my voice sounded.

Paige's eyes snapped to mine. "I'll go with you. Just let me say goodbye real quick."

"No." I shook my head, trying for a reassuring smile. "You should totally stay. I'm just going to go home and go to sleep. Or die on the toilet, and you really don't want to see that."

"I'm not letting you go by yours—"

I cut her off. "Seriously, Paige, I already ordered a ride and everything. Don't waste that dress."

"You're not a waste," she stated firmly. See? Perfect example of amazing friends.

"I know. But it would be a waste for you to leave with me." I left out the part where I would bury myself under all my covers and plan how I could live the rest of my life without leaving the safety of my bed.

She squinted her eyes and gave me an assessing look. "Okay, but text me when you get home so I know you made it safe and sound."

"I will," I promised. My phone dinged, letting me know my ride was close. "My ride's almost here."

She gave me a quick hug, saying one more apology-laced goodbye. I watched her make her way back toward the table, and accidentally made eye contact with Sebastian for a second. His gaze narrowed, propelling me back toward the door and out into the quiet.

I let out a relieved sigh when I saw a silver Honda Accord pull up to the curb. A quick check on my phone confirmed this was my ride. I slid inside the car and greeted my driver.

I wish I could say that when I closed my eyes and leaned my head against the window, the predominant emotion I felt was pride. But mostly, I just felt disappointment. The same sense of disappointment followed me into my apartment as I slipped out of my dress and slid into bed, not even bothering to wash off the makeup. My hand traced up and down my scar in a silent reminder that I was lucky—so lucky—and had survived way worse than a bad night out.

8.

I didn't have much time to wallow on Sunday, which I suppose was for the best even though I totally could have justified a mountain of waffles and a good Netflix binge. Sunday was family dinner day, and truly one of my favorite days of the week. Harrison picked me up around two, and we drove to our mom's house to spend the rest of the day. I was more than happy to slip back into the comfort of routine after last night. There was something to be said about predictability. Even Harrison's not-so-subtle questions was delightfully predictable.

By Monday morning, I barely remembered stupid Sebastian Kincaid and his stupid perfect face, which is exactly what I told Paige when I got her tenth apology text. Well, minus the stupids, obviously.

I stopped to get a latte on my way to work as a reward for only hitting snooze twice as well as for wearing one of my new dresses. I found Monday mornings worked best when they involved a rewards system. I spent the rest of the morning reviewing the data from our latest round of testing on engine components. Numbers were swimming behind my eyelids by the time Janie knocked on my desk to get my attention.

"Hello? Earth to Lennon."

I snapped my head up from my computer and adjusted my glasses. "Sweet mother of pearl, you scared the crap out of me Janie!"

"I thought you were dead." Janie plopped down in one of the

extra chairs in my office. "It's almost one and I hadn't heard from you about lunch."

My stomach rumbled right on cue. "I guess I lost track of time. Did you already eat?"

"Nope. I was waiting on you. I want to hear all the details about Saturday! You and Paige looked ah-mazing, by the way."

I weighed my options. I could tell Janie the same half-truths I'd told Harrison yesterday, or I could tell her the whole truth and relive the embarrassment. Having to make these kinds of decisions was another entry on the growing list of reasons to never leave my apartment, except for work and food. And to pick up my future cat family from the shelter. I sighed.

"It was kind of disaster, but I did discover that I love manicures." I held up my hands and wiggled my fingers.

"What? What happened?" Janie's brow furrowed in concern.

"I'll tell you about it on our way to lunch," I offered, suddenly absolutely starving and needing the fortifying power of carbohydrates.

I filled her in on the events of Saturday while we walked. By the time we made it to the cafeteria, Janie was deciding whether it would be better to murder Sebastian or break his legs. At one point, I attempted to defend Sebastian by pointing out that he probably wasn't expecting to be set up either, but Janie just snorted and pointed out that I didn't react like a gigantic ass clown. I didn't necessarily enjoy being his defender when I was still clinging to my somewhat irrational anger, but I also didn't want to spend the next decade visiting Janie in prison.

While Janie was busy plotting revenge, I scoped out the lunch offerings and filled my tray. I followed Janie to the cash register to wait in line while she highlighted the merits of castration.

"Oh my gosh, it was so romantic! I thought dinner at Basil's was going to be our celebration, so I was just so surprised that he'd booked us a hotel room."

Oh for the love of Cheetos, you have got to be effing kidding me. Why, why, *why* was the universe determined to hate me?

"Oh hey, Lennon," Sam said, smiling at me. "I love your dress."

And I love your boyfriend. "Thanks."

Sam gave me a smile, and I felt a completely unreasonable urge to karate chop it right off her face. She looked at her friend and said, "Lennon is actually the one who introduced me to Theo." Turning back to me, she said, "I was just telling Lauren about our romantic anniversary weekend."

My insides were shriveling up like a grape in the sunshine. I fought the urge to point out that there was food in my refrigerator older than their relationship, but you didn't see me celebrating.

"Oh... uh... that's great."

Janie must have sensed my distress. She whipped around and eyeballed the small space between Sam and me before wedging her body into the gap.

"Hey, Sam, good seeing you." Janie smiled, wrapping a hand around my tray-free arm and yanking me forward. I barely managed to swipe my ID badge and smile in apology at the frazzled cashier. "Happy people are the most annoying people on the planet. Like, keep your happiness to yourself. It's Monday. Don't force your happiness on other people. I mean, do either of us look like happy people right now?"

I wasn't actually sure Janie required an answer, but I shook my head anyway, slumping into an empty chair and setting my tray down.

"So, what do you want to do about this Sebastian situation?" Janie asked, taking a bite of her panini. Her eyes were alarmingly intense.

"Uh..." I picked at my fries. "What do you mean, 'do about'?"

"Are we going to murder him? Because I was thinking it would be better if I unleashed some of my mad Taekwondo skills on him, so he can never play soccer again. Although I'm totally down for the whole castration angle too."

I stared at her, a limp French fry dangling from my fingers. I blinked, waiting for her to add a "just kidding" or laugh, or do *something* that indicated she was just listing punishments as a sign of solidarity.

"Okay, first, you might be slightly deranged, and I'm legitimately worried about what's happening in that head of yours. Second, we aren't doing anything. Sebastian's just a jerk. Third, even though I am seriously concerned for your mental health, I'm still making you an honorary aunt for the colony of cats I'm adopting."

"I'm your ride or die! You say there's a body, and I create a fake identity, use that identity to rent a van because I can't fit a body over five foot six into the trunk of my Prius, and show up with a shovel. No questions asked. But let's circle back to the colony of cats for a second, because that sounds a lot crazier than plotting murder." Janie waved her finger at me for emphasis. I was momentarily stunned by the amount of detail in her plan to dispose of a body. No one can come up with that kind of detail on the fly. I made a mental note to never, *ever* make Janie angry.

"Cats make excellent pets! They're relatively independent but still provide the basic requirements of companionship. And lots of influential people have extolled the virtue of cats. Ernest Hemingway adored his cat. Abraham Lincoln fed his son's cat with a gold fork at White House dinners," I pointed out triumphantly.

Janie rolled her eyes. "Yeah, wow, great examples. Look how well things ended for them."

"I don't really think it was Tabby's fault Lincoln was assassinated." It was my turn to roll my eyes.

"All right, let's slow the crazy train down here—"

"You were the one just casually talking about murder!" I interrupted, throwing my hands up.

"Shhh!" Janie hissed. "Stop screaming about murder before someone reports us both to HR. Now, don't be mad, but I had a little free time on my hands this weekend, so I went ahead and created a profile for you on PairBond."

PairBond was a dating site designed specifically for people

in STEM careers, aka nerds. Janie pulled her cellphone out and slid it to me, actually looking slightly nervous as I picked up the phone.

My eyes bulged when I saw the picture she had chosen for "my" profile. It was a manga character in a tight leather jumpsuit that was unzipped almost to her navel, revealing unnaturally large breasts.

"Janie, why is my profile picture a picture of Kallen Kozuki?"

"Uh, because she's a total badass. And there aren't that many manga characters with red hair. Plus look at her boobs in that jumpsuit! I'd hit that."

I rubbed at my forehead, smearing a little French fry grease on one of my lenses, and sighed. This lunch was getting exhausting. I just wanted to eat my mound of fries in peace—was that too much to ask of the universe? I sighed again, giving the rest of the profile a cursory glance before handing the phone back to Janie.

"Fine. I'll do it, but you are using a real picture of me," I relented, deciding it was better to lose the battle and win the war. I might have a profile but that didn't mean I had to do anything with it.

Janie bounced in her chair, clapping her hands together gleefully. She hit a button on her phone.

"PocketRocket69 is live and looking for love."

I winced. "On second thought, keep the picture."

9.

At Paige's yoga class on Tuesday night I tried to shake off the funk I had been in since lunch on Monday, but even Paige's soothing reassurance that everything was unfolding as it should wasn't enough to lift my spirits. The slew of weird responses I had received from my profile on PairBond wasn't helping the situation. I'd learned that people were still using the abbreviation 'DTF' and that an alarming amount of men thought it was acceptable to send unsolicited pictures of their anatomy. Why anyone thought a picture of their penis would seal the deal was beyond me. Penises were strange-looking, like some weird one-eyed species of naked mole rat without legs.

I knew I was at rock bottom when I seriously considered calling my mom on Wednesday after work for one of her speeches. The tests we'd run on a simulator for one of the thrusters that morning hadn't gone well, and I was scrambling to figure out where we'd gone wrong. I could hear my mom telling me she didn't raise any failures, and she absolutely would not be happy to know I was spending so much time thinking about dating lately. The downside of a Mama Walker classic was that they never lasted less than thirty minutes. She was like a runway train once she really got going.

I decided that what I really needed was to get out of my apartment. A new *National Geographic* magazine had come yesterday, so I grabbed it and one of my favorite issues of *The Watch-*

men, stuffed them both into my bag, and headed toward one of my favorite places within walking distance. Spout was a cozy tea shop about a block away from my apartment building. It was my favorite place to go in the evenings when it was way past the acceptable hour for caffeine. I didn't really care for tea, but they made a cinnamon apple tea that tasted just like hot apple cider, and all their chairs were repurposed wingbacks.

I pushed through the door and made my way to the counter. There were only a handful of people inside, including a knitting group sitting in the chairs around the fireplace. While it didn't necessarily make sense to have a fireplace in this climate, I loved how cozy it made the atmosphere in here whenever they had it lit. Curling up in front of a fireplace with a warm beverage and a good book was one of the things I actually missed about winters in Massachusetts. In fact, it might have been the *only* thing on that particular list.

I placed my order and scanned the room, looking for the perfect place to curl up for a couple of hours. I strategically chose a table tucked into a quiet corner where I could still see the fireplace. Reaching into my bag, I pulled out the magazine and graphic novel, deciding to start with the magazine. My phone vibrated on the table next to my cup. I looked down and saw a text from grandpa and a notification from the PairBond app.

Grandpa: Lennon, do an old man a favor and let me know what the odds are on the Dodgers vs Angels next week.

Me: This wouldn't be for the illegal gambling ring you're running out of the senior center, would it?

Grandpa had been busted multiple time for sports betting at the senior center. He was one bust away from a lifetime ban. I went to ESPN.com and pulled up the stats from last year for both teams anyway.

Grandpa: Of course not. I'm just having a friendly conversation with Saul about baseball.

Me: If you say so. The Dodgers are likely to win if Alexander pitches.

Grandpa: Good, good. How many runs do you think they'll win by?

 Me: That's oddly specific for just a friendly conversation.
 Grandpa: No one likes a snitch, kid.
 Me: Dodgers win by 2 runs.
 Grandpa: That's my girl! Love you.

 I shook my head, switching to the dating app to check the new message. I squeaked when a hand wrapped around yet another penis filled my screen. Hitting delete, I snuck a guilty glance around to make sure no one had seen my screen. I was one dick pic away from deleting this app.

 My attention turned to the *National Geographic* magazine sitting beside my tea. The cover pictured a radio telescope pointed at the night sky with the caption "WE ARE NOT ALONE." I smiled. This was exactly what I needed. Maybe the universe was finally ready to give me a break.

 Grandpa was actually responsible for my love of NatGeo. We used to read them together and imagine all the adventures we would go on when my heart was fixed. Those magazines had been a means of escape for me, and now they were a comforting tradition. Grandpa and I both still read them, and we would exchange notes every month.

 Even though I was excited to read the feature story about scientists' latest efforts to find extraterrestrial life, I started from the first page. I always read each new issue cover to cover, never going out of order. I sipped my tea and got lost between the familiar pages.

 "Is this seat taken?" asked a deep voice with a distinctly British accent. My heart rate spiked in response.

 My eyes slid to take in denim covering muscular thighs and up to heavily tattooed forearms. My gaze flicked upward and then back down to the open magazine in my hands. As if there was some temporary disruption between the optic nerve and the thalamus, my eyes registered Sebastian Kincaid standing beside my table, but my brain could not process the sensory input. I blinked a few times, adjusting my glasses, before looking back up at the man standing beside my table. Sebastian apparently gave up on waiting for a response and slid into the chair across from me, placing a steaming mug on the table.

"What are you reading?" he asked casually, as if it was completely normal for him to be sitting across from me at Spout. As if he just hadn't sent my world toppling off its axis again.

Without taking my eyes of the pages, I lifted the magazine slightly so he could see the cover. My heart was beating frantically in my chest while my mind reeled. What was he doing here? This couldn't be a chance meeting. There was no room between my racing thoughts to form responses let alone to verbalize them.

"*National Geographic*? Huh, I didn't know that was still around. Is that a comic book?"

I peered over the edge of the page, watching as one large hand reached across the table and turned the book to face him. Ink covered his arm, creeping onto hands that were so distinctly male. The ink on his skin contrasted with the ink on the cover, and I wondered what his skin would look like next to my pale skin. And then I wondered why I would be picturing our skin together at all. My hormones may have forgotten about Saturday night, but my brain still remembered.

"*The Watchmen*? This any better than the movie?" He flipped through the pages, stopping at various points to look at something that caught his eye. "I've never been into comics, but I like the Marvel movies."

I flicked my eyes up to take in his face, lingering on those eyes that couldn't quite decide if they wanted to be blue or green, before focusing on a spot by his left ear.

I read a study on what makes a person beautiful. One of the main theories is that we find symmetry beautiful. The more symmetry present in the facial features, the more pleasing we find it to be. Sebastian was the physical manifestation of this theory. His face was a study in symmetry except for a small scar dissecting the edge of his left eyebrow and a slight bump in an otherwise perfect nose. And yet, these slight deviations somehow added to his attractiveness.

I knew what he saw when he looked at me. Rebellious auburn hair that refused to be tamed—neither straight nor curly, just a mess. Green eyes that were a little too large and partially obscured by black-framed glasses. Freckles sprinkled across a too-small nose. Not a single hint of symmetry to be found.

I licked my lips, trying to find some words to offer like a normal human being would. I could hear my heart pounding wildly and felt the familiar somersault movement of my stomach that always came just before a full-blown panic attack. I closed my eyes for a minute, trying to focus on my breathing like Paige had taught me when I'd confessed that I still struggled with anxiety.

"It's good." I finally managed to force the words out on a rushed breath. "Maybe even one of the best. It's actually kind of a deconstruction of superheroes, so it's not like the Marvel universe really. Marvel only explores the flaws of its characters on a superficial level, and the good guys are still good despite their flaws. It's sometimes hard to distinguish between the heroes and villains in *The Watchmen*. But I like Marvel too. Paige will only see the Marvel movies with Chris Hemsworth in them."

Sebastian chuckled. I braved eye contact and noticed the way his eyes crinkled in the corners when he smiled. The effect was disorienting.

"That sounds like Paige. Mind if I take a look?" He held up the issue, one eyebrow canted upward.

"*National Geographic* has been in publication since 1888. It has a global circulation of over six million readers," I blurted out. I felt my cheeks turning red at an alarming rate. My eyes returned to the safe spot by his ear. I cleared my throat before trying again. "You can read it, but it's not the first issue. The storyline won't make sense."

"I promise not to judge it this first go around, yeah?" I could hear the teasing in his voice, but I didn't move my eyes to verify that he was in fact smiling.

I gave a brief nod, turning my attention back to the magazine I was gripping so hard in my hands that the pages were getting crumpled. I loosened my hold and tried to focus on the story I had been reading pre-Sebastian, but it was nearly impossible to focus on the words now. My eyes kept darting away from the pages to Sebastian. Taking in the way he drank his tea and watching his facial expressions every time he moved to a new frame. It had been at least ten minutes and I hadn't moved onto a new paragraph. When I wasn't being a creep, my mind was busy trying to solve riddles. *Why is Sebastian here? Did he know I would be here? Why is he still here? What are we doing? Is there such a thing as drinking tea in a masculine way? Why is watching him drink tea making me squirm?*

I finally gave up the guise of reading and put my magazine down. He was mid-sip, still focused on the graphic novel, so I took the opportunity to openly study him. I tried to decipher some of the tattoos on the arm holding his mug, tilting my head to one side a little to get a better look at the words hidden in between some geometric pattern.

"What's caught your attention?" he asked, angling his arm to get a better look at the spot I was examining.

I swallowed. The frayed piece of string that tethered me to what little was left of my sanity snapped. I started gathering up my things. "I should get going. It was nice seeing you. You can finish that if you want. Give it to Paige next time you see her at yoga or wherever."

I groaned inwardly at the realization that I had just lent a stranger my favorite graphic novel. I shot out of my chair, in an even bigger rush to leave before I offered to loan him a kidney too. I tripped over my shoelaces, bumping into the table and toppling sideways. Sebastian leapt out of his chair with the grace of an athlete and reached out a hand to steady me.

"Whoa, slow down there. Are you—?"

"I have to go now. Have a nice night." I practically yelled it in his face, tearing out of his grip and bolting for the door. I promised myself I would put extra money in the tip jar next time for not picking up my cup, and breathed a sigh of relief when I looked back and didn't see Sebastian following me.

If karma was real, I must have done something seriously

messed up in my previous life.

10.

When I couldn't solve a problem, I found it helped to focus my mind on a task that didn't utilize the same areas of my brain. If I was stuck on some type of equation, for example, I would read a book or color in one of those adult coloring books.

Today, I found myself at a complete and total loss. I had two very different problems and my attention was annoyingly divided. I'd spent all morning inputting data into a simulator program trying to figure out where our original algorithm had gone wrong. I kept coming up with exactly no solutions, which—considering the other half of my brain was fixated on why Sebastian Kincaid had shown up at Spout last night—was not that surprising. I even walked down the street to get another latte to clear my head, but I was too distracted and nothing seemed to help.

I groaned and grabbed my phone. I was tired of being frustrated and there was one problem I could easily solve with a little backup. Pulling up an empty text, I added Paige, Kay, and Janie's contact information to the 'to' line.

Me: Anybody available for dinner tonight?

I set my phone down and tried to refocus on the numbers dancing across my screen. A series of dings had me reaching for my phone.

Paige: Sure! I'm free after 5:30.
Janie: I'm down! What were you thinking?

Kay: Boo, you whores, I am booked solid tonight. Don't have too much fun without me.

Paige: You get to look at Harrison all night so don't expect me to feel bad for you.

Janie: We are accepting stealth photos though. Either end will do. Back and front both work for my spank bank ;o)

Paige: I'm super weirded out by the spank bank part, not gonna lie, butttt if you want to send pictures.....

Kay: I love you perverts but no.

I gagged. I didn't want to hear about Harrison as an object of sexual attraction, and I absolutely did not want to hear about Janie's spank bank reserve. My fingers flew across the screen.

Me: OMG STOP BEFORE I VOMIT.

Me: How about Fusion at 6:30? Does that give you enough time after class, Paige?

Paige: Yep! It's a date.

Janie: Can I ride with you, boo?

Me: As long as you promise not to say the words spank bank ever again.

Janie: No promises. I know where you park your car so I'm not even worried about it.

Me: Stalker.

Paige: Creep.

Kay: You guys are weird.

I smiled and set my phone back on my desk, flipping it over so the screen wasn't visible. The last thing I needed was for a coworker to accidentally get an eyeful of an unsolicited penis. I smiled to myself. I might not be excelling at the dating portion of my life, but I had made a pretty great group of friends.

I tried—really, really tried—to focus on work the rest of the day. I did. But less than an hour later, I found myself typing 'Sebastian Kincaid' into the search bar and anxiously waiting for the results to load. Picture after picture appeared at the top of the page, followed by videos of him on the field. I clicked on a few of the pictures even though I already knew what he looked like. I felt heat creep up my chest and into my cheeks as I took in the picture of him running toward the ball, face serious, as if all his concentration was focused on the ball just out of his reach. His elbow was raised to fend off an opposing player; the motion had twisted his body so that his damp uniform was pulled tightly across his chest, revealing pectoral muscles that had me panting. Every muscle was visible in his legs as they moved him toward his goal. I fanned myself and took a gulp from my water bottle.

"You're worse than Janie," I mumbled. Seeing Sebastian in street clothes was an experience, but seeing him on the soccer field... Holy. Freaking. Crap.

For the sake of my cardiovascular system, I decided to move on to the news links listed below the pictures and videos. The first article that caught my eye was titled "Why Sebastian Kincaid Is a Legend." I clicked on the link and started reading. One paragraph in particular grabbed my attention:

The Man Utd. star might not be the first choice for a football ambassador, considering his bad boy reputation both on and off the field, but he's about to fulfill the role of superhero for the sport in America. Is he up to the task? At 33, Kincaid isn't close to slowing down—quite the opposite, in fact. So it comes as a surprise that Man Utd. would be willing to part with its star midfielder and team captain. Rumors of contract negotiations have been going on for months now, and no one doubted that Man Utd. would do whatever it took to keep Kincaid in Manchester. It came as a complete shock when FIFA announced that Kincaid would be among the players traded with the MLS to help raise the game's profile in America. Kincaid was without question the best player to be involved in the trade on either side of the pond. The MLS sent ten of its own players to the Premier League...

I read several more articles, all claiming he was one of the best soccer players ever, and stored away all the facts I was learning. Why? I had no logical explanation. I told myself that I just didn't understand him. His behavior was confusing, and I didn't like not understanding things. After I found a way to get my issue of *The Watchmen* back, I didn't see any reason for further interaction with him. But a not-so-insignificant part of me knew I was full of it. That part of me knew I was a big old liar, and also knew that, for some unexplained reason, not seeing him again would be... disappointing.

A series of dings from my phone forced me to reluctantly pause my research.

Unknown: I can't tell if this Ozymandias character is good guy or a bad guy? Seems like a bit of a prat. Thoughts?

My brow furrowed in confusion as I read the messages.

Unknown: The guy at the comic book store was no help. I'm on Issue 2. The jury's still out.

Unknown: This is Sebastian by the way. Paige gave me your number, hope you don't mind.

My head whipped up and I glanced around my office. It was like he knew I was stalking him on the internet and caught me red-handed. I cautiously opened my desk drawer and deposited my phone on top of the folders before shutting it. I scolded myself for being so ridiculous, but made no move to retrieve my phone. I closed the browser filled with information about Sebastian Kincaid and returned to work, reassuring myself that answers were just a few hours away.

11.

Janie and I found Paige waiting for us, already sipping on a glass of wine. She waved when she saw us coming, a wide smile in place.

"Hey ladies!" she greeted us. "This was such a good idea, Lennon."

"Thanks." I returned her smile, sliding into one of the open chairs and picking up a menu. "I thought sushi would be a good choice since there are vegan options, and I know we all like it."

Paige laughed, reaching for her glass of wine. "I meant it was a good idea for us all to get dinner, but the sushi was a good call too."

I blushed, a little embarrassed that I had misunderstood her statement. The waitress came by and took our drink orders, and we spent the next couple of minutes debating what to order. After our wine was delivered and we had placed our orders, I decided it was time to get down to business.

I took a gulp of wine for courage and cleared my throat. "So, I actually invited you guys to dinner because I need help."

Paige's and Janie's smiles instantly dropped. Both women set their glasses down and gave me their full attention.

"What's going on, Lennon?" Janie's voice was filled with concern.

"Well, you know I'm not the best with... people. And I'm having a problem with one. A person, I mean." I sighed, frustrated with myself for not being able to articulate the Sebastian situation. "Sebastian showed up at Spout last night, and he sat at my table."

"Whoa, plot twist." Janie's eyebrows shot up. "What was he doing there?"

I shrugged. "I don't know. He asked me a couple questions and I got nervous. I kind of just grabbed my stuff and ran out. I may also have yelled goodbye at him. Loudly."

Paige visibly cringed. "God, Lennon, I'm so sorry. I keep trying to help, but I just make everything worse. I told him to look for you at Spout. It was just a guess, but it wasn't a yoga night and you weren't home, so I figured there was a pretty good chance you were there. He told me he wanted to apologize for being such a jerk. I thought it would be better if I didn't warn you he might show up; that way you wouldn't have time to worry about it or leave. Do you hate me?"

I reached across the table and squeezed her hand. "Of course I don't hate you! I actually thought you probably told him where to find me. He wanted to apologize?"

"He did," Paige confirmed, nodding her head. "He showed up at one of my yoga classes, and I was about to smack him with a rolled-up mat until he explained why he was there. He seemed really sorry, so I told him where to look for you. You deserved an apology from him, too."

"I guess we can cancel Operation Ride or Die," Janie grumbled, taking a drink of her wine.

"Operation Ride or Die?" Paige asked.

"Don't ask," I warned her. "But also, it would probably be a good idea not to make Janie mad. Thank you for clearing this up for me, Paige. I couldn't stop thinking about him. Now I can text him back and let him know it's fine."

Janie and Paige both stared. Paige opened and closed her mouth a couple of times like she wanted to say something but couldn't find the words.

"I don't know where to start with all that," she finally managed.

"I do!" Janie exclaimed. "What do you mean, text him *back*?

Have you two been texting?"

I shook my head. "No, he's been texting me."

I reached into my purse and pulled out my phone. I pulled up the text thread—which now read *Sebastian* instead of *Unknown*—and handed my phone to Janie. She scrolled through the unanswered messages before passing my phone to Paige.

"Why didn't you answer him back? And who is Ozymandias?" Paige asked, sliding the phone back to me.

"I didn't understand why he was being nice to me all of a sudden. I wasn't sure how to respond." I shrugged. "I thought it would be a good idea to get your opinions before I did anything. Now I can text him back and stop thinking about him."

I tapped out a reply and hit 'send,' confident this text would be the end of the entire situation. No more talking to Sebastian. No more internet-stalking Sebastian. No more thinking about Sebastian. No more wondering what Sebastian looked like without a shirt. I nodded my head and took another big drink of wine, suddenly a little less confident in my plan.

Janie grabbed my phone, pulled up the text I had just sent, and read it out loud.

"Hello Sebastian. Paige said you wanted to apologize for Saturday when you came to Spout last night. Obviously, I left before you had the chance to get around to the apology part. I just wanted to let you know that you don't have to feel bad. If you are feeling bad, that is, which I suppose is a prerequisite for a genuine apology. Anyway, apology accepted. You don't need to worry about talking to me anymore. Ozymandias is a critical examination of superheroes. Kind of like Thanos in the new Marvel movies. I hope you enjoy The Watchmen. You can return my copy to Paige when you're done with it. Good luck with your soccer!"

"Good luck with your soccer?" Janie repeated, and then again louder. "Good *luck* with your *soccer*?"

Paige covered her face with her hands and groaned, then huffed out a breath. "Okay, well, that was... it was... gosh. What was it?"

"Was it bad? I don't understand. I accepted his apology so

he doesn't have to feel guilty anymore. I answered his question, and I wished him luck with his career. I even used an exclamation point to clearly indicate enthusiasm, because it's difficult to properly communicate tone through text. Those are all good things," I pointed out defensively.

Our waitress interrupted. "Can I get you ladies another drink while you're waiting? Your entrees should be out in a little bit."

We all ordered another glass of wine. Apparently, I wasn't the only one who felt like she needed reinforcements for the rest of this conversation.

Paige turned her attention back to me. "Okay, so, *technically* that response was fine. You covered all the topics. It just sounded maybe a little... final? Like you were foreclosing the idea of friendship?"

"Exactly!" Paige chimed in. "I think he might have been trying to be friends with you. It seems like he went out of his way to get those comic books and talk to you about them."

I scrunched up my nose in thought. "No, I don't think that can be right. He was just feeling guilty. Apologizing makes the most sense."

"Being friends with you also makes sense," Paige insisted, leaning back to allow the waitress to place her drink on the table. "Thank you."

"Why would he want to be friends with me?" I asked, genuinely confused by the idea. "We don't have anything in common. He's an international soccer star, 'soccer's bad boy on and off the field.' I'm a nerd with poor social skills who falls up the stairs at least twice a week." I took a gulp of wine, ignoring the voice warning me to pace myself. I cringed a little as the alcohol burned a path down my throat.

Janie nodded her head. "It's true. You went down like the *Titanic* the other day. That being said, there's nothing wrong with being a nerd, thank you very much."

"I'm not saying there's anything wrong with being a nerd! I like who I am, mostly. I just mean that there's no reason Sebastian would think, 'Hey, I should be friends with this girl who has fled from my presence in a horribly awkward manner both times we have occupied the same space.'" I held up a finger, indicating I was about to make a point and also that I was starting to feel the effects of the wine. Where was that sushi? "Plus, he's a chick magnet. Paige, you saw what happened at the club. And, I mean, he looks really good in that soccer uniform. His legs have a lot of muscles, and you can see, like, *all* of them in those shorts."

"We don't have a lot in common on paper, but you are basically my BFF. Wait a minute." Paige waggled a finger around near my face. "You seem to know a lot about Sebastian all of a sudden. Did you do some internet stalking, missy?"

"No!" My flaming cheeks gave away the lie. "I did some light research on a problem. I can't help it that the articles had pictures."

Janie dug around in her bag for her phone. "Well, now I feel like I have to check him out."

I tried to swat the phone out of her hand, but her ninja skills were too good.

"I am feeling so much better about my matchmaking skills now. I knew you two would hit it off." Paige smiled smugly, taking a sip of wine. "I just need to work on the actual set-up."

"Wowza." Janie flipped her phone toward us so we could see her screen. "I can see all the muscles in his abdomen. *All. Of. Them.* You weren't lying about the muscles. Paige, feel free to set me up whenever you want."

"What about Greg?" I asked, reminding her of the guy she'd been casually seeing for the last year.

"Greg, Schmeg, have you *seen* this guy? I can't believe I almost had to murder him," Janie answered, eyes still glued to her phone screen.

"I'm sorry, did you just say you were going to have to murder him?" Paige asked, looking appropriately concerned.

Janie just shrugged, still swiping through pictures. "Don't worry about it."

"Can we go back to the part about your matchmaking skills? I feel the need to point out that you were not right in this instance. Are you just going to ignore the whole club disaster?" I asked just as the waitress delivered our sushi rolls.

Paige pointed at me with her chopsticks. "I wasn't wrong. I knew Sebastian was going to be a great first blind date for you. His outgoing personality is a great match for your shyness."

"Paige, Sebastian is not a starter blind date! That's like... like giving a student driver a Ferrari to practice with. You don't do that," I huffed, picking up my own chopsticks. "You give them a beat-up old Corolla, so they can ease into it without pressure. That way if they back into a light pole, it's no big deal. What's another dent?"

"Hey!" Janie said, mouth half full. "Don't talk about my friend that way! You're at least a BMW."

I gave up trying to convince them that Sebastian was probably somewhere across town feeling relieved that I'd let him off the hook, and attempted to steer the conversation toward more neutral territory. I had done the right thing, and I got to have dinner with two of my favorite people even if they were slightly delusional. All was right in my world again. I promised myself I wouldn't give Sebastian another thought, and I almost believed it.

12.

The next morning, I woke up slightly flustered after a very, very vivid dream about non-soccer related activities Sebastian probably excelled at that left me way too worked up to go back to sleep. Making things worse, I had three text messages from Sebastian waiting for me.

Sebastian: Thanks for accepting my genuine apology.

Sebastian: I'm feeling a little cheated though. I had a whole thing prepared. I think I'm going to have to demand a redo. Get dinner with me tonight so I can give you a proper apology.

Sebastian: I just realized how late it is. You're probably asleep already. Have a good Friday and good luck with your science!

I hated that I had a stupid smile on my face the entire time I read his messages. I hated that I was still thinking about those messages hours later. I hated that I was thinking about him at all after I promised myself I wouldn't. And I hated how long it took me to send him a simple response—which I wished I could unsend as soon as I sent it.

Me: Thanks for the invitation but I have plans tonight.

Did I have plans? Absolutely not. Was I emotionally and spiritually prepared for another encounter with Sebastian? God no. Honestly, I thought I might never be able to look him in the eyes again after that dream. My brain was literally exhausted from thinking itself in circles by the time I wandered into Bad Wolf.

Kay smiled at me from behind the desk. "Hey girl, you're

looking a little rough around the edges today. Did you all get carried away last night? I'm super bummed I missed it. We're totally scheduling a girls' night soon."

"I probably had too much wine, but I didn't sleep well. I'm exhausted." I slumped into the seat she had vacated for me.

Her next customer walked in before she could ask the follow-up question she clearly had planned. I got her customer all checked in and turned my attention to the list of supplies Harrison wanted me to order.

"I think Grandpa is gambling again," Harrison stated without preamble. I glanced up to see him leaning over the desk. His casual posture belied the serious look on his face. I turned my attention back to the screen, swallowing down my nerves.

"Oh really? Hmm. Why is that?" I asked, careful to keep my voice neutral and my posture relaxed.

I watched Harrison walk around the desk out of the corner of my eye and silently pleaded with myself to be cool as he swiveled my chair around so I was forced to look at him.

"Lennon, you wouldn't happen to know anything about an illegal gambling operation at the senior center, would you?" His gaze bored through me as if he could actually locate the answers in my brain. *Don't be a snitch, don't be a snitch, don't be a snitch* played on a loop ready for him to discover.

I felt beads of sweat break out across my forehead under his intense scrutiny. I shook my head slowly. "Nope. I don't know anything about an illegal gambling ring."

I forced myself to meet his eyes and gave him what I hoped was a convincing smile. My answer was not technically a lie. I didn't actually know anything about the gambling ring specifically. He scrutinized me for what felt like another ten minutes, but was probably mere seconds, before he released the armrests and straightened.

He crossed his arms and gave me a nod. "Fine. But if the old man calls asking for odds on a game, I hope you'll remind him that he is one bust away from a lifetime ban at the senior center."

I gulped.

"Yeah, of course. No bets."

Harrison the Inquisitor was not done just yet. "You look like shit. What's going on with you?"

"Gee, thanks, Harrison." I rolled my eyes, spinning away from him to face the computer. "Pro-tip: Girls do not like it when you point out how bad they look."

He grunted. "Yeah, don't really need help with women."

I gagged dramatically. "Spare me the details."

"What's going on? Are you feeling okay? Have you been skipping meals?" Harrison walked around the desk so we were facing each other again.

"No, Harrison," I sighed. "When have you ever known me to skip a meal? I didn't sleep well, that's all. Don't worry, though; I plan on sleeping until at least noon tomorrow."

"All right." His voice was laced with skepticism but he let it drop. "Did you eat yet? We're ordering from Frank's."

"Yes! I'll have my usual. Oh! With an extra pickle. And the homemade chips." My mouth was watering just thinking of all that grease. "Make that extra chips."

"How about fruit salad instead of the chips?" Father Harrison asked.

"How about no?"

"I like a woman who knows what she wants," Lou said, emerging from his station. "Wow, Lennon—you might actually want to eat some fruit. You have a very *Dawn of the Dead* look happening right now."

"This place is really doing wonders for my self-esteem," I joked, trying not to smile back at Lou but failing. "Remind me why I come here?"

"For the eye candy, obviously," Lou answered, sweeping his hand from the top of his head downward.

"Yep, that must be it." I rolled my eyes playfully, shooting a smile at the group of girls who were walking through the door.

The shop got busy, saving me from any more questions from anyone, and I managed to eat my sandwich in between checking people in and out and scheduling appointments. A series of dings from my phone distracted me from the phone call I was currently on.

"Harrison's next appointment for a touch-up would be on... Sorry, on the twenty-fourth at six thirty. Would that work?"

Ding. Ding. I eyed my phone suspiciously, like it might turn into a tarantula at any moment. I vaguely registered the voice on the phone agreeing to that time.

"Great. I'll get you all scheduled." I said goodbye and hung up, still staring at my phone. I shook my head in disbelief. Since when had I been scared of a text message?

Since Sebastian Kincaid.

"God, I am absolutely starving!" I jumped in my seat at the sound of Kay's voice. "Whoa, sorry, Lennon. I didn't mean to scare you."

She sat on the couch across from the desk and pulled her sandwich out of a grease-stained bag. "Come to mama, you beautiful sandwich. What were you thinking about?"

I scrunched my nose. "Sebastian Kincaid."

"Who?" Kay asked before taking a large bite of the sandwich.

I gave her a brief rundown of all the Sebastian happenings, from the blind date disaster to last night's texts.

"And this guy plays professional soccer?" I nodded at her question. "Huh. Never heard of him."

"Who plays professional soccer?" Aaron asked, taking a seat next to Kay on the couch. He pulled his sandwich out of the bag and started trying to peel back the wax paper that was grease-glued to the bread.

"The guy Lennon went on a date with last week. Sebastian Kincaid," Kay answered for me.

Aaron's eyes widened and his hands stopped trying to fight the wrapper. "Did you just say Sebastian Kincaid? As in former Manchester United star and current captain of the Novas?"

"Yes," I confirmed hesitantly, a little nervous about the crazy look on his face. "But we did *not* go out a date."

"Holy shit. Holy shit! I can't believe you met Sebastian Kincaid, Lennon! Did you tell him about me? Of course you didn't. Did you get his autograph? Holy shit." Aaron looked like he might be on the verge of losing it. He ran his hands over his close-cropped hair. His sandwich sat forgotten in his lap.

"Quit fanboying. It's embarrassing and he was an ass." Kay swatted Aaron's arm. "I didn't even know you liked soccer."

"That's the dumbest shit you've ever said to me! Do I like soccer? Look at me. I'm Mexican! You know any Mexicans who don't like soccer?" Aaron was shaking his head in disbelief.

"Bro, that's racist," Lou stated, squeezing in between Kay and Aaron.

"It's not racist if it's true." Aaron shot Lou a mean side eye. "Plus, I can't be racist about myself. Dude, there are other places to sit."

"What are we talking about?" Lou ignored Aaron. "Are you going to eat that?"

Aaron picked up his sandwich and took a huge bite, smiling at Lou as he chewed.

"Lennon went on a date with Sebastian Kincaid and now Aaron is turning into a thirteen-year-old girl." Kay filled Lou in on the last five minutes, leaving out almost all the important details.

"We didn't go on a date," I pointed out again, even though the three of them were clearly not listening to me at all. "And he apologized for being a jerk."

My attention drifted back to my phone while they continued to argue on the couch. I traced the edges with my finger, trying to work up the courage to look at the messages I knew were waiting for me.

"Oh, this is just ridiculous," I muttered, finally flipping over my phone. My lips curved into a smile without my consent when I saw the name on the screen.

Sebastian: What are you up tonight?

Sebastian: I let some mates talk me into going to a club because someone had plans. It's weirdly dark and very loud. I had to use the flashlight on my phone to find my way back to the table.

Sebastian: I'm sitting in a club wishing I was back at my place reading The Watchmen instead. You're a bad influence.

Normally, I found it extremely irritating when someone sent multiple text messages to express something that could easily have been said in one message, but for some reason, I found Sebastian's use of excessive messages endearing. What was happening to me? I decided to be an adult about this. I would simply ignore the problem until it went away. Nodding my head to reaffirm my decision, I opened a drawer and deposited my phone in it before sliding it shut. Out of sight, out of mind.

13.

True to my word, I slept until noon the next day. I still managed to make it to Paige's yoga class and to the laundromat. I even went back to the little boutique I'd loved when Paige and I had gone shopping, and picked out some more dresses. I barely checked my phone the entire time—only every thirty seconds or so. But I wasn't hoping that Sebastian's name would appear on my screen with another string of rambling messages. Nope, not at all.

When I got home, I slipped out of my "doing actual yoga" yoga pants and into my "just lounging" yoga pants. My favorite pair was so worn that the fabric was slightly transparent and there was a small hole just above the right knee. I pulled on a large grey T-shirt that Harrison had lovingly dubbed my invisibility cloak. It reached almost to the hole in my leggings. I had no one to impress except Jason, my faithful food delivery boy, and he didn't care what I looked like as long as I tipped him well.

I curled up on the couch, fully prepared to catch up on my *Game of Thrones*, but found myself clicking on a Netflix original teen romantic comedy instead. An hour later, I was cheering on Lara Jean and feeling all the teen-angst feels. I also felt hungry. I paused the movie and headed to my trusty drawer of takeout menus. I dug through the pile of bent and crumpled paper until I found General Chang's menu. I was dangerously close to having the menu memorized, but sometimes liked to pretend that Chinese takeout was a new experience. I couldn't decide what I wanted, so I ordered a little bit of everything. I loved cold Chinese food so eating leftovers was a bonus. Not that there usually *were* leftovers.

My first movie ended and Netflix recommended another teen romantic comedy for me. At some point, I started to have thoughts that were not entirely rational about high schoolers finding their soul mates at the same age I'd been rebuilding alternators with my grandpa in our garage. What if my soulmate had been out there waiting for me while I was passing Grandpa tools? What did it mean that these kids met their great love in high school, and I was twenty-six, living alone and ordering enough Chinese for a family of four?

I rolled over to grab my laptop. I opened a new tab and started searching for cat rescues. Clearly I was destined for a future as a crazy cat lady, so why not finally embrace my destiny? I clicked on Cat Cottage, because I was all about alliteration.

"Aww," I cooed, looking at the glamour shots of available cats. Each cat had its own little profile next to a small collection of adorable, professional-looking pictures. I started clicking on profiles, determined to find my new roommate. A knock at my door forced me to get off the couch for the first time in too many hours.

"Hey, Lennon, how's it going?" Jason asked, handing me two bags packed with food containers.

"Oh, you know, another wild Saturday night." I took the food and handed him a tip. I always gave him a great tip in hopes of keeping the judgment down. I ordered way too much food, way too often, for one person, and I almost always answered the door looking like... well... like I did right now.

"Yeah, looks like it's about to get crazy in here." His eyes scanned my outfit. Jason also had a great sense of humor. I looked forward to our weekly chats. Not.

"Have a good night!" I said, shutting the door and taking my loot to the kitchen. I spread everything out on the counter, then dug around in the cavernous bags looking for the missing egg roll.

A knock at the door interrupted my digging. I smiled and opened the door, fully expecting to find Jason returning with my missing appetizer. Instead, I found a smiling Sebastian Kincaid. My eyes widened to the point that it was almost painful, and my heart attempted to jump out of my chest. I gasped and immediately slammed the door in his no-longer-smiling face.

"Shoot, shoot, shoot. You're not egg rolls. What do I do?" I banged my head against the door lightly, panic and embarrassment racing through me.

I heard a very masculine chuckle coming from the other side of the door. "Are you asking for my opinion? I would start with opening the door and letting me in," Sebastian answered, his voice light with obvious humor.

I took a steadying breath and opened the door. Chewing on my lip, I took in the man leaning casually against my door frame, hands tucked into a pair of jeans that molded artfully to sculpted thighs. I gulped before letting my eyes travel up past a narrow waist to take in the black fabric of a T-shirt stretched across wide shoulders.

"I get the feeling you're trying to avoid me," he said, the smile still in his voice. My gaze darted briefly upward to meet his startling blue-green eyes before settling on a spot just over his shoulder.

"Wh-why do you think that?" I stumbled over my own words, heat flooding my face. He arched one oddly attractive eyebrow skeptically. "I've just been busy with... things. Work! Yep, work. I've been busy with work."

I leaned up against the door trying to mirror his causal pose. I neglected to take into account the fact that he was leaning against a solid, unmoving wall, whereas I was leaning against a partially open door—a door that was now opening rapidly beneath my weight, sending me tumbling after it. I frantically tried to right myself, but somehow the toes of my right foot managed to get trapped under the heel of my left. Foiled by gravity again.

In a move showcasing an athletic grace that was completely

foreign to me, Sebastian grabbed my arm while his other hand stopped the door from slamming into the wall. The warmth of his hand on my arm did nothing to help me regain my balance. I blinked up at him, more stunned by the contact than by the fact that I had almost plummeted to the ground.

"You okay?" he asked, looking down at me. The tiny wrinkles in the corners of his eyes told me that he was amused even though he was clearly working not to let it show.

I nodded. My brain was screaming at me to end yet another slightly humiliating encounter, but my stupid mouth had a mind of its own. "Did you... um... did you want to come in?"

This time his entire face lit up with a grin that hit me like a punch to the gut. "I thought you'd never ask."

He breezed into my shoebox of an apartment like he owned the place, head swiveling to take it all in. I cringed the moment his gaze landed on the smorgasbord of Chinese food spread out on my counter.

"Am I interrupting?" he asked, sounding a little sheepish.

"Interrupting?" I parroted back, because my brain cells were still tangled up with my feet.

He inclined his head in the general direction of the food. "Are you expecting company?"

I finally shut the door and walked to the counter. I proceed to shuffle the containers around like it was my life's work.

"Oh no, this is all for me. I was really hungry when I ordered, so everything on the menu sounded good. I couldn't decide what to get." I shrugged. "I thought I would just get a bunch of stuff and have a little of everything."

Sebastian was watching me with a thoughtful expression. "Good idea."

I shrugged again. "This happens a lot."

I dared a peek at him, watching as he made his way to my side. I reminded myself to breathe as I felt the heat from his body invade my space.

"Does it?" He picked up an open container of lo mein and peered inside. "It's been ages since I've had Chinese food. I try to stay away from the stuff, but this smells amazing."

"Do you want some?" I asked, not wanting to deprive this poor man of the chance to enjoy fried, MSG-coated heaven.

He looked genuinely conflicted for a minute before he gave me a smile that made me momentarily forget my own name. "Yeah, I was going to see if you wanted to grab dinner, but this looks too good. I'll put in a few extra miles tomorrow."

A few extra miles? A few extra miles? Who said things like that? Professional athletes, that's who. Sebastian was a professional athlete who probably treated his body like a temple, while I pretty much treated my body like the garbage can Oscar the Grouch lived in. I added that to the growing list of things we did not have in common.

Wordlessly I opened a cabinet and handed him an IKEA plate before grabbing one for myself. I scooped forks and spoons out of a drawer and set them on the counter. All the while, I silently chanted "This is fine, be normal." I honestly had no idea what I was heaping onto my plate. I was just blindly piling until every inch of white was covered by food.

"I usually just eat on the couch," I said, feeling little tendrils of shame wrapping around me at the admission. "There's not really room for a table."

"Couch is perfect. I rarely sit at my table to eat. It feels weird sitting alone at a big table, you know?" He cocked his head to the side thoughtfully. "I don't know if I've ever eaten a meal at that table."

I made my way to the couch and settled as far as possible away from the other occupant. I did my best to look like this was all a perfectly normal situation but was basically doing a great impression of a statue, "Nervous Girl with a Plate." Sebastian was clearly not having the same issue. He was shoveling forkfuls of food into his mouth at a rate that was both alarming and impressive.

"What are you watching?" he asked, nodding his head at the TV.

I stopped pushing the Mongolian beef around on my plate to

stare at the TV in horror. Red crept up from my chest and spread through my face.

I swallowed. "Erm… just something Netflix recommended. I'm not that attached, though, if you want to watch something else."

Two things occurred to me almost simultaneously. First, I had just admitted that Netflix recommended I watch a teen romance based on my previous viewing choices. Not awesome. Second, I'd just invited Sebastian to hang out for longer than it would take to finish the mound of food he was inhaling. *Very* not awesome.

"I don't mind if you want to keep watching it. I can appreciate a good rom-com. Just catch me up," he said around a mouthful. He must have misinterpreted the look of horror on my face because he added, "Two sisters. I was outnumbered."

I grabbed the remote and switched back to the home screen. "Really, I don't mind. I'm always looking for new recommendations anyway."

"Have you watched any *Stranger Things*? I'm trying to binge-watch it." He shot me a guilty smile that kind of made me feel like vomiting. This man had a pretty devastating effect on my internal organs.

I shook my head. "I haven't seen it yet. I keep meaning to watch it. What do you mean by 'trying' to binge-watch it?"

"It's hard to do a proper binge during the season with practices and games and all that."

My brain caught on the word 'proper' and the way his accent was nothing like Colin Firth's but was somehow impossibly hotter. Mr. Darcy was swoon-worthy, but not "my panties spontaneously burst into flames every time you open your mouth"-worthy. Sebastian's accent definitely fell into the second category.

"Let's start over. You need to get the whole experience."

"Are you sure? I don't want to slow you down," I asked, still unconvinced.

"I'm sure. You introduced me to arguably the best graphic

novel ever made, so I owe you one." He smiled, settling further into the couch, like he planned to stay for a while.

I turned my attention away from the mystery seated on my couch and tried to watch the show. It was actually pretty good, though I think I would have enjoyed it a lot more if I hadn't been a gigantic ball of nerves. Instead, my attention was divided between the thoughts racing through my head and the Chinese food I was storing in my cheeks like a demented chipmunk because I was too occupied by said thoughts to chew and swallow. It was asking too much of even my exceptional brain to perform all those tasks at once.

My laptop lit up with an incoming email and I saw Sebastian's eyes flick to the screen, which prominently displayed an entire screen filled with cat glamour shots. One of those perfect eyebrows raised in question.

"What's all this?"

I frantically tried to chew all the food crammed into my mouth. "Wut? Dis? Uh, is cats?"

If it were possible to die from embarrassment, I would be the deadest of dead. I prayed I would choke on a piece of beef and be put out of my misery.

"I can see that, but why are you looking at..." He leaned forward to see the screen better. "Cat Cottage's website?"

I swallowed the last bit of food and cleared my throat. "I was thinking about adopting a cat."

Or twelve. But I thought I would leave out the part about starting my crazy cat lady future by adopting all the cats I could reasonably fit inside my apartment. I mentally added lint roller to the list of things I'd need to purchase before I picked them up.

"A cat, huh? I'm more of a dog person but adopting is great. Any contenders?" He turned to look at me with a serious expression on his face that was completely disproportionate to the situation.

I shrugged, tearing my eyes from his to look at the screen. "Not really. I think you have to meet them in person. Feel each other out, you know? I want to make sure our personalities are a good match. I don't really know a lot about cats, but a cat seemed like the best pet for my lifestyle right now. Cats are very independent. I mean, I would love a dog, but I don't have a lot of space and going up and down the stairs every time it has to go to the bathroom would be rough. I don't like stairs."

Somewhere an alarm was going off in my head alerting me that this was way too much information in response to a simple question, but Sebastian didn't seem the least bit bothered by it. He listened intently, his serious expression turning into a softer one.

"I would love a dog too, but I'm gone way too much to get one. It wouldn't be fair. I really wanted one as a kid, but my parents were too busy. Always thought they were full of it, but I get it now."

I gave him a smile and small head shake, which seemed to be enough to satisfy him. By some unspoken agreement, we both turned our attention back to the show. Well, I turned half my attention back to the show. The other half was busy trying to steal glances at Sebastian.

One and a half episodes later, my back was aching from sitting so straight for sixty-seven continuous minutes, and my eye muscles were begging me to pick one object to focus on at a time. Sebastian was not suffering from the same level of discomfort. He had gone back for two more helpings of food before placing his dishes in the dishwasher and was currently sprawled on my couch. His arm was stretched across the back of it, bringing his fingers inches away from my shoulder. Did I miss half of what was happening with the Upside Down? Yes. Did I miss a single twitch of those long, strangely attractive fingers? Nope.

My spine breathed a sigh of relief when Sebastian finally stood up and stretched. I carefully avoided looking at him until the hem of his shirt was safely reunited with the waistline of his pants. I really didn't think my fried nerves could handle seeing even a tiny fraction of his abdomen. I was already feeling lightheaded from pretty much skipping dinner. The few bites of food I had squirreled down hadn't done much to curb my hunger, and

Sebastian's presence in my apartment presented a choking hazard too great to risk another attempt.

Sebastian eyed the door. "I should get going." He sounded almost reluctant. I stood up and followed him to the door.

"Well…" I started, suddenly unsure about the goodbye protocol. I made the mistake of looking directly into his eyes. I swallowed. "Thanks for stopping by and eating me… er… eating with me. And introducing me to *Chinese Things*. I mean *Stranger Things*, to *Stranger Things*."

I blinked slowly hoping he would be gone by the time I opened my eyes. When he was still standing there with his hands in his pockets and a half grin painting his disconcertingly handsome face, I considered opening the door and shoving him out.

"Thanks for letting me stay, even though I wasn't egg rolls," he responded, his voice sounding a little tired.

I watched, filled with panic, as he slowly withdrew his hands from his pockets like we were meeting at the O.K. Corral at high noon for a shootout, but instead of guns, there might be hugs or a peck on the cheek. Either of those options could prove to be just as fatal as a gunshot wound. I did the only thing possible in the situation: I stuck out my hand for a good old-fashioned handshake. Sebastian looked momentarily stunned before he slid his hand into mine. My hand was enveloped in his much larger one and he gave it a gentle squeeze, sending warmth up my arm and throughout my body, before he released it.

"Goodnight, Lennon."

"Goodnight, Sebastian," I replied, opening the door for him.

He gave me one more smile as he stepped into the hallway. I shut the door behind him, wondering if I had accidentally wandered into the Upside Down.

14.

Two weeks after Chinagate, I was developing a weird form of Stockholm syndrome. Sebastian was finishing up an "away series," which meant I hadn't seen him since we shared dinner on my couch. However, he was still texting me. Every day. Every. Single. Day. I still couldn't understand what his motivation was, but I had to get him credit for his persistence. The real problem was that I looked forward to getting those messages now. The first thing I did in the morning was look for a message, and I found myself checking my phone with obscene frequency just in case I'd missed the ding. And then, every time my phone did ding, my poor, confused heart would race with anticipation. It was like Pavlov's dogs. If he didn't send me a text until later in the day, I would find myself starting to make excuses for him—he was three hours behind my time where he was at, or he must have an early practice, or maybe he broke both hands wrestling a bear. All totally reasonable possibilities.

Our messages weren't anything life-altering really. He would ask me how my day was going or send me a picture of something random he'd found. One time he sent me a picture of him reading *The Watchmen* in a hotel room. I may have smiled like a lunatic when I opened that message. I wasn't proud of that fact, but there it was. The first day he was gone I asked him a question about soccer, so he made sure to send me a rule of the game or a soccer fact every day. For example, in every other country, soccer is actually football and the field is called the pitch.

I decided that instead of spending the entire weekend staring at my phone I would head over to Cat Cottage to officially start my cat collection. My trunk was jam-packed with all the essentials: food, dishes, litter box, toys, a little palace thing. I was ready to adopt!

Walking into the rescue felt like I was walking into a preview of my future. Cats filled the small space. They came out of corners, over counters, and onto chairs. It would have been like a scene out of a horror movie if it were anywhere else but a cat shelter. Okay, it was still kind of creepy.

"Hi there, welcome to Cat Cottage! What can I help you with today?" a lady asked, rounding a corner with a disgruntled feline yowling in her hands. "All right, there you go, Felix."

She released the cat onto a chair in the waiting room and he proceeded to immediately jump off the chair and run behind the counter.

"Hello. I'm interested in adopting," I responded almost at a yell, trying to make myself heard over all the meowing.

"Wonderful! Have you ever adopted with Cat Cottage before?" She sounded genuinely excited as she walked to the computer behind the counter where Felix had fled moments earlier.

"No. I've never owned a cat actually. This will be my first cat. But don't worry, I've done a lot of research into feline care, and I've purchased everything I should need for him. Or her."

"I'm so glad you've decided to adopt. It's a wonderful option, a fresh start for you both! I'm Helen, by the way. I'll go through the adoption process once we've found a good match for you," Helen said, her voice still vibrating with enthusiasm. "Now, did you have any idea what kind of cat you were interested in adding to your family?"

I didn't think she was looking for "a live one," so I wasn't really sure how to respond. Helen must have seen the confusion on my face, because she took mercy on me in the form of several follow-up questions.

"Was there a particular breed you are interested in? Male or female?"

I shook my head. "No, I'm not looking for anything specific. I'm more interested in personality than breed or sex."

"Okay, I can work with that. What is the most important personality trait to you?" She asked, removing a small black cat from the keyboard.

"Ideally, a friendly cat who is a good balance between independent and affectionate." I answered confidently. I had given the subject a lot of thought. I sometimes worked long hours so having an independent streak was important, but I also wanted a cat who cared if I was still breathing and maybe wanted a good snuggle every once in a while.

Helen hmmed thoughtfully. "I have a couple cats in mind. Why don't we put you in one of our meet-and-greet rooms? I'll bring you in some of the contenders and you can get to know each other."

I followed Helen down the hall until we came to a stop outside a windowed room. Helen opened the door and flipped on the light.

"Here we are." She gestured for me to step into the room. "Now, the door doesn't lock but we keep it shut when we're doing the interviews so no one escapes. If you want to make yourself comfortable in here, I'll go round up the cats."

I stood in the middle of the room and took in my surroundings. There was an armchair in one corner of the room and a small box overflowing with a variety of cat toys. A cat climbing contraption was stationed in the corner diagonally across the room. I didn't really know what to do with myself, so I took a seat in the chair to wait. My right leg bounced nervously. Why I was nervous to meet cats was beyond me, but I did feel a bit like I was waiting for a job interview to start.

Over the next forty-five minutes or so, the room slowly filled with cats of every size and color. Some of them were super sweet and playful, while some were shyer and took their time feeling me out. I liked some of them—I liked most of them, really—but something was missing. I didn't know what I was expecting—a spotlight to shine down from the heavens and illuminate the right cat for me?

"How's it going in here?" Helen asked, poking her head into the room.

"Good. They're all really great." I stroked a grey cat who had crawled onto my lap. He was sweet, but not mine. "I don't know how to choose one."

As Helen stepped into the room, an orange blur snuck in behind her and proceeded to leap onto my lap, scaring away the grey cat. I looked down to see the most unfortunate-looking creature I had ever seen staring up at me. Its tail—well, the part still attached—twitched back and forth.

"Boomer!" Helen lunged forward to retrieve the cat, who was now in the process of trying to crawl up the front of my shirt.

"It's fine," I reassured Helen while prying Boomer off my front. I held him at arm's length, taking him in. In addition to half a tail, he was missing part of his left ear and a considerable number of whiskers. Bald spots littered his back. He let loose a throaty meow and attempted to reattach himself to my shirt. "What happened to this guy?'

"We don't know. He's a stray who just kept showing up at our back door. That's how he got his name—Boomer's short for Boomerang. He was in worse shape when we found him, if you can believe it. He's a real character." Helen reached out to take Boomer out of my hands. "Sorry about that. He's always ending up where he isn't supposed to be. He's one of our permanent residents."

"Permanent residents?" I looked at the furry little mess. His eyes locked with mine and he gave another meow.

"Yes. Due to his condition, we don't anticipate that he'll be adopted. He's already been here for almost two years," she answered, trying to contain the cat who was attempting to wriggle out of her grasp.

The heavens might not have opened up, but something inside me screamed that this was my cat. I looked at him one more time, like I was asking for permission. He meowed in what I was going to take as agreement.

"I want to adopt Boomer."

Helen looked momentarily stunned. "Oh! Well... are you sure?"

I nodded confidently. "Positive."

"Okay, all right. Let's just get your application all filled out."

15.

One harrowing car ride later, Boomer was happily exploring his new surroundings, and I was silently thanking Harrison for insisting I get my brakes checked regularly. Turned out Boomer could have his own show in Vegas as a magician. The little minx got out of the carrier and insisted on trying to sit on the steering wheel while I was driving. In the words of my mother, I got "real close to Jesus" on the drive home. Despite the multiple near-death experiences on our drive, I did not regret my choice at all.

I gave Boomer a tour of his new home, then got busy trying to get dinner ready before Sebastian's game started. The Novas were playing in Boston tonight, and even though I didn't fully understand what was happening on the field, I enjoyed watching them play. If I were being completely honest, I enjoyed watching *Sebastian* play. He was so intense on the field that it was almost like watching a stranger in a Sebastian suit. Serious soccer Sebastian, relaxed on the couch Sebastian—all variations of Sebastian were quickly becoming an unhealthy addiction.

My culinary skills were nothing to brag about, but I could make a mean spaghetti. I dumped the frozen broccoli florets into the boiling water and stirred the sauce. I was firmly convinced that adding broccoli to anything made it a well-rounded meal. Kraft macaroni and cheese with broccoli, nutritional and delicious! Ramen with broccoli, easy and packed with vitamins!

I stepped over Boomer, who was sunning himself in the last of the evening sun directly in the middle of the floor, and turned the TV to the station televising the game. I'd been informed by Aaron earlier that hardly any stations had televised American soccer until the player swap thing. Thankfully, I had easily been able to find stations broadcasting the Novas. You know, now that I cared about soccer and all. I turned up the volume waiting for my favorite part of every game.

The camera zoomed in on Sebastian exiting a large bus. He was wearing a tailored black suit that hugged his muscular frame in a way that I was positive meant he hadn't purchased it off a rack at Macy's. Dark sunglasses covered the eyes I knew crinkled at the corners when he smiled, and his hair was styled like he was going to a photoshoot, not to play soccer for ninety or so minutes.

"Good grief, Charlie Brown, that man can wear a suit," I said to Boomer, which was roughly the equivalent of talking to myself since he did not currently appear to be conscious. My mouth was watering, and it was not a result of the pasta cooking in the kitchen. I was staring so intently at the screen—hoping the camera would catch him walking from behind, like the pervert I was turning into—that I almost screamed when the timer went off, sending Boomer twelve feet into the air.

"Sorry, buddy! If you liked human males, you would totally understand what just happened," I explained, moving quickly to turn off the timer. "And for the record, it's totally fine if you're into boy cats. Cat love is cat love. I will love you no matter what."

I threw everything into the bowl and settled onto the couch, fully prepared to cheer on my new favorite team while scarfing one of my favorite carbohydrates. Boomer hopped on the couch next to me and proceeded to attempt to attack every noodle that dangled from my fork.

"Bad kitty! Keep your paws off my pasta," I scolded, but he was undeterred. I sighed. "Roommates."

The game had been underway for less than ten minutes when some blond man who looked like he was at least a distant relative of a Viking kicked Sebastian in the knee. It was a cheap shot: Sebastian had already kicked the ball to someone else.

"Hey, rude! Give that guy a card, ref person!" I yelled around a mouthful of pasta, jabbing my fork in the general direction of the TV. Man, I was really turning into a super fan!

Boomer meowed his annoyance while simultaneously trying to grab noodles directly from the bowl.

"I know, right? We do not like that guy."

The rest of the game felt like a constant battle between Sebastian and Viking guy. Or good and evil if you wanted to be dramatic about it, which I did. With twenty minutes left in the second half, Viking guy elbowed him in the head so hard that it knocked Sebastian off his feet.

I gasped. I may have held my breath for the entire minute it took Sebastian to get up. He immediately charged Viking guy before his teammates intercepted him and were able to drag him off the field. A guy in a suit attempted to examine Sebastian, who was busy yelling in the general direction of Viking guy.

Even though I knew it was stupid because there was no way Sebastian was checking his phone during a game, I grabbed my phone and quickly typed out a message.

Me: You need to calm down so that guy in the suit can examine you for signs of a concussion! That was a hard hit to the head and you need to cooperate.

After hitting send, I noticed I had several messages from PairBond. I figured I wouldn't miss anything important in the game since Sebastian was temporarily sidelined. I opened the app and clicked on the message tab. I had two new messages. The first one was from a user named H2OhYeah, which I deleted solely because of the username. I estimated there was at least a seventy percent chance the message contained a dick pic, based on that name. The next one was from a user named DarWinning. I decided this message was probably safe and opened it.

Hey,

I never know what to write in these things, but your profile was really interesting. Are you into manga? I dabble myself. I'm more into online gaming though. Starcraft is my vice of choice. Anyway, I'd like to get to know you if this message didn't completely scare you away.
Patrick

I was smiling by the time I finished reading. *I finally got a message that's not creepy or completely off-putting. I should write him back.*

I knew I should respond. It was the logical thing to do. My gaze drifted back to the TV screen, searching involuntary for a glimpse of Sebastian. The reasonable Lennon, who understood the way the real world worked, silently reminded me that he was not for me.

I clicked on Patrick's profile and scanned his information. He was two years older than me and a biomedical engineer. I read through his interests and was pleasantly surprised at the number of things we seemed to have in common. Suddenly determined, I clicked 'reply.'

Hi Patrick,

I used to watch some manga, mostly when I was in high school, but it's not really my thing. To be honest, my friend signed me up for this and made my profile. She's pretty into the whole manga scene. I do like Starcraft though! I don't play as much as I used to anymore. I went on a serious bender in college once. My friends had to stage an intervention. I don't really know what else to say? Your profile says you're a biomedical engineer. That sounds pretty interesting! I'm an aerospace engineer, so we're both engineers. What do you specialize in?

Lennon

I hit 'send' and turned my attention back to the game just as play started again. The Novas won 2-1, but I couldn't muster up the appropriate amount of enthusiasm. I didn't even wait to see if Sebastian would be interviewed. Instead, I turned the channel to PBS and cleaned the kitchen. After everything was loaded into the dishwasher, I curled up on the couch to finish watching the documentary filling the room with soothing tones. Boomer curled into a little ball by my abdomen and I felt his soft purrs humming through me.

    I was well on my way to sleep when my phone dinged. I cracked an eye to see who had messaged me. I told myself I wasn't disappointed to see Janie's name on the screen, and if I was disappointed, it was only because I was hoping to hear from Patrick. I was in no way disappointed that the message was not from Sebastian. And even if I was just the teeniest, tiniest bit disappointed, it was only because I was concerned that he might have sustained a traumatic brain injury. Yep, I was just a world-class friend. Closing my eyes, I laid my head back down and silently acknowledged that what I was, in reality, was an extremely subpar liar.

16.

Sunday morning there was a message waiting for me from Sebastian when I woke up. Seeing his name on my phone got my heart going faster than a shot of espresso, and I was seriously concerned about what that fact meant for my well-being.

Sebastian: You watched the game?

Me: Are you okay? Were you concussed?

Sebastian: I'm fine. The team doctors cleared me. It's not the first shot I've taken to the head.

Me: That guy was such a jerk! What was his problem?

Sebastian: He's a really physical player. It's nothing personal, but he's not my favorite person either.

Sebastian: So, what did you think?

Me: I think you should get a second opinion. You were too busy yelling to be properly examined. You should be more cooperative during neurological exams. There is very strong evidence that repeated concussions can cause serious cognitive and memory issues similar to those in Alzheimer's sufferers.

Sebastian: Thank you, Dr. Walker. I meant about the game?

Me: Oh, I don't have any doctorates. I just have two masters, so I don't go by doctor. The game was good. I still don't understand all the rules but I yelled at the TV a lot. More than during Jeopardy and Wheel of Fortune combined.

Sebastian: What am I going to do with you, Lennon?

I wasn't sure how to respond to his last question. I blamed

the lingering confusion for how I ended up agreeing to have dinner with him on Monday evening.

Naturally, I tossed and turned all night, and woke up Monday feeling like I needed either six more hours of sleep or a time traveling machine. It didn't help matters that Boomer slept directly on top of me. I woke up at one point thinking I was having a heart attack, only to open my eyes and come face to face with Boomer purring contently on my chest. Meeting his glowing cat eyes with my own, half awake, almost gave me an actual heart attack.

I hit snooze one too many times and ended up having ten minutes to get ready. I managed to pull a navy A-line dress over my head and drag a brush through my hair with two minutes to spare before rushing out the door. I threw my hair up into a messy bun as I ran down the stairs, promising myself I would leave work early to get ready for dinner.

I was a jumbled mess of nerves the rest of the day. It didn't help that we were still having issues with the first stage engines. Issues that meant my four o'clock meeting was two hours long instead of the projected one hour, so of course, *of course*, I had no time to go home to get ready for dinner.

Why I was surprised that the only place I could find to park was seven blocks away from the restaurant was beyond me. I half-jogged, half-limped the entire seven blocks in what would probably have been record time if I'd had anything to compare it against. It wasn't until I staggered the remaining feet to the doors, a panting, sweaty mess, and saw the sign for valet parking that I seriously considered turning around and going back home. Of course the swankiest restaurant in LA would have valet parking! I whimpered to myself silently as I pushed through the doors into the air conditioning. It didn't escape me that the hostess was eyeballing me like she was weighing whether she would have to call the police to come return me to the asylum or if she could just throw me a roll and I would scurry back outside. I adjusted my glasses and tried to gather up what little dignity I had left, reminding myself that this place probably had an awesome wine list.

"Hello." I cleared my throat, focusing on the woman's immaculately manicured nails. "I'm meeting someone here, but I'm not sure if he made a reservation."

"I'm afraid we're booked solid tonight. If you don't have a reservation, there's no way we can fit you in. Sorry," she replied, in a tone that led me to believe that she was not in fact sorry.

"Could you check for a reservation please? It would be under Sebastian Kincaid." I tried to peer over the stand to look at the tablet she was currently typing away on.

"Yeah, nice try. I really don't want to have to make a scene, but I will have you removed from the premises if you don't leave immediately."

"What? But I'm meeting him here." I held up my hands, backing away from the desk slowly.

She rolled her eyes, finally lifting her gaze to give me a once-over. "Listen—"

Her mouth clamped shut at the same time her eyes widened. My back collided with a solid object and an "umph" escaped my lips. I turned around to apologize, but my apology was forgotten when my eyes landed on the well-defined pectoral muscles and broad shoulders that were mere inches from my face. My gaze roamed the muscled planes of this stranger's chest until they met very familiar eyes.

"Oh, hi." I smiled at Sebastian in genuine relief. "Do you have a reservation? This lady is like a dragon guarding its treasure and I am starving. She takes her job very seriously."

His lips tipped up at the corners. "I have reservations. Let's get you fed."

One of his hands gently turned me toward the hostess stand before settling on the small of my back, propelling me forward. My feet were trying to resist the motion, not wanting to have a rematch with the hostess who was definitely not the mostest.

"I thought you were hungry?" Sebastian's voice was a breath against my ear, and I had to fight against a shiver.

"I am, but we could just get a cheeseburger or something.

Have you had In and Out yet? It's an American institution and you really should—"

His chuckle cut me off. "Lennon, it's fine. I made reservations."

"Mr. Kincaid." The hostess greeted him by name, suddenly all smiles. "We have your usual table ready for you."

She motioned us forward while clearly trying to size me up. She probably assumed I was part of some adopt-a-nerd program and Sebastian was my mentor. We made our way silently to the very back of the restaurant, where a table for two sat tucked behind a small stained-glass partition, creating a secluded little space. I slid into the seat nearest to me, relieved to be sitting down.

"Here we are. Please let me know if there's anything I can get you. Enjoy." She handed us each a menu and shot one more quizzical glance my way before leaving the small area.

"So, you come here often?' I asked, immediately flipping to the drinks portion of the menu.

"I wouldn't say often, but I have been here a few times. They're really good about privacy, which is nice if you want to have a meal out without being mobbed by people."

I peeked at him over the menu. "Are we in some sort of VIP room?"

"It's one of the perks that comes with the whole professional athlete bit." He looked a little sheepish as he said it, and a faint hint of pink dusted his cheeks.

"Nice," I said, taking in the immaculately decorated space. "I think she was going to call the police on me, so that's good."

Sebastian coughed, setting his water glass down. It took him a few seconds to recover enough to ask, "What are you talking about? Why is that good?"

"She must have thought I was some crazy stalker, so she threatened to call the police. That's good for you, right?"

He rubbed one hand roughly over his mouth. "Was she rude to you?"

I gave his question some thought. She hadn't been friendly

or helpful, but was she rude? I imagined myself in her position, seeing me rush through the door looking disheveled and completely out of place.

I finally settled on an answer. "No. She wasn't rude, just doing her job."

Sebastian looked like he wanted to say more, but was interrupted by the waiter who introduced himself, took our drink orders, and disappeared, all in a very efficient manner.

"You know, I don't think I've ever had such a hard time convincing a woman to get dinner with me. It's been very... humbling," he said, his voice light with humor.

"I don't think I believe you. The part about being humbled, I mean. The part about the other women is very believable. And I wasn't being difficult."

"I asked you to dinner once and you were busy. You ghosted me. I had to ambush you at your apartment." He ticked off each item on his fingers as he went. "You finally caved, but only after you thought I suffered a head injury."

"When you put it like that, I think I'm the one the hostess should have been protecting. Geesh, you're kind of a stalker." My brain finally caught up with my mouth and I felt the blush rushing up my neck. Why was I joking with this perfect man about being a stalker? How low was my blood sugar that I was making jokes? Where was that wine?

As if on cue, Ian returned with our drinks and took our orders. I made Sebastian order first, because I was still debating between the filet and the scallops. I needed an extra minute to reread the mouth-wateringly delicious descriptions of each dish one more time.

"I'll have the salmon, but with extra vegetables instead of the risotto, please. And no butter on the vegetables," Sebastian said, handing Ian his menu.

"And for you, miss?" Ian turned to me.

"I'll have the filet, medium, please. And instead of the asparagus may I have the gouda mac and cheese? It sounds pretty amazing."

Ian smiled conspiratorially. "Good choice. It's my favorite thing on the menu. I'll put these in for you. Is there anything else I can get for you?"

We both shook our heads and Ian disappeared, leaving us alone again.

"Mashed potatoes *and* mac and cheese?" Sebastian asked. "Are you carb-loading for something or just opposed to vegetables?"

"I prefer to avoid vegetables, and let's be honest, who's going to choose asparagus over *gouda* mac and cheese?" I was practically drooling at this point, visions of cheesy noodles dancing through my head.

"People who are concerned for their health?" he fired back, looking way too pleased with his response.

"I ate really healthy as a kid, so I got it all out of the way when I was young."

Sebastian was clearly skeptical. "I'm pretty sure that's not how it works."

"Eh," I responded, waving a hand. "Who's to say?"

"Oh, I don't know, anyone in absolutely any of the health fields. Doctors, dieticians, nurses—"

"And all of those people would be crying over their asparagus watching me eat gouda mac and cheese," I interrupted. "If you stop now, I might let you have a bite. But just one bite."

"Very generous of you," he responded, taking a sip of his whiskey.

I was momentarily mesmerized watching the muscles of his neck work as he swallowed.

"Thank you, I thought so," I finally managed, my voice sounding slightly thin even to my own ears. I took a sip of wine. It was crisp and buttery all at the same time, and I couldn't remember ever having such a delicious wine. In all honesty, I usually couldn't tell the difference between a five-dollar glass of wine and a fifty-dollar glass of wine, so I usually just went with whatever was on sale at the grocery store. This wine might just make me a believer.

"Tell me about your day," Sebastian said. His fingers were lightly tracing the rim of his glass, but his eyes were focused intently on my face. A little too focused for my emotional well-being and ability to form coherent thoughts.

"Well," I said, training my eyes on his hand, "it was long. We're having a problem with our first-stage engines. They're designed to operate at full throttle during certain phases of the mission, like liftoff, but then throttle down after, until separation when..."

I glanced up at his face, afraid I was boring him. He was probably looking for superficial details, not a full dissertation on engines.

"When...?" He nodded his head, encouraging me to continue.

I let out a little sigh—part frustration, part relief. "After separation, the center engine should throttle back up to full thrust, but it's not. We've been trying to figure out what's causing the malfunction in the center engine, and... *nada*. I was in meetings all afternoon, which consisted mainly of people pointing out what we already know."

"I think it's safe to assume that you are an incredibly intelligent woman, Lennon. I have complete faith in your ability to solve the problem."

My chest swelled with pride even though I knew he was just trying to be comforting. "That's a very nice thing to say. Spatium is filled with people a lot smarter than me, though."

"I find that hard to believe. Explain these engines to me, but like I'm a football player who barely passed algebra."

We spent the rest of the dinner discussing engines and soccer. I did, in fact, let Sebastian have a bite of my mac and cheese, and because I was feeling very generous, I even let him have a second bite. Also because he moaned his appreciation the first time and I definitely wanted to hear that sound again.

Sebastian offered to drive me to my car after dinner when I explained that I didn't use the valet service. I had attempted to sneak away while he was handing his ticket to the valet, but I should have known better. I was not fast enough to sneak away from him unobserved, especially after a large meal and wine.

By the time we reached my parking spot, I was scrambling for ideas to keep the night from ending, because I was actually enjoying this thing that I had spent so much of the day dreading. In the end, I settled for a "goodnight" and a promise that we would have dinner again soon.

17.

As it turned out, dinner with Sebastian would end up being the highlight of my week. The issue with the engines was becoming a dark specter hanging ominously over the rest of my life and sucking the joy out of everything. I had reached the level of stress where I was beginning to lose sleep. I was already planning to call Harrison to let him know I wouldn't be pulling my usual Friday night shift when I received a delivery confirmation notice. I leapt out of my chair with a burst of energy that I wouldn't have thought I was capable of a minute ago, and jogged to Janie's office.

I knocked once, swinging the door open before she had a chance to reply.

"It's here! It's here!" I squealed, bouncing on the balls of my feet with excitement.

Janie looked up from her computer. "What are you talking about, crazy lady?"

"The LEGO Hogwarts Castle was just delivered! It's finally here! All 6020 pieces of it!" I was smiling so wide my face hurt. This bad boy had been on back order for months and it was finally here. Thank Dumbledore, Paige was home to sign for it!

Janie spun around in her chair yelling "Yes!" like a maniac, finally at the appropriate level of enthusiasm the situation demanded. She stopped spinning to face me with an equally wide smile of her own.

"Are you thinking what I am thinking?"

I nodded my head and we shouted in unison, "LEGO NIGHT!"

Someone in the hall shushed us so I stepped into her office, closing the door behind me.

"My place at seven? We can order pizza and play the HP soundtrack while we build it. Or we can start an HP movie marathon!"

"This is going to be epic," Janie said, rubbing her hands together. "I'll stop at the store and pick up snacks. Snacks and energy drinks. We're going to need caffeine for sure."

"Perfect!" I exclaimed, checking my watch to see what time it was. "I'll see you in three and a half hours."

Walking back to my office, I couldn't help but think about what a weird week it had turned into. It was like two fun bookends with lots of crummy books in between them. It had started Monday when I had dinner with Sebastian, and now I was looking forward to a night of LEGOs with Janie for a pretty great Friday night.

I sat down in my chair with a renewed sense of determination. I pulled up a blueprint I had been staring at diligently for the past hour, but I was distracted when the screen of my phone lit up. Thinking it was a message from Janie about our plans for the evening, I grabbed my phone, but was surprised to find a notification that I had a new message from Patrick on PairBond.

Lennon:

Sorry for the delayed response. The project I'm assigned to at work has turned into one unexpected problem after the next. I was really glad to get your message. I specialize in biomedical electronics but have been known to dabble in biomaterials. We're working on developing a chip that can send signals from your spine to your prosthetic limb. I'm one of those lucky people who really love their jobs. Well, most days.

I hope you're not the judgmental type, because I have to confess that I once got way too involved in World of Warcraft. I went a week without showering and knew it was time to go cold turkey. My college roommates were really big into it too, so there was no hope of an intervention. I probably would have failed out of college if I didn't smell so bad. I got a good whiff of myself one day and knew it was time to quit. Thank goodness for olfactory senses! What do you like to do now that you have kicked the gaming habit?

An aerospace engineer is pretty impressive! What kind of work do you do? I generally think of NASA when I hear anything with the word space in it, but I realize there are lots of commercial possibilities for an aerospace engineer. Although, it would be really awesome if you worked for NASA.

Patrick

I read his message twice, a goofy smile on my face both times. Patrick seemed like someone I could potentially date. We had a lot of similar interests; we were both engineers. He seemed to have a sense of humor, which was definitely a bonus. On paper, we were a great match. I pulled up his profile and clicked on his pictures. I fought down a wave of disappointment when his pictures didn't make my heart feel like it was fluttering around in my chest like Sebastian's did. There was absolutely no reason why I should be comparing the two men. It was completely ridiculous and illogical. Patrick was attractive in his own right with his thick, wavy blond hair and horn-rimmed glasses partially obscuring brown eyes. Maybe Janie and Paige were right about this whole online dating thing?

Patrick:

Don't worry, I can totally relate! I have spent all week trying to figure out what the issue is with one of our engines. The first stage engines don't want to cooperate. I work at Spatium. It's my dream job and I love it! I keep reminding myself how much I love this job when I have weeks like this one. We do have a contract with NASA though! It's the project I'm working on actually. I am secretly hoping that I'll get to meet an astronaut.

The project you are working on sounds so interesting and pretty exciting! I took a couple biomedical engineering courses in college and really enjoyed them. If I wasn't so in love with aerospace engineering, I definitely could have been swayed. Also, the faculty member who headed the program was very intense and made me very anxious every time we interacted. I don't know if I could have survived more than a semester under her supervision.

I don't know that I have what would constitute hobbies. I like graphic novels and attend yoga once a week. My friend Paige is an instructor. I help my brother at his tattoo shop as well. Oh, and I recently acquired a cat! His name is Boomerang, but I call him Boomer unless he's in trouble—which, as it would happen, is most of the time. I adopted him from a shelter and he is of indeterminate breed. He also appears to have engaged in and lost multiple street fights. What do you enjoy now that you are showering regularly?

Lennon

I read the message twice before hitting send, trying to catch anything that would make Paige or Janie cringe. Another good thing about online dating was the anonymity. If I completely embarrassed myself, I would never have to look the other person in the eye again.

I made a mental note to call Harrison so he would know not to expect me tonight, and I sent Sebastian a text wishing him good luck at his game. I might be in charge of an engine that spontaneously shut off, sending a multi-billion-dollar rocket plummeting back to Earth, but things were looking up!

18.

I had a little pep in my step as I climbed the stairs and made my way to Paige's door. I didn't even contemplate what I would do if she wasn't home. I'd probably call maintenance and tell them I smelled smoke coming from her apartment. I knocked on her door, straining to hear any signs of life inside. I heard footsteps and breathed a sigh of relief.

"Hey girlie, what's up?" Paige greeted me cheerfully.

"Hi Paige, I'm here to pick up my package. Thank you so much for signing for me!" The words came out in an excited rush. I was trying not to be rude, fighting the impulse to grab the box and run back to my apartment chanting, "My precious."

"Oh duh! I forgot about your package. Sorry, it was long day." She turned to retrieve a brown box from her table.

Do the right thing, Lennon, ask her why her day was so long. I took the box from her hands and paused to really look at her. She seemed uncharacteristically deflated. Paige wasn't shallow. She felt the full range of human emotion, I knew that. It was just that she always seemed to face the world with a smile. It was one of the things I envied and admired about her. I felt more like the little black rain cloud that followed Winnie the Pooh around. Sometimes I forgot that Paige was susceptible to melancholy too.

I clutched the box and prepared to be a good friend. "Why was your day so long?"

Paige looked down at her feet and let out a breath that

sounded frustrated, and suspiciously watery. "Nothing. Well, not nothing. I got in a fight with my mom, but I don't really want to talk about it right now, if that's okay? I really appreciate you asking, though."

I glanced down at the box in my arms and then back at Paige. "Umm... did... would you like a hug?"

Paige's head shot up and she nodded. "Yeah, a hug would be really great, actually."

I set the box down and wrapped my arms around Paige. She squeezed back, resting her head on my shoulder. She let out another watery sigh before breaking out of my arms.

"Thanks, Lennon. I really needed that. What are you up to tonight?"

I motioned toward the box on the floor, keeping my arms available in case she needed another hug.

"Well, this box just so happens to contain the Hogwarts Castle LEGO set." I paused, waiting for some sort of excited utterance from Paige, and plowed on when she didn't make a peep. "It's been on backorder forever and it's finally here!"

"Uh, so you're playing LEGOs tonight?" Paige asked, a quizzical expression on her face.

"It's not *playing*. It's putting together a complex model. Totally different."

"Clearly," she said with mock seriousness.

"Anyway, Janie is going to come over and we're going to get started *building* this *model*." I paused to make sure she noted the extra emphasis. "We're ordering pizza and Janie is stopping for snacks, which means we're going to have a ridiculous amount of food. Hey! You should come! I mean, if you don't have plans."

"I don't think I have ever play—built with LEGOs, but you know what? I'm in. I was just going to mope on my couch with a bottle of wine and that's not really constructive. I mean understandable and maybe necessary, but not constructive."

"Great! Not the moping with an alcoholic beverage part, but the joining our party is great. I'm going to get changed and clear off my coffee table, but you can come over whenever you want."

I thought for a moment and then added, "Just be careful when you open the door; Boomer's fast."

Paige laughed. "I still can't believe you adopted that mess. Don't get me wrong, I love my furry nephew, but that cat is a mess with a capital M."

We said our goodbyes and I made my way back to my apartment to get set up. I inched open the door just wide enough to sneak through, keeping my eyes trained on the floor for any signs of Boomer attempting to dash through my legs. As much as I was just dying to recreate the scene from Wednesday where I'd chased him through the hallway in nothing but an oversized shirt and my underwear while praying no one came out and saw me, I didn't have time for his antics tonight. I heard a meow from my bedroom and rushed in, quickly shutting the door behind me.

I greeted Boomer and threw on my Hufflepuff sweater and leggings. I even added my stripped Hufflepuff knee socks to complete the themed look, because what else do you wear when you're building Hogwarts? I had just finished feeding Boomer when Paige walked through the door with two bottles of wine in her hand.

"I wasn't sure if a LEGO party called for a red or white wine, but I do know that it calls for wine." She waved the bottles back and forth. "Do you want a glass?"

"Yes, please," I responded, picking up the remote and turning the television to the channel broadcasting Sebastian's game. "White, preferably. Red makes my neck hot and itchy."

"You know you're probably allergic, right?" she asked, getting two wine glasses out of the cabinet.

"It's a distinct possibility. You know, oral immunotherapy for peanut allergies is showing some promise. It's still in the clinical testing phase but it's had a 60-80% desensitization rate in patients," I said, clearing off the coffee table.

"Yeah, I don't know what any of that means, but good for them. I don't know if I could live without peanut butter."

"It's a procedure for people with severe allergies to peanuts where they slowly introduce small amounts of peanuts in a clinical setting. The goal is to increase the threshold that triggers an allergic reaction. So maybe if I slowly increase the amount of red wine I drink, I'll gradually become less bothered by it," I rambled on while unpacking the set from its box.

"Open up, nerd, I come with snacks!" Janie's voice boomed from the other side of the door.

I got off the floor and rushed to open the door. Janie's arms were loaded down with bags, but I could see she was decked out in Slytherin gear.

"Can I Slyther-in?" She wiggled her eyebrows. "These bags are getting heavy and I skipped arm day for the last, like… oh… twenty-five years straight."

"Very punny," I deadpanned, reaching to take some of the bags. "Hurry up and get in here before Boomer escapes."

"I still can't believe you adopted that mutant," Janie said, kicking the door closed behind her.

"I know, right?" Paige chimed in from the kitchen. "That cat has been to hell and back."

"Oh, hey, Paige! I didn't know you were into LEGOs."

Paige laughed, reaching for a third wine glass. "Yeah, that's because I'm not. I'm here for the company and the snacks. I was told there would be pizza, too."

"Pizza has chee—" I elbowed Janie in the ribs before she could finish saying 'cheese.' "Owww! What's with the flying elbows there, Skeletor?"

I gave my head a tiny shake and then nodded toward Paige. "I already ordered the pizza. Paige had a rough day so she's going to hang out with us instead of wallowing. Right, Paige?"

"Yep, hanging with friends is better for your emotional health than watching Bravo and drinking straight from the bottle while thinking about the Stepford wife who gave birth to you. Do you want red or white wine?"

"Uh, red, it'll pair nicely with Sour Patch Kids," Janie answered, pulling out an assortment of snacks from her bags. "What's with the sports? I thought we were listening to the HP soundtrack."

"What's HP?" Paige asked, taking a seat at one end of the coffee table.

"Is that a joke?" Janie gasped, one hand splayed dramatically on her chest. "Lennon, she's joking, right? Please tell me she's joking."

"HP is an abbreviation for Harry Potter," I explained, choosing to ignore Janie's theatrics entirely.

"Ah, okay, I'm not down with the lingo you cool kids are using these days," Paige joked, taking a sip of wine and picking up a LEGO piece to examine. "How do you even know where to start with this thing?"

I took a folded piece of paper out of the box and waved it in the air enthusiastically. "There's a blueprint!"

"No one should ever be that excited over instructions," Paige mumbled. "I should have brought over the boxed wine I keep for emergencies."

Janie and I looked over the instructions and then divided the castle into sections. We gave Paige the least complicated part, and the responsibility of keeping Boomer away from the table. Turned out that cats liked knocking things off tables for no discernable reason.

"You never answered my question about the sports game currently playing on your TV," Janie said, not bothering to look up from the section she was working on.

"Oh, sorry. It's just that I usually watch Sebastian's games. I don't really understand all the rules, but I'm learning. I recently discovered that offsides occurs when a player is closer to the opponent's goal than both the ball and the second-last opponent and someone passes him the ball. Sebastian explained how a corner kick works at dinner Monday. I don't know if I'm a sports fan, but it is more enjoyable to watch a sporting event when you have someone to root for. It's almost over though. We can turn the music on after."

I noticed that Janie and Paige had both stopped working on their sections and were looking at me with astonishment.

"Let's unpack that, shall we?" Janie asked, her attention drifting back to the piece in her hand.

"Yes, Janie, I think that's an excellent idea." Paige voiced her opinion while trying to separate Boomer from her leg. "Boomer, quit trying to climb me!"

"There's nothing to unpack. Sebastian and I appear to be friends, something which, while I am still confused about, I have accepted as a fact. Part of being a good friend is supporting your friend in their endeavors. Sebastian's profession is soccer, therefore I am taking an interest in soccer." I tried to sound very matter-of-fact, hoping it would put an end to this particular topic.

"And you two have been hanging out regularly?" Paige asked over Boomer's agitated meow.

"I wouldn't say regularly. We exchange texts and we met for dinner once." I provided the details, mostly truthful but leaving out Sebastian showing up at my apartment. For some reason I couldn't quite understand, the night Sebastian and I had shared Chinese while watching Netflix felt important. Like a memory I didn't want to share with the outside world lest that somehow tarnish it.

"And you want to be just friends with Sebastian Kincaid, the world's hottest soccer player and, though I haven't done the research necessary to support this claim, probably the hottest male on this planet?" Janie asked, sounding more than a little skeptical.

"Yes." I decided what I needed here was some sort of diversion. "So Paige, what's your favorite Harry Potter book?"

I was using my knowledge of Paige's reading habits to theorize that she hadn't read a single Harry Potter book. It was low, but I was desperate—Janie approached interrogations with the tenacity of a KGB agent.

"Uh…" Paige stalled, looking around the room for a lifeline. "*The Wizard Saves London?*"

"Ohemgeezus. You haven't read a single Harry Potter book, have you?" Janie demanded, looking as astounded as she sounded.

"No," she answered, cringing. "I thought the series was for kids."

"Wow, Lennon, we have a total HP newb on our hands. We have to pop Paige's HP cherry. Don't worry, we'll be gentle."

"Some of what you said sounded kind of disturbing, but we should totally have a Harry Potter marathon! It'll be so fun!" I reached for a handful of cheeseballs. "But first, we have to make Paige get sorted. It's essential for a marathon."

"Agreed." Janie nodded. "All newbs must be sorted. Are you in?"

Paige shrugged, looking a little nervous. "I guess?"

Janie and I spent the next hour filling her in—or torturing her, according to Paige—with all the essential details of Harry Potter. Even the arrival of pizza didn't provide her with a reprieve. I made her take the sorting quiz on my tablet. Paige was a Hufflepuff like me, and I was not the least bit surprised. 'Patient and kind' described Paige perfectly.

But I *was* surprised when my phone dinged with a message from Sebastian.

Sebastian: what are you up tonight?

Me: Janie and Paige are over helping me put together the Hogwarts Castle LEGO set! It's been on backorder for months and it finally arrived today!

Sebastian: When you say LEGO set, do you mean an actual LEGO set? It's not American slang for something?

I looked up from my phone, an idea forming in my head. "Would you guys mind if I took a picture of you with the castle for Sebastian?"

"We would be happy to be in a picture for your *friend*," Janie responded, emphasizing the word friend. Paige nodded her agreement. I snapped the picture just as Janie held up her fingers in a peace sign. "Gotta represent."

I sent the picture to Sebastian, and tried not to be disappointed when my phone didn't immediately ping with a response. When I didn't hear from him almost an hour later, after

Paige and Janie had gone home, I told myself he was probably busy with post-game stuff.

It wasn't until I slid into bed that I allowed myself to admit I was afraid Sebastian wasn't responding because I had done something wrong, offended him with my nerdiness. I knew it wasn't "cool" to get excited about LEGOs on a Friday night. Even though I really, really didn't care that I was perpetually labeled a nerd like it was some sort of incurable disease, it didn't mean that I wasn't capable of being hurt. I rubbed the puckered skin that divided my chest in half. My other fear, if I was being completely honest, was that Sebastian hadn't responded because he was on a date or picking up girls at a bar.

"Why am I doing this to myself?" I asked Boomer. He cracked one eye in acknowledgement and then promptly went back to sleep. Cats.

"You know what, Boomer?" He cracked open both eyes this time and stretched. "Good, this is important. You have to hold me accountable. I need to stop worrying about something that is not a realistic possibility. Sebastian is my friend. We are friends. So what if I have a physical reaction to him? It's simple biology. That's it. My body is recognizing him as an ideal candidate to pass on superior genetic material so my offspring have the best chance of surviving. And hey! I have plenty of practice ignoring arrhythmia, right? The smart thing would be to focus my energy on Patrick, so that is what I am going to do from now on. Thank you, Boomer, this has been a very productive chat."

I looked over at Boomer, who was now belly-up, snoring softy on the pillow next to mine. Sighing, I nestled further under the covers. I ran my fingers along that ridged line dissecting my chest one more time, a silent reminder that life could be so disappointing, unfold in ways you didn't expect, but that it was all still so worth it.

19.

When I woke up the next morning, two text messages from Sebastian were waiting for me. He apologized for not responding right away. He'd been exhausted after the game and fell asleep on the couch icing his knee. I fought down the urge to revel in the knowledge that he was alone and not ignoring me. Friend. Friend. Friend.

I texted my *friend* back that I understood and hoped his knee was feeling better today. A very friendly response to my friend. And if I watched his game that evening, it was a purely academic endeavor undertaken only because I had no plans.

When Harrison picked me up for Sunday dinner, I was just finishing up another email to Patrick. We were officially at least pen pals. Neither one of us had broached the topic of meeting face to face, and I was relieved. I liked the idea of exchanging some more messages with him before we met in person. It allowed me to collect as much data on him as possible so that when we did meet, I would have a list of conversation topics fully prepared. I realized I would have to admit to Janie at some point that her online dating theory was actually very solid, if you had the patience to tolerate an insane number of creeps and penis pictures. So, so many. Some that would haunt me until my dying days.

"How was your Friday night?" Harrison asked, after a few minutes of comfortable silence while I searched through radio channels. "We missed you."

I yawned. "It was really fun. We made pretty good progress on Hogwarts, and Paige admitted that LEGOs are strangely soothing. I had to build a fort to protect the castle from Boomer though. He keeps knocking things off the table."

"You mean one of your wizards couldn't protect it with a spell?" Harrison said, his voice filled with mock surprise.

"Ha ha ha. So funny." I nudged him lightly on the shoulder. "How were things at the shop?"

"Busy. Been thinking about bringing in some new people," Harrison replied, turning the radio back to the rock station he preferred.

"Really? That's awesome, Harrison! Are you thinking about adding another artist?" I reached over, switching the radio back to my indie station.

"You know the driver gets to pick the music, right?" He switched the radio back to his station. "I'm leaning more toward finally getting a permanent replacement for Marty. I don't want to be doing all the office shit and we need someone at the front desk. Lou fucks everything up and I don't have the patience for it. Teddy is barely less of a fuck-up, but he's getting booked more regularly now. I'm still looking at the numbers. I haven't made any final decisions."

"You know, I could drive. My car gets much better gas mileage."

Harrison grunted. "Pass. I don't feel like spending two hours with my knees in my chest."

I rolled my eyes. "Anyway, I think it's great that you need to hire more people to manage the shop. You've done a really great job growing Bad Wolf. I'm so proud of you."

"All right over there, calm down." He groaned. "Jesus Christ, are you crying?"

I sniffled, shaking my head. "No."

"Lennon, come on. Don't cry. What just happened? Are you getting your period? Here," he said, putting my station back on the radio. "We can listen to your shitty indie garbage."

"No, I'm not about to get my period, Harrison," I said, suddenly annoyed. Nothing, I mean *nothing*, switches a woman from sad to angry like a man asking if she's about to get her period. As if our uteruses are entirely responsible for our emotions! "I'm just really freaking proud of you."

"Thank you," he responded, his voice sounding a little gruffer than it normally did. I nodded in acknowledgment and leaned my head back against the headrest, closing my eyes.

"Lennon." A warmth landed on my leg, sending my whole body swaying gently. "Lennon, we're here."

I jolted upright, a sharp pain shooting up my stiff neck. "Did I fall asleep?"

Dumb question, judging by the drool I felt gathering at the corner of my mouth. I tried to stealthily wipe the drool off by faking a yawn. Was it even possible to attractively sleep in a car? I had spent a lot, *a lot,* of time sleeping in cars during my two and a half decades, and never once had I woken up looking like Sleeping Beauty. I always woke up looking like Maleficent—after she unleashed her inner dragon.

Harrison confirmed my suspicions. "Snoring like a lumberjack."

"I do not snore," I mumbled, unbuckling my seatbelt and exiting the car. I could hear Harrison snort over the sound of the door shutting.

As soon as we entered the house, we were greeted by two of my favorite sensory inputs: the sound of baseball and the smell of garlic.

"Harrison? Lennon? Is that you?" Mom called from the kitchen. Who else she was expecting was a mystery. She turned the corner, a wide smile on her face and arms open ready to sweep us into a hug. "How are my babies?"

"Good," Harrison and I answered in unison, as we were smashed together between two arms that absolutely did not look like they were capable of crushing bones but had been known to squeeze the life out of her children.

"Dad! Kids are here!" she yelled directly into our ears. I could see Harrison's wince mirroring my own. She released us from her clutches and we dutifully followed her into the kitchen. "Dad!"

"I heard you, Susan!" he shouted from his recliner in the living room. I didn't even need to be able to see into the room to know that was exactly where he was, and that he would be watching whatever game was playing. "The whole neighborhood heard you."

"Hi, Aunt Jen," I greeted the woman standing at the counter slicing a cucumber for the salad sitting in a bowl at her elbow. Her bright red curls bounced with every slide of the knife. My eyes scanned the room looking for her husband, who was arguably one of my top three favorite men on the planet. "Where's Uncle Frank?"

"They're behind at the shop, so he's working late," she offered, her tone sounding apologetic on his behalf.

"It's good that they're so busy." Harrison stooped down to place a kiss on her cheek.

Aunt Jen and Uncle Frank were not biological relatives. Jen and my mom had been best friends since first grade. Grandpa always said Jen was over so much that they ended up putting bunk beds in mom's room and he claimed an extra dependent on their taxes. They had gone to college together and opened up the diner together. When our sperm donor disappeared the first time, Jen and Frank had stepped in to help my mom with Harrison. They even bought a house four down from ours. The last and final time our sperm donor had disappeared, my mom was six months pregnant with me.

I had no memories of him, obviously, but every single memory of my childhood featured Aunt Jen and Uncle Frank. Along with my grandpa, we became a weird family unit. When I was little, I liked to think my dad was a CIA agent who had been called away on a secret mission. Now that I was older, I liked to think he was roadkill. Although, to be honest, I didn't think about him very often anymore, because my slightly dinged-up heart had always been filled with so much love.

The day I'd gone in for my big heart surgery all five of them had crammed into my preoperative room, and it hadn't felt like there was anyone missing. I remembered opening my eyes and looking for my mom and grandpa, never once thinking about the man who should have been there. And when they left to take Harrison back to the hotel and get a few hours of sleep, Aunt Jen and Uncle Frank stayed with me. Aunt Jen refused to let go of my hand the whole time, as if she needed the constant reassurance that I was still there. I barely ever thought about my dad, before or after, because there were too many people busy filling up the hole he'd left in my life.

Those same people were currently filling the seats around the kitchen table, loudly chatting about their weeks while shoveling lasagna into their mouths. I smiled, thinking that if happiness had a sound, it would sound an awful lot like Sunday dinners at the Walker house.

20.

Uncle Frank showed up after dinner and asked Harrison to walk him through the new billing software he had installed in the shop. As much as Grandpa had been involved in both our lives, Uncle Frank had played the leading role in modeling an adult male for Harrison. We had hit the jackpot for father figures to stand in for an absentee father. I still remembered the sight of Grandpa and Uncle Frank in the bleachers on Friday nights, cheering on Harrison like he was their own son, both men wearing buttons with his face on them.

I ended up in the garage with Grandpa helping him rebuild an engine for a '39 Ford convertible he was restoring with some of his buddies from the senior citizen—you know, when he wasn't busy running an illegal gambling ring. I was perched on my usual stool, holding a flashlight and handing him tools, while he grumbled obscenities in the general direction of what would be the radiator. I *hmm*ed in agreement when he called out requests for a tool or more discernable complaints.

He stood up straight without warning and gave me one of his signature squinty-eyed glares. "What's on your mind, kid?"

I was still "kid" at twenty-six. "What do you mean?"

He grunted. Harrison had come by his extensive repertoire of grunts honestly. "I can hear that big old brain of yours churning from over here. You've handed me the wrong tool twice now, and agreed that I should expand my gambling operation to the assisted living facility across from the senior center."

I sat up straighter. "Grandpa, you absolutely cannot expand your gambling ring! It would definitely be illegal, and I'm pretty sure it would also be very unethical to fleece old people out of money."

"I *am* old people. And no one's getting fleeced out of any money," he said, wiping his hands on an oil rag. "We don't gamble for money."

"What do you gamble for, then?" I asked, not even attempting to hide the skepticism in my voice.

"Don't worry about it." That reassurance actually made me worry a lot more. "Quit trying to change the subject. What's got you all tangled up over there?"

I sighed. "I'm not tangled up. I was just thinking."

He waved the rag around. "About?"

"I guess I was just wondering about attraction." I clarified, "Attraction between people, not magnets."

Grandpa swallowed hard a few times before he managed a response. "Oh God, I was sure your mom would have covered this with you. Okay, I'm going to need to sit down for this. I should have had more of that wine at dinner, but your mom's always on me about drinking. Gotta hide the good stuff in the garage. Do you want a drink? I think we should both have a drink for this."

He was dragging over a stool and a bottle of what looked like whiskey. He sat down on the stool, placing the bottle on the bumper of the car. I watched, confused, as he took a fortifying breath.

"All right, okay, so when a man and woman—or, uh... a woman and woman, although I'm not going to be much help there—anyway, when two people love each other or have had too much to drink or are just, uh... attracted to each other in a healthy and consensual way—"

My head whipped back so fast I almost fell off my stool. "Grandpa, stop! Are you trying to give me the sex talk?"

He scrubbed two hands down his face. "Well, yeah, I thought that's what you were asking about."

Through the horror at the thought of my grandpa giving me a sex talk, my love for him grew impossibly bigger.

"Mom already had the talk with me." I left out the part where I also had firsthand experience in that topic. Although, considering the experience, additional input couldn't hurt. "I was just... I guess I was wondering how you know if you're attracted to someone or you're just having a physical response based purely on biology."

"Is there a difference?" he asked, looking beyond relieved.

"I think so. For example, you can be attracted to someone purely on a physical level but think they have a terrible personality. Our bodies have been programmed through centuries of evolution to look for mates who possess qualities that will ensure offspring survive to pass on our genetic material. None of that has anything to do with personality. You can be attracted to someone physically, but understand intellectually that they would not make an ideal life partner."

"Uhhh, let's see here." Grandpa cleared his throat. "I think your theory is a little bit flawed there, seeing as how we're not fighting mammoth on the plains of Africa anymore, but I think you gotta have both things to make a relationship work, if that's what you're asking. There has to be a physical spark there, but you also gotta like talking to the person."

I chose to ignore the statement about mammoths on the plains of Africa. "How did you know Grandma was the one for you?"

My grandma had died suddenly when I was eight, of an aneurysm that had gone undetected. A total fluke. I was just young enough that my memories of her were all a little fuzzy. She was Grandpa's great love. As far as I knew, he never dated after she passed away. I never heard him so much as mention another woman, even though we all encouraged him to date.

"Well, now that's a harder question to answer than you'd think. It's hard to put that feeling into words. But you know, I didn't have it all figured out when I met your grandma. I almost broke it off with her, actually. Dumbest thing I ever almost did."

"You did? Why?"

"Oh, I had this big crush on a girl all through school. Never gave me the time of day until about two or so months after I started dating your grandma. Sara, that was her name. Anyway, Sara started taking an interest in me and, well, one thing led to another and I decided I was going to break things off with Grandma." He smiled at the memory. "I walked her home that day, just waiting for the right moment. She smiled up at me when we got to her house and I just knew that there *was* no right moment, because that smile was my whole world right then. I can barely remember what Sara looked like, but I can close my eyes and still see your grandma smiling up at me like it was just yesterday."

I swiped at the lone tear that managed to escape. "I really love that story."

"The point is that Sara was very pretty and had a great personality, just like your grandma did. Love is more than attraction, but I don't think you can have one without the other, either."

I slid off my stool and wrapped my arms around him, squeezing him tight and ignoring his muffled protest. "Thanks, grandpa. I love you."

"I love you too, kid." He patted my back before releasing me. "Now, can we get back to this engine?"

I thought about what he'd said the whole ride back and while lying in bed that night. It was not even remotely helpful. I thought about the two brief relationships I had in college. I met my first boyfriend in my biochemistry class. I knew I didn't love him, but I didn't know *how* I knew it wasn't love. I liked him. He was smart and funny and cute in a nerdy way. But in the six months we dated, never once did I ever consider the L word. My second boyfriend was a different story. I thought I could maybe love him. I thought the liking I felt for him could grow into love with enough time and effort. He did not agree. I was upset when he broke up with me, but I could honestly say I hadn't been devastated.

It occurred to me briefly that maybe I didn't have the ability to love. That maybe my heart was more broken than a cardiothoracic surgeon could repair. Frustrated, I gave up trying to fall asleep and decided working on the Hogwarts castle would be a more constructive use of my time. I made my way into the living room and flipped on the light. Boomer was curled up sleeping on top of the empty cardboard box I covered the castle with to protect it from him. Sighing, I lifted him up and placed him on the couch behind me, ignoring his loud, unhappy noises, and removed the box. I worked for a while, the silence and comfort of following a clear plan helping to calm my mind. Then my phone rang, startling both me and Boomer. I glanced at the screen and saw Sebastian's name. I hesitated for a beat before answering.

"Hello?" I said, the word coming out more questioning than usual.

"Hey, I hope I didn't wake you up." His voice sounded rougher, like he was trying to sleep and wasn't having any luck either, and it made his accent seem impossibly more attractive.

My mind wandered to tornadoes. The Enhanced Fujita Scale had been designed as a rating system to measure wind speed and the level of damage associated with those speeds. I thought a similar scale, rating the various presentation of Sebastian's accent, should be created to better help people prepare for the accompanying damage of each. For example, sleepy Sebastian's accent leads to moderate damage of the cardiovascular system, usually preceded by some sort of unexplained reaction in the gastrointestinal system. This was more damaging than calm Sebastian, which led to a much milder, though still dangerous, reaction in the pulmonary system, generally referred to as a sigh.

"No," I finally responded, focusing back on the actual conversation. "I was just working on Hogwarts."

Sebastian's chuckle seemed to travel through the phone and settle directly into my chest. "How's it coming?"

"Good. Boomer keeps trying to knock pieces off the table and just generally wreaking Godzilla-like havoc, but I've been covering it with an empty box and that seems to be working."

Boomer chose that moment to let out an irritated part-meow, part-growl, like he knew what I was saying and wasn't ready to give up the fight.

"What is a Boomer?" Sebastian asked, sounding genuinely confused.

"Oh, Boomer is a cat. Well, my cat to be more precise." I reached behind me and gave him a little scratch on the head.

"You got a cat? When?" His voice was a weird combination of curious and angry.

"Umm, a little over a week ago now. I adopted him from the Cat Cottage—remember, the place I was looking at when you introduced me to *Stranger Things*?"

"You should have told me," he chastised, though his voice had lost that small hint of anger from moments earlier. "How are you two getting on?"

I thought about chasing the cat down the hall in my underwear, the way he seemed to enjoy suffocating me while I was asleep, and getting out of the shower to find everything that had been on the counter was now floating in the toilet.

"We're… getting used to each other," I said, eyeballing the cat in question who was watching me talk with a twitch of his tail, which I was quickly learning meant he was plotting something. "It's an adjustment, but we're making progress."

He chuckled again and parts of my body sighed. "I can't wait to meet this cat. I was actually calling to see if you were busy tomorrow evening?"

"Oh. Why didn't you just text me?" I asked, caught off-guard by his question.

"I wanted to actually speak with you," he confessed, his voice softening with the admission and adding another rating on the scale. "I haven't spoken to you all week."

My heart galloped wildly in my chest before I could tell it to calm itself down. *Friend. Friend. Friend,* I reminded it.

"We had dinner Monday," I pointed out. To my *friend.*

He let loose a long, suffering sigh. "I remember. Are you

going to answer my question?"

"I am busy tomorrow evening, but…" I hesitated, then said, "I don't have plans Tuesday evening."

"Tuesday evening will work. I'll text you the details later. Have a good night, Lennon."

"Goodnight, Sebastian," I responded, ending the phone call. I stared at the phone in my hand before turning to look at Boomer.

"What just happened?" I asked him.

He stretched out one little paw toward me like he was about to offer me some small amount of creature comfort. This was it! We were finally connecting on an emotional level, enough for Boomer to be able to sense when I was upset. This was the moment I had imagined when I'd first started planning my future as a cat lady. I leaned toward his paw slowly, not wanting to ruin the moment with any sudden movements. I kept my eyes locked on his, hoping to communicate that we were in this thing together. Just before his paw connected with my shoulder, it flicked once, twice, sending a pile of LEGOs onto the floor. He meowed, curling back into a ball and closing his eyes.

I slumped in defeat. Why were all males so confusing?

21.

The next day I showed up at Paige's yoga class, hoping to finally get a chance to ask her what was going on. She had been sad and distant since her fight with her mom. Even more concerning, she had become uncharacteristically militant about her vegan diet. When I asked her if she wanted to come over and binge-watch Bravo shows, she told me she didn't have time. I even tried to lure her back to my apartment with the promise of cookies from Lola's, but she wouldn't take the bait, so I had resorted to exercise and bribery. I was at the very bottom of my bag of tricks. I was getting seriously concerned we would have to stage an intervention if she didn't break soon, since having Janie kidnap her seemed like the option of last resort.

Tuesday started with a bang. Literally. My alarm startled Boomer and he flew around the room, knocking everything off my nightstand in the process. Did I think it even remotely strange that I apologized to the cat dangling from my curtains while I cleaned up the mess left in the wake of his terror? Not even a little bit.

I should have recognized that my wake-up call was an omen of things to come, but I was too excited about seeing Sebastian later to recognize it for what it was. The first sign that the day might not be all rainbows and sunshine was the loud, gurgling death of my coffee pot. Harrison had been trying to get me to replace my trusty machine with a Keurig for years, but I was loyal to my classic piece of machinery. We had been through so much together! I made the sign of the cross and whispered, "RIP, old friend," before hustling out the door hoping to have time to stop for coffee on the way.

Every single person in the city seemed to be getting coffee this morning; I gave up trying to find a short line by the third place and accepted that I was going to have to drink the extremely subpar, mostly-water drink that the people on my floor called coffee.

As if being deprived of a decent source of morning caffeine wasn't bad enough, the lunch situation was an actual tragedy. I had just enough time between my morning meeting and my afternoon team session to grab a quick lunch with Janie. The daily menu board proudly announced that it was "Tofu Tuesday."

"Tofu Tuesday?" I turned to Janie in horror. *"Tofu Tuesday?* What fresh hell is this?"

I tried so hard to convince myself that the tofu nuggets tasted just like my beloved chicken nuggets, but my body refused to accept such treachery. Even Janie looked like she was struggling to swallow her all-soy burger. I ended up eating a lunch composed of the reject items left in the vending machine. Then Sebastian sent me a text telling me to be ready at six—and to wear athletic gear. My excitement over seeing him turned to dread. Nothing good ever came from the words 'athletic gear.'

I was busy trying to push down the butterflies in my stomach with chips when a knock at my door had me glancing at the clock. Ten minutes till six. Sebastian was early. I made my way to the door, keeping an eye out for Boomer, and opened it to find Sebastian smiling at me. My eyes traveled up the length of his bare shins to the pair of athletic shorts and across his broad shoulders, which always seemed to be testing the strength of whatever material his shirts were made of. I swallowed, offering a weird wave instead of saying hello. My brain cells were apparently too busy greedily taking in eyefuls of the masterpiece standing just outside my door.

"Hey, Lennon." His smile hitched a little at the corner making the chips in my stomach want to make a sudden, violent reappearance.

A thud from somewhere in the apartment got those pesky brain cells back on track. I grabbed his arm and dragged him into the apartment, quickly shutting the door behind him.

"Hi," I finally answered, taking a look around the apartment to see if I could find the source of that ominous thud.

Sebastian looked mildly amused and definitely confused. "Everything okay?"

"Oh yeah, yes," I said, turning my attention back to him. "I was thinking, though, maybe we could grab dinner instead of... whatever it is you had planned?"

"You'll like what I have planned, I promise," he reassured me. Those little crinkles at the corner of his eyes made me light up somewhere in the general vicinity of my ovaries.

"I'm sure I will, but I definitely won't like it as much as I like dinner," I pointed out. "Plus, I haven't eaten yet."

He picked up the half-empty bag of chips on the counter. "The crisps should hold you over until dinner."

"My blood sugar is low?" It sounded weak even to my own ears, but I was getting desperate.

"You're not diabetic," he began, but then his attention shifted to his leg. I followed his eyes to find Boomer trying to climb his right leg, one of his front paws making a swipe for Sebastian's shorts.

"Oi, what the bloody hell is that?" Sebastian yelled, his finger pointing at the cat now fighting to hold on.

I dove for his leg and struggled to detach Boomer's claws from the hem of his athletic shorts before his hind claws could find a new home in Sebastian's flesh. Finally freeing his claws, I clutched Boomer to my chest and stood.

"*That* is Boomer. He's my cat." Boomer let out a deranged meow from my arms. His one free arm pointed in Sebastian's direction, claws on full display.

"That is not a cat," Sebastian accused, pointing at the struggling cat in my arms. "It's... it's a... a bloody *gremlin*, is what it is!"

"He is not a gremlin!" I gasped, offended for both of us. Although, honestly, he did look a lot like a gremlin, now that I thought about it. "You're going to hurt his feelings."

Sebastian pinched the bridge of his nose. "Is this the cat you adopted from the Cat Cottage?"

"Yes," I answered, bending slightly to release Boomer now that Sebastian seemed to be recovering and I wasn't so worried about Boomer getting kicked across the room like a soccer ball.

"Lennon, love," he said, eyeballing the fury menace inching on his belly toward him. "You quite literally got catfished."

"Catfished?"

"Yeah. They lured you in with all those pictures of normal-looking cats and sent you home with... this thing." He pointed at Boomer, who let out an insulted hiss as if he actually understood the insult. "It doesn't even have both ears!"

"*He* has one and a half ears, which is a perfectly respectable number of ears. And just because he's a little banged-up doesn't make him deserve a good home any less than a cat with both ears and all of his tail."

He sighed. "Fuck, sorry. You're right. That wasn't very well done of me."

I watched as he crouched down and stuck out his hand. Boomer inched toward him eventually nudging it with his head. Sebastian scratched him behind the ears, and I resisted the urge to sigh. I wasn't familiar with the proper execution of a swoon, but if Sebastian kept talking to Boomer like that, in a voice too low and deep for me to make out any of the words, I was pretty sure I was going to discover it very quickly.

"He likes you," I pointed out in a voice that was a little too high and squeaky.

"The little blighter's all right when his claws aren't in your leg," Sebastian grumbled, standing up. "We should get going."

It was my turn to grumble. "Fine."

Sebastian just laughed. "Try not to sound too excited."

"I'll do my best," I declared dramatically, slipping on the

sneakers that had spent most of their short life in the way back of my closet.

22.

I used most of the car ride trying to explain to Sebastian that I was not athletic. I promised him that I wasn't just trying to be humble. I told him that athleticism and I were polar opposites, but it somehow led to me explaining that the phrase 'polar opposites' referred to diametrically opposite points on a sphere. And then a small—teeny, really—speech about how the north and south poles are polar opposites but they both get the same amount of sunlight. So, clearly, I was nervous.

By the time we arrived at a large park filled with soccer fields, I was already working myself into a solid anxiety sweat. Sebastian bore it all with a smile and a patience that made me wonder why he had decided to make me his friend. Was he trying to make his clique more well-rounded by adding a socially awkward nerd who tended to sweat profusely when she got nervous? Was there some kind of quota system I wasn't familiar with?

I got out of the car and walked around to Sebastian, who was pulling a large duffle bag out of the trunk.

"Are we going to play soccer?" I asked, warily eyeing the bag he threw over his shoulder.

"No," he responded, shutting the trunk and turning to shoot me one of those ridiculously disarming grins. "We're going to play football."

"God, you're such a snob." I rolled my eyes but couldn't keep a small smile from sneaking out.

"And you're such an American. Let's go, I reserved Field 6 for us."

He started marching confidently in the direction of the fields while I lingered, half-stalling and half-admiring his backside in his well-fitted shirt and shorts. I figured I deserved one small moment of joy before I was murdered, and more than likely humiliated, in front of a professional athlete and a handful of teenagers. With one more sigh, I scurried after Sebastian.

He dropped the bag from his shoulder onto the ground and bent to unzip it, producing a soccer ball—just as I'd feared.

"Hey, did I ever tell you that I never played sports?" I asked, eyes laser-focused on the ball. He was holding it as if he had been born with a ball in that very hand.

"Once or twice, yeah. Calm down. I wasn't expecting Sam Kerr to make an appearance," he said, in what I could only assume was an attempt to reassure me.

"I don't even know who he is," I whined.

"*She*," he responded, tossing me the ball. I barely managed to catch it before it connected with my stomach. I let out a very attractive 'oof' anyway. "Is arguably the best female footballer in the world."

"Well, good for her." And then I added under my breath, "I have two degrees from MIT."

"Who's the snob now?" Sebastian fired back good-naturedly. "I thought you might like to learn some skills, now that you're an official footy fan. We've only got the field for an hour so quit wasting time."

My first instinct was to exclaim "only an hour!" An hour of playing soccer might actually kill me. It might as well have been forty-eight hours in the desert naked with no water or sunscreen. But I told myself that I needed to stop being such a whiny brat and make an honest effort to at least try to enjoy this evening. Sebastian had obviously put some thought into this whole thing, and not many people got to learn soccer skills from a professional player. I adjusted my glasses, smoothed the flyaway hair off my face, and plastered on a smile.

"Okay, show me what you got, hot shot!" I sang, my smile widening at my rhyme.

"Let's start with the basics. Have you ever kicked a football before?" He took the ball from my hands and placed it on the ground in front of me.

"Nope. This is officially the closest I have ever come to a soccer ball." I tried to sound more excited about that fact than I felt.

"You didn't ever play football in PE class?" He sounded genuinely shocked and possibly outraged.

This would have been the perfect opportunity to tell him that I'd only attended public school for two years and had been excused from the physical education requirement due to having recently had open-heart surgery. Instead, I replied with a simple "No," lying by omission. I wasn't trying to hide my childhood heart defect or the impact it had on my life. It was just that the past and I had a complicated relationship.

On the one hand, I was pretty proud of my comeback. I hadn't just survived; I had built a really great life for myself despite being dealt a crummy card. On the other hand, the whole thing was like a gigantic raw wound that never seemed to be fully healed. I'd spent more than half my life one way, and in some ways I was still figuring out how to reconcile old Lennon with new Lennon. Talking about it always left me feeling exposed. It didn't help that people never seemed to be entirely sure how to react. They either started treating me like I was a fragile piece of china or like a survivor who needed to be championed. Complicating matters with Sebastian was the fact that I still believed his desire to be my friend was based on some combination of guilt and pity.

"All right then, give it a go," he said, placing his hands on his hips.

I adjusted my glasses, sizing up my opponent. Kicking a ball—how hard could it be? It was a simple physics equation: Force is equal to mass multiplied by acceleration. And I was great at physics! I closed my eyes. *My foot is one with the ball.*

Sebastian cleared his throat. "You are aware that you have to move to kick the ball?"

I opened one eye. "I'm envisioning success, and then I will project my vision into reality."

His chest vibrated with suppressed laughter. "Right then, carry on."

For reasons I will never fully understand but will always blame Sir Isaac Newton for, I decided I needed to get a running start. I took a few long strides backward and then charged. I squinted my eyes, focused on my goal, and drew my leg back. I swung it forward with all the force my puny muscles could muster up, but instead of kicking the ball, my toe connected with the ground just in front of it. The next few seconds were just a blur of blue and green and my own limbs flailing as I flew forward toward the ground. I wheezed as my abdomen made contact with the ball, forcing the air out of my body in a whoosh. I was vaguely aware of Sebastian shouting something and then the sound of running feet.

"Lennon, holy shit, are you okay?" His concerned voice came from somewhere above me. All I could see from my position folded over the soccer ball was grass and a hint of blue sky being reflected in the lenses of my glasses.

"That depends. Am I dead?" I asked, rolling onto my back to take in his frowning face staring down at me. He was partially blurred thanks to my crooked glasses.

"No." Sebastian reached down to fix my glasses, bringing his worried face into focus.

"Then no." I groaned, squeezing my eyes shut. "I am going to close my eyes, and when I open them, I would really appreciate it if you could pretend to be Saint Peter welcoming me to my eternal home."

"I didn't peg you as religious," he commented, sounding curious, not judgmental.

"Seriously, how is that your follow-up? I'm not, but this seemed like a good time to find Jesus," I pointed out, opening my eyes to take in his now smiling face.

Staring into his eyes seemed to have the same effect on me as landing on the soccer ball. It stole the breath right out of me. I needed to break eye contact for my sanity. I turned my head slightly, the new angle bringing an impressive polyester-covered bulge directly into my line of sight. I swallowed, darting my gaze back to his face. I could feel heat start to creep up my neck and into my face.

Sebastian stood slightly and offered me his hand. "Up you go."

I slid my hand into his and let him pull me up. My heart gave a little tug at the contact and I couldn't stop myself from thinking that it would be nice to hold his hand for longer than it took to get me upright. *Friend, amigo, ami, amico*, I silently reminded my imagination in every language I could think of, because it didn't seem to be getting the message in English.

Sebastian patiently demonstrated the right way to kick a soccer ball, which did not actually involve running or toes. I finally got good enough to kick the ball back and forth with him, and I celebrated each kick that actually reached him like it was the game-winning goal in the World Cup.

After kicking the ball around until I was pretty confident, Sebastian suggested we play a game of one-on-one. I laughed like a hyena until I realized he was totally serious. When I told him I thought this was a bad idea—I might accidentally trip him or something, and I didn't want to be responsible for injuring the star of the Novas—he just laughed and shook his head. The game consisted mostly of me running after Sebastian and taking swipes at his legs, but I laughed the whole time while he alternated between shouting insults and encouragement. I finally called it quits, flopping down on the ground somewhere around Sebastian's twenty-third goal.

"I give up, you win!" I called from my spot on the ground. I watched as he dribbled the ball down the field, stopping it just before it collided with my head. I winced, earning a laugh from him.

"Do you mind if I run over and say hi to the kids?" he asked, nodding his head in the direction of a small crowd that had gathered to watch our game. Judging by all the pointing and frantic hand movements, someone had recognized Sebastian.

"Nope, I'm just going to lie here until I can feel my legs again. Go greet your adoring fans." I waved my hand in the general direction of the crowd.

He chuckled. "Okay, I'll be right back. There's water in my bag if you can drag yourself over there."

I picked up the ball and threw it at his back as he jogged toward the group. Missed by a mile.

I sat up and watched him interact with the group, which was mostly kids. An adult produced a Sharpie and he started signing anything they could find. He posed for pictures and shook hands with the few adults in the group. It was strange to watch him slip into superstar mode. Sometimes I forgot that the man who had crouched on the floor to talk to my cat was the same man featured on the cover of sports magazines. It was another reminder that my heart needed to get on the same page as my head.

With one last wave, he jogged away from the group back to me. Once again, he stuck out his hand to help me up, and once again, I noticed how much I liked the way my hand felt in his.

"Sorry about that," he said, shooting me an apologetic grin and bending down to pick up the ball.

"Don't be sorry. It's really great that you take time to meet fans." I gave him a reassuring pat on the arm, mostly as an excuse to touch him again. "I bet you made their day."

"It's a bit easier to manage over here. Football's not as popular, so I don't get recognized as often." He shrugged, steering us in the direction of his bag. Dropping the ball next to it, he bent down and retrieved two water bottles, passing me one.

I took a gulp of water, watching Sebastian over the top of my bottle. His throat worked as he drank, the movement distracting me and apparently making me forget how to swallow. I choked, gasping for air in between violent coughs. I fully admit that there was a moment in which I hoped I had inhaled enough water to actually drown. Sebastian watched me with concerned eyes, muscles coiled like he was ready to spring into action at any moment.

"Are you okay?" he asked, once my coughing died down enough that I could hear his voice. My cheeks were a deep shade of red, from the exertion of coughing as well as a large dose of embarrassment. Stupid laryngeal pharynx, dropping the ball.

"Yep." My voice came out sounding like a frog being strangled, and I cleared my throat. "I can't believe I'm going to say this but that was fun. I had a good time."

Sebastian smiled so widely that his blue-green eyes were almost eclipsed by those familiar lines at the corners. I sighed, a little out of relief and a little from feeling the full effect of that smile.

"I'm glad. I was a bit nervous there after your first go at kicking the ball."

I groaned, dropping my head back to look at the sky. "Can we just agree to never speak of that again? Even better, let's just forget it ever happened."

He laughed, shaking his head back and forth. "Sorry, love, not going to happen."

I sighed, watching him pack up his bag. "Where's the Tardis when you need it?"

"Tardis?" Sebastian asked, glancing up at me.

I pretty much shrieked, "Are you kidding me right now? How can you be British and not know about Dr. Who?"

"That's a show, right?" he responded, sounding completely serious, much to my horror.

"This is a tragedy. Since you introduced me to soccer, I will return the favor by introducing you to one of the best shows..." My voice trailed off as my eyes landed on the small bag in Sebastian's hand. "Sebastian, why are you holding a bag of... of... are those gummy..."

Heat rushed to my face and I couldn't seem to force the word from my mouth. Mercifully, Sebastian finished my sentence for me.

"Yep, someone sent me a bag of gummy dicks." He opened the little card attached at the top of the bag and proceeded to read it dramatically. "'Eat a bag of dicks, you dick. Signed, the Big Bad Wolf.' I've gotten a lot of weird hate mail, but this is my first bag of dicks. The guys at the security desk handed it to me on my way out. They thought it was a riot."

I laughed a little maniacally as my brain raced. The Big Bad Wolf? It couldn't be. Harrison would never have sent Sebastian a bag of gummy wieners. He hadn't even been in the room when I'd told everyone about meeting Sebastian at the club. But 'the Big Bad Wolf' seemed like an awfully big coincidence. And Harrison wouldn't send gummy wieners—but Lou absolutely would, and he would know how to find a place that sold them. At least Sebastian didn't seem the least bit fazed about the whole situation, which was actually kind of strange. I would probably have been alarmed or surprised, or maybe even mad, if someone sent *me* a bag of those particular pieces of anatomy with a note saying... what that note said.

Later, after Sebastian had dropped me off and my sore legs convinced me I should take the elevator, I reflected on what a strange day it had been. I'd played a sport (well, sort of, but I did sweat a lot!) and didn't hate it, and I was fairly confident that my brother's employees had sent my new friend a bag of gummy dicks. What a time to be alive!

23.

Thankfully the rest of the week had very few surprises in store for me. Sebastian's game this week was at home, which seemed to mean he had a lot more time to send me texts. He also sent Boomer an apology box filled with cat toys and catnip. I was honestly pretty hesitant to give Boomer any of the nip considering what an unpredictable character he was, even stone cold sober. A large part of me really wished Sebastian would stop being so likeable, that he would go back to the arrogant jerk from the club. All this attention was making it hard not to like him more than I should. I'd had plenty of guy friends in the past but—as horribly superficial as it sounded—not a single one of them had looked like they'd just descended from Mt. Olympus.

And then there was Patrick. We were emailing daily and had exchanged phone numbers in the last email. Things were definitely getting serious with him. Well, as serious as things could get via email. But despite the fact that Patrick was absolutely perfect for me, my brain seemed to want to classify him as a friend, and Sebastian as a potential mate.

Then there were the work issues, which I was trying to convince my brain were the actual important problems in an effort to stop feeling like a boy-crazy teenager from one of the romantic comedies that were quickly becoming my new favorite things to watch. We ran a new test in the program simulator with the adjustments we'd made from the last one, and our rocket made it exactly 23.017 minutes before it exploded. 'Exploded' was almost too tame a word for this fiery ball of disaster. If we didn't get the issue solved soon, we were going to have to push back the scheduled start for construction of the first prototype. The whole project would be delayed.

By the time Friday rolled around, I was stressed out and looking for some not-so-innocent individuals to take my frustration out on. Lucky for me, I spotted the perfect candidates sitting on the couch as I pushed through the doors of Bad Wolf. Lou and Aaron turned to look at me as I stomped across the room.

"Did you send Sebastian a bag of... of... penises?" I asked, the last word coming out much quieter than the eight before it had.

Aaron let out a loud groan and reached into his back pocket. I watched curiously as he pulled out a wad of bills and handed them to Lou.

"Nice doing business with ya." Lou saluted him, reaching for his own back pocket.

The pieces clicked into place and my anger ratcheted up to the point where I thought I might explode like our rocket.

"Did you bet on whether I could say pe... that word out loud?" I shot a withering glare, or what I hoped was a withering glare, at the two men on the couch.

Lou groaned this time, stopping his hand's progress toward his wallet and handing the cash back to Aaron.

"You bet on me twice!" I yelled, throwing my arms up wildly in frustration.

"Lenny-poo, it was a slow night," Lou said, using a placating tone, as if it being a slow night explained the whole thing. I reminded myself not to fall for the goofy grin that made it almost impossible to stay mad at him. Sensing my irritation was still firmly in place, Lou continued, "And he needed a big ol' bag of dicks."

"He did. I don't care if he's arguably the best soccer player in the world right now. The guy's a dick," Aaron added, not taking his eyes off his sandwich. I felt a momentary pang of happiness that Aaron would help send a bag of dicks to his man-crush. "And technically, Lou came up with the idea but Harrison actually sent them."

I rolled my eyes. "Of course he did. I expected more from both of you, though."

"Hey, Kay tried to start a rumor online that he has herpes," Lou said, sounding genuinely upset by the idea that I could be disappointed in him.

My head swiveled toward Kay, who was seated behind the front desk. "You did?"

She shrugged, her eyes never leaving the computer. "I sure did. A bag of dicks is temporary but herpes is forever."

I placed my head in my hands and groaned. "Why did you guys feel the need to do all this? He apologized."

"Uh 'cause you're our friend, Tater Tot, and no one messes with you. Well, unless it's one of us." Lou responded so quickly that I knew he truly meant it. Everyone nodded their head in agreement.

I had to blink back the wave of tears that had suddenly rushed to my eyes. I cleared my throat, hoping to dislodge all the emotions that were currently clogging it.

"Thank you, I guess? It was very unnecessary, and frankly, a little weird, but I appreciate you guys looking out for me. Just please maybe don't send anymore gummy genitals to anyone without asking me about it first."

My words were met with grumbles and mumbled "Fine"s. I figured that was as much of an agreement as I was going to get from this bunch. All the fight I had blown through the doors with left me. It was easy, so easy, to think about all the things your life was missing and all the things you would change about it, to dwell on the negatives. Sometimes I forgot to think about all the really great things and people my life was filled with. It felt melodramatic to say that I had come too close to dying to need reminding to be thankful, but I *had* come close enough that I shouldn't need it.

I looked at Aaron, who had turned his attention back to his

sandwich. "Speaking of Sebastian, I was wondering if you would want to go to a Novas game with me."

Aaron's gaze swung to mine, brows drawn down in confusion. "Sure, we can try to get tickets to one of their home games. They're hard to score this year, but I might know someone who can hook us up."

"Great! I was going to bring Paige or Janie, but you actually *like* soccer." I smiled at him. "And don't worry about the tickets; Sebastian said he would send them."

Aaron choked on his food, coughing and sputtering so hard that Lou slapped him on the back a few times.

"Sebastian Kincaid is giving me soccer tickets?"

It seemed petty to point out that Sebastian was actually giving *me* the tickets, so I just glossed over that. "He told me to pick a game and he would get the tickets. I thought I would ask you first, so you could pick the game you wanted to see. I obviously don't have a preference."

Without missing a beat, Aaron responded, "Seattle FC. They play here in two weeks."

"Okay, I'll let Sebastian know. Is my brother in his office?" I asked, even though I knew the answer was more than likely yes. If he wasn't with a client he was usually holed away in his office, trying to get caught up on administrative stuff.

Lou and Aaron nodded, Aaron still wearing a dreamy expression. Even though a lot of my irritation had fled after Lou's comment about friendship, I still felt the need to let Harrison know that I was not at all happy about his interference with Sebastian. I loved Harrison—he was the best big brother any girl could ask for, but he did need a reminder every once in a while that I was no longer a child.

"Great. Kay, I'll be back to relieve you in however long it takes me to kill my brother," I yelled over my shoulder as I marched down the hallway. I heard Lou's "Godspeed" just as I turned the handle on the office door.

24.

Did you want to grab dinner sometime?

I read and reread the sentence. And then I read it again. Each time I read the words, fresh tendrils of fear climbed up from my stomach and wrapped themselves around my lungs. It was ridiculous to feel so anxious about the idea of meeting Patrick. We had been texting all weekend and everything about our conversations had been easy. He was proposing dinner, not marriage.

"Hey, do you..." Janie paused midsentence, sitting down in the empty chair on the other side of the desk. "What's wrong? Are you feeling okay?"

I groaned. I must have looked as anxious as I felt.

"I'm fine. Patrick sent me a text asking if I wanted to get dinner sometime," I explained, my fingers tracing the edge of my phone screen.

"What?" she exclaimed, leaning forward in her seat. "Lennon, that's great news! Why do you look like a Dementor just sucked the soul out of your body? You should be doing a happy dance and planning an epic outfit that will knock Patrick's pants off."

"I'm just nervous about the idea of meeting him in person. Things have been going so well communicating by email, and we just started texting. Why mess with a good thing?" I resisted the urge to add that I was afraid he wouldn't measure up to Sebastian when we met in person, and it would put an end to whatever we had going on.

"Uh, because your phone can't give you orgasms?" Janie stated, as if the answer was obvious.

"*Orgasms?* I can barely handle the idea of dinner with him, let alone any activity that could result in an orgasm." I lowered my voice when I realized I was practically shouting about orgasms. "Are you trying to make me more nervous?"

Janie slapped her hands on my desk and leaned forward. "Listen up, Lennon. You are going to put on your big girl panties, and you are going to go on this date and have a really good fucking time. He's going to buy you dinner and maybe you two will have a couple drinks after. Things might be a little awkward at first, because first dates are always a little awkward. But you'll get past it and enjoy yourself so much that you might even let him touch a boob when you say goodnight."

I sat in my chair, momentarily shellshocked by her aggressive pep talk. I said the first thing that popped into my head.

"Just one boob?"

"It's a first date. Two boobs would be trashy." She paused before adding, "Unless he takes you someplace really good for dinner."

Against all odds, I did actually feel inspired by her speech. Maybe Harrison had groomed me to respond to the overbearing, militant approach?

"You know what? You're right." I picked up my phone and responded to Patrick, simply stating that I would love to get dinner. "Done. What were you about to ask me when you came in?"

"Oh! I wanted to see if you had any plans this week. I thought we could try to schedule another dinner with Paige and Kay," she said, settling back into her seat. "The dojo is hosting a tournament this weekend, so most classes have been canceled. I'm a free bird pretty much all week."

"I would love to have another girls' night!" I answered enthusiastically. That would be a dinner I had no anxiety about attending. "Actually, it might be a good time to stage an intervention for Paige."

"Why? What's up with Paige?" Janie sounded concerned, but also surprised.

"I'm not sure. She got in a fight with her mom, I think, but I can't get her to talk to me about it. She's been acting strange ever since." I went on to list all the ways Paige's behavior had been off since the phone call with her mom and all my efforts to get her to confide in me.

Janie was quiet for a minute. "That is all very un-Paige-like. Do you have any idea what the fight could have been about? I can't remember Paige ever mentioning her parents."

"I have no clue. I know Paige isn't very close with her parents. I think her dad's some big plastic surgeon in Beverly Hills." I searched my memory for any helpful details Paige might have provided about her parents, but I couldn't come up with anything else.

"Well, this is just one more reason we need a girls' night," Janie agreed.

We made a plan of attack for getting Paige to agree to dinner, since she had refused all my other attempts to get her to do anything, then Janie had to leave for a conference call. I told her I'd talk to Paige at her yoga class tonight.

I had my speech all prepared as I unrolled my mat in the back of the studio later that night. Assuming I survived the intermediate-advanced class, I was going to ask Paige to dinner under the guise of needing dating advice. No way would Paige turn down a friend in need. Paige was busy talking to a group of women, but she excused herself and made her way over to my spot when she saw me.

"Hey, Lennon, what are you doing here? This isn't your normal class," she asked, a curious smile on her face. "Not that I'm not happy to see you."

"I thought I might spice up my normal routine and try something more advanced." I tried to sound convincing while saying quite possibly the most un-Lennon-like phrase I had ever uttered.

"Okay," she responded, sounding not at all convinced. "This is actually kind of perfect timing. Do you think I could stop by after class? I've been meaning to ask your help with something for a while now."

"Yes, definitely!" I responded with a frightening amount of

enthusiasm. I reeled in the crazy. "I would love to help."

"Thanks. I really appreciate it. Enjoy the class, and remember, don't be afraid to ask for modifications for any pose that's too advanced, okay?"

My mouth said "Yes" even though I had absolutely no intention of asking for a modification and drawing attention to myself in this Lululemon-wearing crowd. I was fully prepared to do the minimum necessary to blend in, and reward myself with pizza rolls after.

25.

I limped home an hour later with a full body cramp and a craving for pretzels. As usual, I had been a sweaty mess by the end of class while everyone else looked refreshed and energized. I fed Boomer and dragged my carcass to the shower while the oven was preheating. Boomer was sliding his arms under the gap between the door and the floor while meowing his displeasure at being shut out of the bathroom. Such a soothing soundtrack for a relaxing, post-workout shower. I turned off the water and stepped out of the shower, wincing at the flash of pain the movement caused. I opened the door for Boomer, who proceeded to jump up on the toilet lid and glower at me as I toweled off and combed my hair.

I made my way to the kitchen after putting on my pajamas and dumped an entire package of pizza rolls onto the tray. The knock on my door came just as I was piling the steaming rolls onto a plate.

"It's open!" I yelled, assuming it was Paige. I grabbed a container of ranch dipping sauce I'd swiped from the cafeteria and made my way toward the couch. "I hope you're hungry for a gourmet dinner."

Paige laughed as she joined me on the couch. "God, I haven't had pizza rolls in forever."

I smiled as she took one off the top of the pile and popped it into her mouth. She moaned. "How is something so disgusting so delicious?"

"I don't know what you are talking about. Pizza rolls are quality food packed with goodness. You should try them with ranch." I waved the container in her direction and watched as she dipped one in the sauce. I was hoping this was a good sign that she was feeling better. We ate a couple more rolls in silence before Paige wiped her hands off and got down to business.

"Promise me you won't laugh when I tell you this," she demanded, suddenly super serious.

"I promise," I answered truthfully.

"I want to go back to school." She braced herself for my response, which made me feel like absolute garbage.

"I would never laugh at you for wanting to go back to school! I think that's great. Why would you think I'd laugh at you?"

She shrugged. "You're so incredibly smart, and I'm a high school graduate who teaches yoga and sometimes models. I know it's kind of ridiculous to be trying college at twenty-five."

I sat my plate down and turned to face her on the couch. "Paige, you are smart too, and you can do absolutely anything you want! I have never, not once, thought you were dumb. Going to college doesn't make you intelligent, and it's not ridiculous to want to go back to school—at any age. It's awesome and brave."

"Thank you for saying that." Her posture relaxed noticeably but her eyes were suspiciously shiny. "I talked to my mom about it and it didn't go well. I let her get to me even though I know better."

"What happened?"

Paige let loose a watery sigh. "My mom's always had this idea of me becoming an actress or a supermodel. It's the only time she takes an interest in my life, which is why I was in beauty pageants all growing up even though I hated them. When I told her I wanted to go back to school, she was so upset and disappointed. She told me I would be wasting my time, because I never did well in school and was too pretty for it anyway. Instead, she suggested I let my dad fix some of my trouble areas, because I have a very all-American, girl-next-door look and that's not what people want right now. They want the Kardashian look. Then it was the usual lecture about my weight, skin, and hair."

I instantly hated Paige's mom with an intensity I hadn't known I was capable of. I could not imagine a mother ever tearing down her own child, making her doubt herself. All my life my mom had gone out of her way to make sure her children knew that they could do absolutely anything. My very first day of high school was the first day I'd ever heard my mom swear. I cried telling her about eating alone at lunch, and how the girls I asked to sit with had treated me. She sat me down and told me those kids were all a bunch of losers who would never amount to anything, and I was too damn special for them and they knew it. The fierceness in her voice had healed some of the hurt and reminded me that everything wasn't as awful as it felt at that moment.

"Okay, well, your mom is kind of the worst." Paige laughed a little at my words, so I continued. "Although people do seem to be really into the Kardashians. But I think you should follow your heart, and if it's telling you to go back to school, you should go for it. I'll be here to help however I can. I feel very confident that if you can master King Pigeon pose, you can do anything."

"Thanks, Lennon." She gave me the first genuine Paige smile I had seen in at least a week. "The thing is, I don't care what she thinks anymore. Or I'm trying not to care, anyway. I've spent twenty-five years trying to be her version of the perfect daughter, and the idea of trying for the next twenty-five years is horrifying. I hate acting and modeling, and honestly, I'm not great at it either. As much as I like teaching yoga, it's not what I want for my life."

"You're pretty much one of the best human beings I know, so I don't think you should try to be anyone else's version of Paige. I like my Paige." I hoped she felt the sincerity of every single word.

"But will you still like me after you help me with my calculus homework?" Her eyes looked pleading and slightly panicked.

"Totally! It's going to take more than calculus to break up this friendship," I reassured her. I'd spent many years helping with—and then just *doing*—Harrison's math homework. If we still loved each other, there was no chance calculus could come between me and Paige.

Over the remaining pizza rolls, Paige told me about the classes she was planning to take and her game plan. She was going to get all the core classes out of the way at the community college, then see about finishing her degree at a traditional university. I offered lots of encouragement and promises to help. I think we were both feeling relieved by the time Paige left. She even sounded excited about a girls' night.

My phone rang from the couch, causing my heartrate to accelerate in response. The only two people who actually called me were my mom and Sebastian, since Patrick and I were still strictly texting, and my mom would still be working. I tried to make my way toward the couch casually, as if every cell in my body wasn't screaming for me to move faster.

"Hi," I breathed into the phone, trying not to sound giddy. I sounded like I had a wheeze instead.

"Hey, what're you up to? You sound out of breath," Sebastian asked. I could almost hear the smile in his voice, which did absolutely nothing to improve my current state.

"Ummm, just..." My eyes searched the room until they landed on the furry bump behind the curtain. "Chasing Boomer around. You know how he gets after eight o'clock."

His rich chuckle hit me right below the sternum. "How was your day?"

I took a second to reflect on the day. I know the expected reply was to give a generic "good" or "fine" and then reciprocate with the same question, but I didn't feel like social niceties were always conducive to meaningful exchanges. So I went with the truth.

"I don't know. It was kind of weird." I felt the strain of holding the phone up to my ear with my noodle of an arm and added, "And a little painful."

"Painful?"

I fought back a sigh at how concerned he sounded. Why, oh why, was my body working against me?

"I'm fine. I think. I went to Paige's intermediate-advanced class this evening. And then I ate a lot of pizza rolls."

"That was a bold move. Just felt like a little light torture on a Monday?"

I could hear rustling in the background, and I instantly imagined him shirtless in bed. I was developing a very active imagination at twenty-six, and it was apparently dirty.

"Ugh, no. I needed to talk to Paige, and she's been avoiding me. So it was more about desperation than the desire to be tortured." I tried to focus on the conversation instead of the images of shirtless Sebastian floating around my brain.

"Are you two having a row?" His question was followed by more of the distracting rustling.

"Having a row?" I asked, my mind still more focused on trying to discern the source of the rustling.

"Are you fighting?" he clarified.

"Oh no, we aren't fighting. I think she just needed some time to process some stuff, and I was worried about her. We talked tonight though, so my plan worked." My ears still strained to hear the background noise. Did naked have a sound? *Focus, Lennon, focus.* "How was your day?"

"Long. Practice was grueling, I had meetings all afternoon, and then a photo shoot. I'm absolutely knackered," he said, his words ending on a yawn.

My mind was running through a list of all the really important questions, like: What kind of photoshoot? Was it for underwear? Were you in underwear? Can *I* see you in underwear? Thankfully, there was some part of my brain that was still functioning rationally and forced an appropriate response out of my mouth.

"I'm sorry you had a long day. Afternoon meetings are always the worst, and I'm sure they are extra miserable after a long practice. What was the photoshoot for?"

Please say underwear. Please say underwear. Please say underwear.

"Rolex. Not my favorite, but better than standing around in my knickers." I disagreed strongly but kept my lips zipped. "I didn't call to complain, though. Wanted to see if you picked a game yet."

"Yes! I did, actually. The game against FC Seattle—or Seattle FC; I can't remember where the FC part goes—if that's okay."

"That's fine. Should be a good game." I heard him trying to muffle a yawn. "Sorry."

The ticket. As in singular. As in, one for me and not one for Aaron. I couldn't think of a single good reason why I had assumed Sebastian would be giving me two tickets, and I had already invited Aaron. I closed my eyes and let out a breath. I had to ask. I *had* to. Aaron would be so disappointed if I didn't, and I really didn't want to go to the game alone. Just the thought of it sent a shudder through me.

I braced myself and forced the words out. "I have a favor to ask, but I don't want to sound rude or greedy."

"I have a favor to ask, but I don't want to sound rude or ungrateful."

"A favor?" he asked, a hard edge to his voice that made my toes curl into my slippers.

"I know, it's already so nice of you to offer me a ticket and I guess I should have clarified the details with you first. It's just the idea of all those people, strangers, packed into a stadium makes me really nervous, and it's been such a long time since I've been to a sporting event that I'm afraid I won't know what to do—"

"Lennon, sweetheart, take a breath. Do you want an extra ticket? Is that what you're carrying on about?"

"Would that be okay?" I asked, hoping the answer was yes. If not, I would have to find another pair of big girl panties for this game, and I was blowing through my supply of them at an alarming rate.

"Yeah, of course it's okay." His voice had lost that hard edge and he sounded almost amused. "There's plenty of room in the box."

"The box?" I asked, hoping he couldn't hear the increasing anxiety in my voice.

"Yeah, there's a suite or box for family and friends of the team."

A suite? That didn't sound ideal. I would definitely be forced to interact with the other occupants, and I wasn't sure how I would explain my presence in that particular group. And then there was the hot dogs. I remember how unnaturally delicious the hot dogs had been at the baseball games Grandpa had dragged me to when Harrison was unavailable.

"Oh, a suite. Are... are there hot dogs in the suite?"

"Hot dogs? I've no idea. I'm sure they can bring you a hot dog if you fancy one." His voice sounded incredulous and amused.

Silence stretched across the line, taking us from one awkward second to the next. I didn't know how to ask Sebastian for what I really wanted. I'd never been in this situation before, so I wasn't sure what was acceptable. I chewed on my lower lip, wondering how I could explain myself without sounding unhinged or ungrateful.

Sebastian made a sound, halfway between a sigh and a chuckle.

"What's on your mind, Lennon?"

"Can I sit in the stands?" I blurted it out so quickly that the syllables all ran together. I took a deep breath, trying to slow my proverbial roll. "I really, really don't mean to sound ungrateful. But I went to baseball games with my grandpa growing up and I remember how good the hot dogs were at the game. I did some research and concluded that the atmosphere of the stadium setting was likely what made the hot dogs taste so good—you know, the way you become an instant member of a group sharing a common objective."

Aaron would probably cry and then murder me if he knew I

was attempting to turn down tickets to the family and friends' box.

"I want to start with the hot dog experiment, but I feel like you need me to tell you that I can get you tickets in the stands first so you can relax." The calmness in his voice managed to soothe all the raw edges of my nerves. "I'm not mad, love. If you'd be more comfortable sitting in the stands with your friend, that's perfectly fine. Now tell me about this experiment."

It did not escape me that he had used two terms of endearment during our conversation. I was greedily gathering them up and storing them like a skinny squirrel in the fall. I might have to ignore them now, but I could dig them up to enjoy later. So I told Sebastian about the late summer afternoon Grandpa, Harrison, and I had spent eating various combinations of different manufacturers' hot dogs and buns, all cooked different ways. The experiment lasted until Harrison puked because he insisted on eating the entire hot dog instead of just a couple of bites of each combination.

We spent another thirty minutes talking, while I tried to ignore the fact that Sebastian had chosen to spend the end of his long day talking to me.

26.

We settled on a Mexican restaurant that was centrally located between Spatium, the yoga studio, and Kay's apartment for our girls' night. Janie and I were the last ones to arrive because of traffic, and between Janie's driving and the stress of LA rush hour, I was thinking the fishbowl-sized margaritas advertised on the board above the hostess station sounded like a very good idea.

Janie and I slid into the open side of the booth, and I swear I experienced a moment of sheer euphoria knowing I had survived what Janie had called "evasive maneuvers" but would be more accurately described as reckless operation of a motor vehicle. We each placed an order for a fishbowl margarita and took a minute to peruse the menu, silently acknowledging our mutual understanding that the business of ordering food needed to be handled before we got down to the business of talking.

Orders placed, I tried to sneak the index card I had written a list of items to discuss at dinner on out of my purse, but it slipped out of my grasp and landed next to Janie's foot.

"What's that?" Janie asked, bending down to pick it up.

I made a swipe for the card, but it was too late. Holding the card just out of my reach, she took in the list I had spent an embarrassing amount of time procrastinating on earlier in the afternoon, when I should have been busy reviewing a thruster blueprint that was hot off the press.

"Is this... a list of things to discuss tonight? Did you really think we would run out of things to talk about?" she asked, sounding surprised.

"No! I just didn't want us to miss something important, and I also didn't feel like doing any actual work."

Janie snorted, handing me the index card. "Now *that* I can relate to. Your explosions are starting to give me hives."

"Explosions?" Paige asked, her eyes wide and eyebrows raised high.

"Our last test launches with the simulator software have all ended with something exploding." I sighed. "Think Fourth of July in space."

Paige and Kay grimaced.

"Yep, but instead of going *boom* those explosions go *ka-ching, ka-ching, ka-ching*," Janie said, absently scratching her wrist. While she was distracted I snatched the card back and returned it to my purse. But Janie wasn't ready to let it go. "Anyway, the first item on the Lennon's list was updates on Kay's life, because she missed the last girls' night. However, I would like to make a motion to move Paige ordering extra cheese on her quesadillas to the number one slot. Paige, what's with the cheese?"

Paige took what I imagined was a fortifying breath and filled Janie and Kay in on her decision to go back school and the ensuing fight with her mom.

"Wow, Paige, that's great! I mean, obviously your mom is a total bitch, but I think it's amazing that you're going back to school. And that you're back on the dairy."

Kay echoed Janie's congratulations, and assured Paige that she was one of the three people on this planet who didn't need plastic surgery.

"Thanks, ladies. I've had to drop some of my normal yoga classes, so I'm hoping I saved enough to make this work. Obviously, my parents aren't an option for help. I hear eating ramen for every meal is basically a rite of passage for college students, though," Paige replied with what sounded like forced cheerfulness.

I made a mental note to make sure she was not actually eating ramen. As much as I loved ramen, I had a feeling Paige was more worried than she was letting on.

"Oh my gosh, Paige!" I sat up, suddenly remembering the conversation I'd had with Harrison. "I can't believe I didn't think of this sooner! It's perfect! Harrison is looking for someone to help him around the shop."

"Oh no—" she began, but Kay interrupted whatever argument she was about to make.

"I love that idea! He would totally work around your class schedule, and you'd get to work with me."

"*And* you'd get to work with Harrison every day." Janie sighed dreamily. "That is a job perk I could really get behind. Or under, or on top of."

I groaned. "Please stop before I barf up the salsa and am scarred for life."

Janie shrugged, taking a sip of her margarita.

"I don't know. I'm not sure I'm even qualified to work there," Paige responded, thankfully ignoring Janie's comments about Harrison even though I was pretty sure seeing him every day would end up in her pros column.

"At least think about it," I urged. "Bad Wolf could use another woman around to keep the guys in line."

"Amen to that," Kay said, lifting her glass with both hands. "I think you're more than qualified too. You'd be a great fit for the shop."

"Since we're all in agreement that Paige is awesome, let's move on to the next item on the agenda," Janie said with mock seriousness.

"No, no, no!" I cut her off, slapping my hand over her mouth. "Did you memorize that freaking list?"

All Janie could do was nod and mumble around my hand.

"Kay, what's new with you?" I asked, hand still firmly in place over Janie's mouth.

"Nice try. I want to hear whatever it is you're willing to use force to prevent from coming out."

Paige nodded. "You did put it on the agenda."

"No one was supposed to see it," I grumbled, dropping my hand. "And it wasn't an agenda."

"Lennon has a date with Patrick on Friday!" Janie blurted out as soon as my hand left her mouth.

There was a full minute of pandemonium as all three women talked excitedly. I made no effort to even attempt to follow along. I focused on shoveling the complimentary chips and salsa into my mouth instead.

"Are you excited?" Paige asked.

Kay followed with, "Where are you going?"

Janie felt the need to add, "Do you have condoms?" even though she'd told me the first-date limit was one boob grope.

I swallowed my current mouthful and then attacked their questions in the order they were asked.

"I don't know, Arthur's, and of course not."

"You'll love Arthur's," Paige assured me. "They have the best breads."

"How can you not know if you're excited?" Kay asked.

"Because it's Lennon," Janie said, nudging me with her shoulder.

I rolled my eyes. "I am excited to meet him, but I'm also pretty nervous."

"It's totally normal to be nervous about a first date," Kay assured me. "I mean, it's been about a decade since I had a date, but I think I remember being nervous."

"Men are just intimidated by your awesomeness. Pretty sure Lou would go out with you in a heartbeat," I pointed out.

It was her turn to roll her eyes. "I would rather die alone. Lou would go out with a broom if it had boobs."

"That's probably true." As much as I loved Lou, there wasn't much I could say in his defense when it came to women. "I've already started making a list of possible topics of conversation based on Patrick's interests and our shared interests. I also did some research into the area of biomedical engineering he specializes in, so I can meaningfully participate in any conversation about his work. I think all that's left to do is pick out an outfit."

"Oh, that's an easy one. You'll wear the emerald wrap dress with the capped sleeves." Paige's tone was confident and commanding. "That was not a suggestion."

"Emerald would be a great color for you," Kay added, squinting like she was trying to picture me in the dress Paige described. It had been safely housed in the garment bag I'd brought it home in after Paige convinced me to buy it.

"It's not too much for a first date?" I didn't want to end up looking like I was meeting the queen instead of a man I'd met on the internet. I didn't know what the expectations were for this type of first date. My last boyfriend I met in class when I was wearing sweatpants and a T-shirt. Our first date was a game night at his friend's apartment, to which I wore nicer sweatpants and a sweater.

"Nope, it's perfect. You're a total knockout in that dress," Paige assured me.

"Oh, while we're on the topic of clothing. Would it be weird to get a Nova jersey with Sebastian's name and number on it to wear to the game? He offered to let me sit in the family and friends' box, but I thought that would be weird. It would be normal friendship stuff to wear his jersey, though, right?"

I was too busy eyeballing the tacos al pastor the server had just placed in front of me to appreciate the fact that silence had descended around the table. I took a bite and looked up to find three pairs of eyes staring at me.

"Wut?" I managed around a mouthful of perfectly marinated pork.

Janie blinked at me no less than five times before she managed words. "Hold the mothertrucking phone. Sebastian wanted you to sit in the WAGs box?"

I shook my head. "No, the suite for family and friends."

"So the WAGs box." Paige's eyes seemed to widen with each word until I was worried they might pop out of her head. I moved my plate closer to me just in case they rolled my way.

"I feel like we're speaking different languages here. What am I missing?" I directed my question at Kay in the hopes that she would be the other sane person at this table and could translate whatever language Paige and Janie were speaking.

"WAGs is an acronym for 'wives and girlfriends.' Also a terrible reality show that I don't think lasted long," Kay explained. "It's used exclusively for the wives and girlfriends of professional athletes."

It was my turn to blink furiously while my mind worked to reconcile this new information with what I believed to be true.

"Okay, well, wives and girlfriends fall into the categories of family and friends respectively, so I suppose both statements can be true." I shuddered involuntarily. "I'm even more thankful I asked to sit in the bleachers now. Though Aaron's going to be extra mad if he finds out I turned down those tickets."

"Why would Aaron be mad?" Paige was looking at me like we were still speaking different languages.

"Because Lennon gave him the extra ticket." Kay followed up this statement with a slightly deranged laugh that was, concerningly, echoed by Janie.

"Oh, this is going to be good," Paige grinned.

I wanted to ask what she meant by that, and why Kay and Janie were exchanging conspiratorial looks. There was also the one thing I couldn't bring myself to write down earlier, the thing that was occupying way too many of my in-between thoughts. Did it mean anything that Sebastian had called me 'love' and 'sweetheart'? But just like every other time my mind started to wander down that particular road of what-ifs, I chastised myself for spending so much time thinking about Sebastian.

The Lennon who believed in science and thought rationally knew that if you had to look that hard to prove something existed, in all likelihood, the thing didn't really exist. You were just creating evidence to support a theory you wanted to be true. I needed to focus, to spend my energy on what the evidence supported: Patrick. Given the fact that he had asked me out on a date, I knew he was interested in at least pursuing a romantic relationship with me. I didn't have to wonder 'what if' or search for hidden meanings where they likely weren't. So I steered the conversation away from me altogether.

27.

And just like that, it was D day.

Date. Doom. Death. Diarrhea. Or dick, as Janie had so helpfully reminded me via text twice already. Three times if you count the post-it note attached to the box of condoms I found on my desk this morning. 'Ribbed for her pleasure,' and extra-large because Janie was an eternal optimist.

Despite the daily affirmations that Paige had been sending me since Wednesday, I didn't feel smart, beautiful or fun. I felt incredibly nauseated. I took another large drink straight from the bottle of Mylanta I was currently on track to finish by the end of the day. I was alternating between drinking antacids and ingesting them in chewable form, depending on the setting. For example, it would have been extremely weird to pull out my bottle of Mylanta and start chugging during the long meeting we had just before lunch, so I'd switched to the cherry-flavored chews to keep down the rising panic that was threatening to exit my body in violent fashion.

I watched as the clock on my monitor changed from 5:29 to 5:30. *It's time.* I let out a nervous burp and took another swig of Mylanta just as my phone dinged. I looked at the screen. It was Janie.

Janie: Girl, time to get that D! Meet you in your office in 10.

I sighed. The only D I currently wanted to get was Doritos from the vending machine, but I stood and grabbed the dress hanging off the back of my door, thankful for the first time that my office didn't have any windows. I quickly unbuttoned my shirt and shrugged it off, and then slipped off my skirt before pulling the green dress over my shoulders. I tied the little inside strings super tight, then wrapped the thicker outer bands together, securing them with a bow over my left hip. I looked down to survey how much of my cleavage was on display, and tugged the material together enough to hide the top of my scar poking out above it. I was sure nothing would kill the mood quicker than a story about open-heart surgery. That was definitely more of a second-date topic. This dress really did make it look like I had something to work with and the band around the waist gave me the appearance of having hips.

Janie burst through the door without even bothering to knock. "That dress is killer!"

"I could have been naked!" I shielded my cleavage with my hands for absolutely no reason. "But yes, it's a really good dress."

Janie swatted at my hands. "Don't hide that light under a bushel, let it shine! What are we doing about your hair?"

I reached up instinctively to smooth down the flyaways. "What's wrong with my hair?"

Forty minutes later, my hair had been styled by Janie, my makeup had been touched up, and I was standing outside of Arthur's trying to force myself through the door. I was a seven-layer bar of nerves covered in emerald-green icing. Nerves on nerves on nerves.

"It's just a date, Lennon, you can do this," I reassured myself, wiping an alarming amount of moisture from my hands onto my dress. "Bad idea! Shoot."

I waved the bottom of my dress back and forth, trying to create enough air circulation to dry the small wet smudges left behind on the fabric.

"Lennon?"

The sound of my name had me spinning around mid-swish. I turned around fully, mortification very evident on my face and neck, and faced the man who so closely resembled the pictures on his profile.

"Patrick?" I stuck my arm out so fast for a handshake that I ended up almost punching him in the chest. Off to a good start. "Hi, it's nice to finally meet you. That feels weird to say since we've been talking for a month now."

He smiled and slipped his hand into mine. "It does, but it's nice to be able to talk face to face. I hope you're hungry."

Patrick released my hand and opened the door for me. I stepped into the restaurant and tried my best to look more "happy to be here" and less "deer in the headlights."

"I actually skipped lunch today too." I paused as Patrick gave his name to the server. "My friend Paige—I think I've mentioned her before—told me Arthur's has the best bread."

"It's really amazing. They bake all their bread here, so it's always fresh and warm." Patrick smiled at me, seeming completely at ease.

I was so focused on staying calm and not tripping over my feet that I literally noticed absolutely nothing about the restaurant by the time we reached the table. I could not have answered the question if someone asked me what color the walls were. The host pulled my chair out for me and I slid into it with all the grace of a drunk hippopotamus. I picked up the menu and gave it a quick glance. According to the research I had done on dating etiquette, I should select something that could be easily cut into smaller pieces and wasn't messy. Chicken wings were a definite no. Pasta fell into an ambiguous territory that made me think it would be wise to avoid if possible.

"Do you recommend anything?" I asked Patrick, glancing up from the menu.

He really did look just like his pictures, except it seemed he'd spent extra time styling his blond waves, and he had shaved the light beard covering his face in most of his pictures, revealing a strong jawline with the hint of a cleft in his chin. He was taller than me by a few inches, and lean but not thin, like maybe he went to the gym once or twice a week. He definitely didn't have Sebastian's—I pumped the mental brakes on that train of thought.

"I've had the pork chops and the sea bass, both of which were really good. I don't think you can go wrong here, though." He smiled at me over his menu and I made a valiant attempt to meet his gaze. "I should probably try something new, but I'm going to go with the pork chops."

"Why mess with a good thing?" I offered. I was so nervous that nothing sounded good and I was a little worried that I might actually end up barfing.

"Exactly." He nodded. "I try to be really adventurous but sometimes it's good to stick with something you know you'll like."

I placed the menu in front of me, giving him my full attention. "What's the most adventurous thing you've eaten?"

He didn't miss a beat before responding. "Odorigui."

"You ate live seafood?" I couldn't keep the horror out of my voice.

"Yeah, I had live ice gobies when I was in Japan. The whole thing was really awful." He shivered at the memory. "I would not recommend it."

I tried to shift the conversation to less disgusting territory. "What made you travel to Japan? I've always wanted to visit but haven't gotten the chance."

"I actually minored in Japanese. I was there as part of an immersion program for a semester. It was an awesome experience."

"Wow, that's amazing! I regret not spending a semester abroad when I was in college," I admitted, just before the waiter returned to take our orders.

The conversation flowed so easily for the rest of the meal that I didn't once feel the urge to pull out the index card with my list of potential topics. It was like catching up with an old friend you haven't seen in a while. Dinner turned into dessert and then into a drink, and I was almost disappointed it was over as we walked in companionable silence to my car.

"This is me," I said, coming to a stop next to my car. We stared at each other silently, Patrick with his hands in his pockets and me shifting my weight from foot to foot. This was the most awkward part of the date since meeting outside the restaurant, and my mind was scrambling for a way to break the silence.

"God, I'm terrible at this." He let out a self-deprecating laugh. "I had a really nice time."

I gave him what I hoped was a reassuring smile. "I had a really nice time too, and for what it's worth, I think you're doing a great job."

"I'm glad you think so, because I'd very much like to see you again."

"I'd like that too," I responded, as I pressed the unlock button on my key fob.

Patrick shifted forward, one hand coming out of a pocket to open my door. I stepped forward to avoid getting hit by the door and effectively caged myself in—not that I felt threatened, just a little nervous about the physical closeness. Patrick's eyes searched my face before drifting to my mouth. His head dipped down and I closed my eyes reflexively. I felt the soft press of his lips against mine and I fought the urge to stiffen in response. It had been a long time since I'd had a first kiss. His lips moved across mine, and I relaxed into his touch as his other hand found my hip. Our lips met once, twice and again before he broke the kiss and smiled down at me.

"Let me know you make it home okay," he said, helping me into the car.

I nodded mutely.

"Have a good night, Lennon."

He shut the door and stood back. I fumbled with my keys for a second and robotically fastened my seat belt. I gave a small wave and pulled away, sneaking one last glance at him standing on the curb, watching me drive off.

I drove silently for a couple of minutes, trying to turn off my brain. It wanted to analyze every second of that kiss.

"Stop trying to ruin this for me!" I yelled at my brain and turned the radio up, trying to drown out my internal monologue "I'm just going to enjoy the fact that I had a good first kiss and an even better first date with a really nice guy."

I had a feeling I was going to have to relive the whole thing with Paige, Kay, and Janie later anyway. I drove home feeling a little weird but also pretty dang proud of myself. Tonight, I, Lennon June Walker, made dating my biotch.

28.

I rode the good-date high for most of the next few days. I woke up Saturday morning to find a sweet text from Patrick telling me again what a good time he'd had. Just as I had anticipated, Paige knocked on my door around eleven and dragged me to brunch, where she made me go over every second of the date. I didn't think I'd ever had post-date brunch with a girlfriend and I kind of loved it. Also, mimosas.

Patrick and I exchanged texts the rest of the weekend, and I was genuinely disappointed that he was going to be out of town next weekend for a bachelor party. He was leaving Tuesday, so we wouldn't have a chance to squeeze in another date before he left. We did make tentative plans for the following week, but now that I had flexed the old dating muscles, I was ready to go.

As someone who is highly motivated by food, the promise of a food truck festival on Wednesday kept me going through all the disasters of a still-exploding engine and some very concerned meetings with higher-ups at the beginning of the week. Spatium had arranged for a bunch of food trucks to set up in the little green space outside the building, which was usually filled with picnic tables and a few hammocks for people who wanted to spend their lunch breaks outside. I had been watching them transform the space all week to accommodate the food trucks, so by the time Wednesday rolled around, I was more than ready to get my stress-eat on. I even remembered to grab my tennis shoes on my way out the door this morning—the shoes that had been in the exact same spot by the door since my soccer lesson with Sebastian.

As soon as the clock on my computer flashed the magic numbers 1-2, I was reaching for the shoes I had stashed under my desk and slipping off my flats. I snapped a picture of my sneaker-clad feet and sent it to Sebastian.

Me: It's food truck festival Wednesday and I came prepared! This is the first time these bad boys have seen any action since our game. I like my odds of winning at a food truck festival better than my odds of beating you at football.

I was about to slip my phone into my bag when a strange guilty feeling made me pull it back out and send a similar message to Patrick. I knew it was silly to feel guilty about sending a text to Sebastian and not Patrick. We were just friends. I never felt guilty about sending a text to Paige or Kay. The only difference between them and Sebastian was that Sebastian just happened to have a penis and these veins in his forearms that did things to me.

"Hey, what the hell!" Janie yelled, throwing open the door to my office and almost causing me to throw my phone at her head.

"Geez, Janie! You almost gave me a heart attack!"

"You've been harassing me all week about this food truck festival and you're the one who's running late? I skipped breakfast to prepare for this, and I think I should warn you that I'm straight up hangry."

"Sorry!" I scrambled out of my chair and grabbed my purse, slightly afraid of upsetting a hangry Janie. "I had to send a message really quick."

I turned off my light and jogged down the hall after Janie, who was already halfway to the elevator. We made our way out of the building, and both paused to take in the glorious sight of three tidy rows of food trucks occupying the green space.

"If heaven had a smell, it would be fried food," Janie said on a dreamy sigh. She wasn't wrong.

"I think I can actually feel my salivary glands kicking into gear." I tore my gaze from the trucks and asked, "Are we sticking with our original plan to get the lay of the land before we make any decisions?"

"Yes, definitely," Janie nodded, making her way toward the first row of trucks. "Maybe they'll have samples a la Costco?"

We wandered down each row, reading menus and creepily eyeballing other people's selections before making our own choices. Janie went with what looked like just a gigantic pile of shaved meats from Off-Beat Street Meat, and I chose a gourmet grilled cheese sandwich from Cut the Cheese—in large part because they had tater tots as a side. A girl can always be swayed by a good potato.

Are you sure that's a Rueben?" I asked as we sat at a picnic table tucked under one of the tents that had been erected for the event. "It just looks like weird meats on a plate."

"You just worry about you." Janie gave me a look that made me clamp my mouth shut. Note to self: Hangry Janie was kind of terrifying.

A series of dings coming from the general direction of my purse had me doing a one-handed dive for my phone. No way was I putting down a tot to check my messages.

Patrick: Good luck and Godspeed! I am seriously considering switching careers so I can work for Spatium.

I smiled and then moved to the next message.

Sebastian: That's one field I wouldn't want to face you on. Keep me updated on your progress.

He attached a picture of himself sitting in an ice bath, and I zoomed in trying to catch a peek of absolutely any part of his skin visible between cubes.

"What's with the goofy smile you're rocking over there?"

I looked up from my phone to see Janie looking significantly less scary, with an empty plate in front of her.

"Oh—uh, I was just reading some texts from Patrick and Sebastian."

I took a quick picture of my plate and sent it to Sebastian with a "Round 1 goes to Lennon" caption.

"Girl, go on with your bad self!" Janie said right before a burp escaped. "I'm kind of disgusted with myself for that, but also kind of proud."

"I'm pretty proud of you myself. I honestly didn't think you could handle that much meat."

Janie threw her head back and laughed. "Speaking of handling meat, look at you juggling men. The professional athlete, the suave engineer—which one will she choose?"

"I am not juggling men!" I launched a tot at her, and she managed to catch it with her mouth. "Sebastian is just a friend."

"Yeah, mmmkay. Do you smile like a horny little clown when you read my texts too?"

"I do not smile like a horny little clown at his texts!" I said defensively.

"You're right. Sometimes you make these lovesick puppy eyes and sigh dreamily while you try to get a glimpse of that dick in an ice bath—which, by the way, is not the best setting for a dick pic." She held up her hand, moving her thumb and pointer finger closer together.

"How am I friends with such a pervert? You seemed like such a nice girl when we met."

"Lies. I come as advertised. Speaking of come—" I groaned but Janie was not deterred. "I think you should take both vehicles for a test drive before you make a purchase."

When I didn't respond, she felt the need to clarify. "I'm talking about sex."

I rolled my eyes at her.

"I'm not having sex with anyone. Wait, that's not what I meant. I'm having sex with Patrick." Janie's eyebrows hit her hairline. "Ugh, that's not what I meant either! No one is having any sex. Can we just move on please?"

"Speak for yourself." She held up her hand, stopping the words of protest before they left my mouth. "I'm going to grant you a temporary reprieve, because I have a full stomach and am feeling generous."

"You are a wise and benevolent queen," I said, voice oozing with sarcasm.

"And don't you forget it, my little peasant. Anywho, I was talking to Will after class last night and he's trying to organize a big LOTR game night at his house next weekend. I said I'd put out some feelers with my peeps. Would you be interested in going? It should be pretty fun. LARPing optional, obvi."

"Yes! I'm totally in, and it just so happens, I ordered a new LOTR shirt last month. I've been dying to wear it someplace that will appreciate its awesomeness."

"Perfect! I'll get you more concrete details once it's a sure thing. Feel free to invite one of your boy toys. The more the merrier, I always say."

"I have literally never heard you say that," I pointed out. "Are you ready for round two?"

Thankfully, Janie was too busy eating the rest of lunch to mention Patrick or Sebastian again, but I couldn't seem to shake the feeling of guilt from earlier. I knew for a fact that I was not dating two people. I didn't even think I was technically dating one person. Some part of me recognized that the problem was that my heart and my head were not at all on the same page. If I could step through a wardrobe and into a world of magic, I would choose Sebastian—and that was a problem, since I currently did not have access to a magic portal.

Later that evening, I made a quick stop at the grocery store to grab some essentials—ice cream and cat food. Cart filled with a bag of cat food, an assortment of cat treats, and a pint of ice cream for me, I made my way toward the checkout lines. As usual, the line for the self-checkout was longer than most of the normal lines, so I wandered into the "ten items or less" line and perused the candy lining the shelves. A magazine cover caught my eye and I yanked it out of the slot to get a better look.

I knew that face. The grin, the tattooed forearms. The headline read, in bold letters: *Sebastian Kincaid Spotted with Mystery Woman*. The pictures were clearly taken from a distance but the images were easy enough to make out. My heart sank. Sebastian was leaning in close to a tall blonde woman whose back was to the camera. The series of photos showed the leaning turn into a hug and then a kiss on the cheek. I absently rubbed the scar on my chest through my dress. The brief blurb under the pictures was speculation about who the blonde could be, and whether this was a new girlfriend or just the flavor of the month for the British playboy.

    I placed the magazine back in its spot and turned abruptly, squeezing past the man in the suit behind me and heading directly to the frozen foods aisle, where I added two more pints of ice cream to my cart.

29.

I wanted to pretend like my heart wasn't even a little bit broken over the pictures, but it felt like those stupid pictures were playing on a highlight reel in my mind the rest of the week. A courier dropped off tickets with VIP access to the game on Saturday, and instead of feeling excited, I kind of felt like crying. I knew I was being an idiot, but I couldn't make it stop.

Aaron held down the excited front for both of us, though. Kay sent me a picture of him wearing his VIP pass around the shop on Friday afternoon. It was actually pretty adorable. We made plans to meet at the shop Saturday afternoon, and then share a ride to the stadium, since the shop was closer than either of our apartments. He talked about the game non-stop Friday night until even good-natured Lou looked like he was ready to strangle him. I doubted Aaron would be getting any sleep tonight. He reminded me of a kid on Christmas Eve.

I woke up Saturday morning to persistent meowing and cat paws to my face. I cracked open an eye and glared at Boomer. He sat down on the pillow next to me and started licking his paws like he hadn't just cat-slapped me awake.

"It's not time for breakfast." I rolled over, fully prepared to go back to sleep for at least another hour.

Just as I was drifting off to sleep, Boomer landed on my head with a loud meow. He made circles on my cheek and shoulders until one of his paws was hopelessly tangled in my hair. I sighed.

"All right, you win. Ouch! Boomer, sit still, you're pulling my hair out." I withdrew one arm from out of the blankets and rolled over just enough to reach the stuck paw. I got to work untangling it while Boomer made hysterical cat noises directly into my ear. "None of the Disney princesses had to deal with this from their animal friends. They swept their floors and made their beds, not ripped chunks of hair out of their head."

I got us untangled and dragged myself out of bed to make us both breakfast. Boomer promptly scarfed down his food and found a sunny spot to pass out in. A nap didn't sound bad to me and I still had an hour before I needed to start getting ready. I tried to sleep, but as soon as my body was still, my mind got busy worrying. Large crowds were not my thing, and it felt like every minute I spent lying on the couch made my anxiety worse. I gave up, deciding that spending a little extra time on my appearance today wasn't the worst idea anyway.

I styled my hair into controlled waves instead of the usual chaos and applied a little more makeup than I might have on a normal Saturday. I pulled on the Novas jersey I'd ordered with Sebastian's name and number on the back, and a pair of jeans I hadn't worn in forever—so long that I had to do the shimmy-and-prayer routine to get them on. I completed my new 'footy fan' look with a Novas baseball cap to keep the California sun out of my eyes, and a soccer scarf draped over my shoulders, which the internet told me was necessary to call oneself a true FC fan. The internet had also informed me that FC stood for football club, so I was basically fluent in all things football now.

I headed toward the shop and found Aaron already outside pacing back and forth like he couldn't physically contain his excitement. I checked my phone to make sure I wasn't late and saw that I was a good fifteen minutes early. I waved when he turned to pace back in my direction.

"Hey, you're early!"

"Yeah, I was worried about traffic." His gaze traveled over me. "Look at you, all fanned out."

"I wanted to blend." I turned around enough to show him

the *Kincaid* lettered across my back. "And show my support for my favorite player."

He smiled, flashing those almost too-white teeth. "Favorite player, huh? You know a lot of other players?"

"Do you think I'm just hanging around with professional athletes now?" I pulled out my phone to order our ride.

He huffed out a laugh. "I meant, can you name another player on the Novas?"

"Oh, of course. There's a... there's the guy with... *Malone*!" I shouted triumphantly. I remembered seeing that name on the list of jersey names when I was shopping online.

"Calm down over there, Supernova." He snorted a little at his own terrible joke. "Are you ordering us a ride or do you want me to do it?"

"I got it. You can buy our first round of hot dogs."

"First round?" he asked, sounding incredulous. What an amateur.

Our car pulled to the curb a few minutes later, and we rode to the stadium, each of us fidgeting with a different type of nerves. My anxiety reached almost hysterical levels when I caught my first look at the crowds gathered around the stadium. My fingers tapped out a nervous rhythm on my jeans-covered thigh. The car came to a stop and Aaron I stepped out into the throng of people. The words 'teeming masses' came to mind.

"There's a lot of people here. I thought soccer wasn't that popular," I stated, trying to make my voice sound light instead of slightly panicked.

"The Novas have a pretty big group of diehard fans, and their popularity exploded when they got two players from the FIFA trade. Seattle got a player from Barca, so it should be a pretty exciting match."

"What is Barca?"

His excitement was infectious, even though I didn't understand what he'd just said.

"FC Barcelona. Spain has two powerhouse teams, FC Barcelona and Real Madrid, and you don't play for them unless you're the best of the best. So I am obviously stoked about watching Ramos play even though he's playing for Seattle."

I watched him as he steered us toward the entrance Sebastian had told us to use. He did look excited. Something about watching him like this made him seem less intimidating and more human. It also slowed the pace of my racing heart. Facts. Aaron was giving me facts. I could be distracted by a little information-gathering.

"You really like soccer, don't you?"

"Yeah. I played all the time growing up, in leagues and in the neighborhood. My *abuela* is a huge Barcelona fan, which makes absolutely no sense since she was born in Juarez and has never stepped foot in Spain. We got cable growing up just so she could watch their matches, so I wasn't complaining." He shot me one his half-grins and I actually managed to smile back at him as we stepped into a line of people.

I thought of another question to ask him to keep my mind focused on anything besides the crowd that felt like it was starting to surround us from all directions. The noise got louder the closer we got to the stadium.

"Is your scarf for Barcelona?"

He lifted one frayed end. "It's about fifteen years old but yeah, it is. Abuela got it for me on my thirteenth birthday. It's lucky."

"That was really nice."

We shuffled a few more feet forward.

"Not really." He chuckled at my bewildered expression. "I was a huge Manchester United fan. She acted like I had betrayed the family. '*Como pudiste hacerme esto, mijo?*' The old woman loves her telenovelas as much as she loves her FC. Joke was on her though, United signed Ronaldo that year."

I laughed along even though I had no idea who this Ronaldo character was. I asked Aaron a few more questions while we slowly marched toward the lady taking tickets. It was a good distraction. We finally reached the entrance and handed our tickets to the lady who greeted us. She looked at them and asked us to stand to the side just inside the gate, then spoke into her walkie-talkie.

"If you two wouldn't mind standing right there, someone will be along in just a second to take you to your seats." She smiled at us and then turned her attention back to the line.

I looked at Aaron who looked bewildered but was also wearing a huge smile.

"Is this normal?" I asked, watching the people who were in line behind us walk through the entrance and into the stadium.

He shook his head. "Nope, definitely not normal—but then I've never been a VIP before. This is so fucking awesome."

My stomach did a series of tumbles that did not feel awesome, and my heart followed its movements. It seemed like people were filling all the empty space around us and I could barely hear myself think over the music coming from the overhead system. I took a few steps closer to Aaron, basically plastering myself against his side, gaze still laser-focused on our shoes.

I felt him looking at the top of my head. "You okay?"

I nodded, giving him a sad imitation of a smile. "Yeah, there's just so many people."

He threw an arm around my shoulders and hauled me the few remaining inches into him.

"I got you, Lennon. This is going to be fun. It'll seem less crazy when we get to our seats, and hey, we can get those hot dogs."

"Hello, folks!" A middle-aged man greeted us before I could answer. "May I have your tickets, please?"

We handed them over and he scanned them quickly, smiled, and waved us forward. Aaron chatted with our guide while I took everything in, including all the vending places we passed. Once we were out in the open, things were a little less loud and chaotic.

Aaron elbowed me in the side and gave me crazy eyes. We walked down row after row until we were almost to the field. Finally, our guide stopped and gestured toward two seats in the middle of the second row.

"You two are right through here. A waiter should be around shortly if you'd like to order a drink or something to eat, but you're of course welcome to grab something inside and bring it down. Enjoy the game."

Aaron nodded a lot and I said a thank-you. The row was completely empty, so we were able to walk through the row to our seats without a problem. We sat down, both of us wiggling a few times to get comfortable, and looked out over midfield where a couple of players were stretching.

"Lennon," Aaron said, never taking his eyes off the field, "I think this is the best day of my life."

30.

A waiter did in fact come by a few minutes later to take our order. Looking around the rows of seats behind us, it was very obvious that we were not seated with the general public. I turned around to face the field and watched as more players jogged onto it to stretch or kick a ball back and forth. My eyes eagerly scanned every new player, looking for Sebastian. I squinted into the distance toward two men who were standing near a row of benches on one side of the field. My gaze lingered on the heavily tattooed arms of one, and the uniform that clung to a now-familiar body.

I smiled. Nudging Aaron, I pointed toward the two men.

"Look, Aaron, I see Sebastian!"

Aaron looked in the direction I was pointing. "Holy shit, you're right! It looks like he's talking to Sully. I don't think I've ever been so close to the field that I could actually read the name on the back of a jersey."

The rows around us slowly filled up with people. Most people wore Novas shirts or jerseys, but I noticed a few Ramos jerseys in the mix. Luckily for Aaron, the people who ended up next to us were huge soccer fans, so he spent most of the warmup talking soccer with our neighbors. I mostly visually stalked Sebastian's movements and shoveled food into my mouth. I had already downed a hot dog and nachos by the time the warmup clock on the scoreboard reached zero. I would have been two hot dogs in, but bless his heart, Aaron thought I'd ordered the second hot dog for him. I let it slide, because the waiter announced our food and drink had been 'taken care of' when Aaron attempted to pay for our first round of sustenance.

The players jogged off the field as the announcer started running through first lines and the crowd cheered. I winced at the sudden change in volume. I felt my fingers tap-tap-tapping on my leg and tried to will myself to calm down. This was fine. My amygdala needed to stop sending out distress signals. People were excited for a soccer game. This was not about to be a survival situation. I was not going to have to fight for my life gladiator-style.

I watched the promotional video playing on the scoreboard in an attempt to distract my hypothalamus with something shiny. I smiled like a lunatic every single time Sebastian was shown in the video. By the second video, I could understand why sports played such a significant cultural role through our species' history. One of my anthropology professors hypothesized that games or sports are a social mechanism that promote group unity through social intercourse, and provide members of society with a singular event to help them deal with the excessive amount of emotional stress that comes with being a human. Watching this video and its effect on the crowd did more to make me believe this theory was correct than all the scientific articles we'd read for class, especially since I was starting to feel the same overwhelming sense of excitement clearly being felt by the other members of this group.

The video ended and the crowd erupted. I looked at Aaron, hoping for a clue about what was happening. He must have read the expression on my face, because he pointed to an opening on the field where a couple of men were now standing with cameras pointed.

"The teams are getting ready to take the field."

The crowd erupted again when the announcers introduced the Novas. I jumped to my feet and clapped because herd mentality and all. I booed when they announced Seattle even though it felt mean. The teams lined up and faced an American flag that was being stretched out by a group of kids in soccer jerseys. The national anthem began to play. Instead of being patriotic, I was focused on Sebastian in his soccer uniform. It felt like he was looking right at me, which was a ridiculous thought since I was one tiny dot in a crowd of thousands of dots. But did that stop me from giving him a tiny wave anyway? Nope. I even threw in an extra-dopey smile just in case. I could have sworn I saw familiar crinkles appear in the corner of his eyes, but it was probably just the adrenaline doing things to my brain.

I snapped a picture of all the players lined up and the nice lady in front of us volunteered to take a picture of Aaron and me when she saw I was struggling to take a selfie that included more than just his chest and half my glasses. I sent them to the group text, which Janie had inexplicably named "Bonerfied Babes."

Me: Just two footy fans at a match!

Paige: Omg you look so good in all your new gear! Love the hat!

Kay: I hope you have an awesome time girlie! Aaron is never going to shut up about this. NEVER. You're lucky I love you.

Janie: At what point in the game do they start taking off their shirts? I need to know when to turn the game on.

I scrunched up my nose reading Janie's text.

Me: I don't think that is a thing?

Janie: It should be. I'd be the #1 fan if they lost all that clothing.

Paige: This is a sporting event, not a strip club, Janie.

Janie: But can you imagine how much better it would be if it was a little bit of both?

Kay: She's not wrong....

Janie: Let's compromise. Lennon, you can make it up to me by sending a picture of Aaron without his shirt on.

Me: Make what up?

Janie: IT, LENNON.

I smiled, shaking my head, and turned my attention to the start of the game.

I spent the next ninety-some minutes on a freaking roller coaster of emotions. I cheered, I gasped, I hugged Aaron, I yelled at the referees for being blind, and I nervously crammed peanuts into my mouth when Seattle got a goal kick approximately eight-seven minutes and thirteen seconds into the game. Thankfully, our goalie was amazeballs and made blocking the shot seem easy. Also, I said things like "our goalie" now.

I tracked Sebastian the entire game, and oh my ovaries, watching him play made my pituitary gland light up like a pinball machine. Holy hotness, Batman. I imagined it was like the chemical version of Fourth of July in my brain, with bright explosions of dopamine and serotonin. This Ramos character from Barcelona was no joke either. He was very good and very aggressive, and as long as it wasn't directed at Sebastian, I did not hate it. At all.

By the time the game was over and it was time to wait for Sebastian—and the other players, if you actually cared about anything else—the primal instincts that had helped *Homo erectus* beat out the other anthropoids were woke. I barely heard anything Aaron said as we walked down to the VIP tunnel to wait for Sebastian with the small crowd. I was a tangled mess of hormones that no amount of logic was going to calm down, and I was ready to give the hormones what they wanted. Who was I to stand in the way of biology?

The atmosphere in the hallway changed as soon as the door opened and the first player stepped out. Aaron was practically vibrating next to me and just generally losing his proverbial crap. It was weirdly adorable but also making me feel even more like barfing, which might have actually been good because there was a real chance that I would start humping Sebastian's leg like a dog in heat if I didn't cool down. I was one hundred percent absolutely positive that humping a player's leg would get me arrested and banned for life. Oddly enough, I was more worried about the lifetime ban than I was about a night in jail. Janie would totally bail me out once she found out it was for a lewd act.

And then Sebastian pushed through the door.

I have never been one to believe in magic or fairy tale nonsense. I liked to escape to other worlds in books, but I realized that it was just that, an escape. I was practical, logical. Sometimes to a fault. But, as I took in Sebastian in a fitted navy suit with his freshly washed hair pushed back from his forehead, it was like every single molecule that composed my corporeal form screamed *MINE*. For the first time, I was forced to acknowledge the truth. I might be a little in lust with my friend.

I knew every single one of my emotions was written on my face when Sebastian's gaze swept through the small crowd and landed on me—the happiness and the wanting. He smiled the big, beautiful smile that lit up those blue-green eyes and wreaked havoc on all my organ systems. I bounced from foot to foot impatiently, while he stopped to sign autographs or snap a picture on his way to me. Us. On his way to *us*. I had temporarily forgotten Aaron even existed, let alone that he was standing right next to me.

"He looks really good in that suit, doesn't he?" Aaron whispered, giving me a gentle nudge with his elbow.

I glanced over at him briefly and honestly, based on the current look of longing he was wearing, I felt like he might be a little bit in lust with Sebastian, too.

"Yes, how weird of you to notice," I replied. I felt strangely territorial, considering I knew for a fact that Aaron was extremely heterosexual.

With one last flick of his pen, Sebastian closed the remaining distance between us. Before I could get out the brief soliloquy I had been practicing, Sebastian's hands were on my shoulder, pulling me close as he leaned down and kissed my cheek. Just the faintest touch of warmth on my skin and all the thoughts in my head scattered.

"Hi," I sighed, looking up at him.

"Hi," he repeated, looking back at me with those smiling eyes. He gently pushed me back a few inches, his eyes traveling from my Converse-covered feet to my newly-acquired hat. "You're all kitted out like a proper fan."

I turned fully out of his grasp and pulled my hair over my shoulder so he could see the *Kincaid* lettered across my back.

"Yep, and I'm sporting my favorite player's number."

"I'm chuffed, even though I'm fairly certain I am the only player whose name you know." His deep voice was laced with humor.

"Ha. Wrong." I smiled up at him, fully prepared to use the knowledge Aaron had imparted earlier. "I know Malone, Ramos, and Harris."

"A whole three, I stand corrected."

Aaron did some sort of throat-clearing choking thing that had both Sebastian and me turning toward him.

"Hey, hi," Aaron said, sounding breathless, his eyes wide in awe.

I tugged him a little closer. "Sebastian, this is my friend Aaron."

The smile slowly faded off Sebastian's face as his eyes landed where my hand still rested on Aaron's arm. All traces of the happy, teasing Sebastian were gone and the same Sebastian I'd met that first night at the club stood in front of me. Eyes narrowed and jaw tense, Sebastian finally dipped his chin slightly at poor confused Aaron. His jaw was so tense I was concerned for the integrity of his teeth.

"Nice to meet you, mate."

He did not sound happy to meet him at all. The three of us stood lost in a Bermuda triangle of tension, until I finally did what I do best when I am anxious and have no idea what to do: ramble at approximately the speed of light.

"Aaron is the friend I was telling you about. He works at Harrison's tattoo shop as an artist, giving people tattoos. I told you I had a brother, right? An older brother who's a really talented artist, which is pretty hilarious when you think about it since art was the only class I ever almost failed. The sides of my pot collapsed in the kiln. His name is Harrison, just in case I never told you about him. Fun fact: My mom is a huge Beatles fan, so she wanted to name her kids after the Beatles, but she thought Paul and John sounded too Catholic so she went with their last names instead, which is great because I'm a girl and John is not a good name for a girl." I took a deep breath. "Anyway, back to the subject, Aaron's a really big socc—football fan, so I thought he might like to see a game. He's been serving as my unofficial interpreter while you were busy playing. Manchester United is his favorite team so ignore the scarf. His abuela gave it to him as a joke and it's lucky."

It was either stop talking or pass out from lack of oxygen, so I managed to zip my lips. I shot a quick glance at Sebastian. He was giving me that soft, patient smile that simultaneously made my heart stutter and my cheeks heat. He tugged the brim of my hat gently and then turned the full force of that smile on Aaron. Poor, poor Aaron; he didn't stand a chance. He bloomed like a morning glory in the sun.

"You're a United fan?" Sebastian asked Aaron, who was nodding too furiously to form words. Sebastian looked over his shoulder. "Right. Come on then."

We followed Sebastian a short distance until we reached another man in a suit. I didn't recognize him, but based on the gasp from Aaron he was a player he liked. The player lifted his gaze from his phone and smiled at Sebastian, his gaze traveling to take in Aaron and me. Cue my new signature move, the awkward half-wave, half-hand-flop.

"Harris." The two men exchanged some sort of handshake/back-slap situation. Sebastian placed his hand low on my back and guided me forward. Reflexively, I grabbed Aaron and tugged him forward with us. "Tom, this is Lennon and her friend Aaron."

All I could think about was Sebastian's hand, slowly creeping from my lower back to the small dip of my hip and making its home there. Tom shot a smile and wink my way.

"Lennon, it's a pleasure. How'd you enjoy your first match?"

"I had a really good time. The hot dogs were as good as I remembered and our seats were amazing. You guys played really well too." I figured I should add something about their performance in there, since I was ostensibly at this event for the game. "Aaron's a really big fan, so I think that made everything more enjoyable."

I hoped the last part would get Aaron to return to planet Earth and join the conversation. I mentally high-fived myself when he responded without missing a beat. I stood listening to the three men talk football, adding a comment here or there, but mostly focused on the small circles Sebastian's thumb was tracing on my hip.

What a strange and wonderful day.

31.

I stopped in front of Paige's door for the second time in three minutes and then pivoted and walked the four feet back to my door.

"You are being ridiculous."

I marched back to her door. I raised my fist to knock.

"Are you actually going to go through with it this time? Because it was cute the first two times but now I'm just getting worried."

I jumped at Paige's voice coming from the other end of the hall.

"Holy macaroni, Paige! You scared me."

Paige laughed, walking down the hall to join me in front of the door. She slid her key into the lock and ushered me inside.

"I feel like Boomer is starting to rub off on you. I need to get you inside and close the door before you escape."

"Har-dee-har-har." I sat down on her couch while she hung her purse on the coat rack and then joined me.

"So, what's up?"

"I hope you won't be upset, but I talked to Harrison yesterday about hiring you to do all the office work at Bad Wolf. Your classes don't start for another couple months so that gives you plenty of time to adjust. I bet you could even teach and work at Bad Wolf until school starts," I said, hoping she wouldn't be angry with me for talking to Harrison without getting her permission first.

"Lennon, I don't know about this." I fought to keep the alarm off my face. Paige must have noticed my reaction. "I really appreciate your effort. I do. I promise I'm not mad. It's just that I really don't think I'm qualified to do any type of office work."

It was my turn to rush to reassure her.

"Yes, you are! You would be a huge asset to Harrison. I wouldn't have suggested it if I didn't think you could do it. And I'll teach you how to use all the software programs you might not be familiar with."

"I don't know. I don't want to embarrass you."

My head snapped back like her words were a physical blow.

"*Embarrass* me! Paige, you could never embarrass me. Why would you even think that?"

She let out a tiny puff of air that could have been a sigh and tugged on the end of her ponytail.

"I'm not smart. No, it's okay. I'm not being mean, just honest. You're a genius, so I'm sure learning a new program is easy for you, but to me it sounds really freaking hard."

I crossed my arms and glared at her in my best disappointed-mom act.

"First of all, you *are* smart and I will do something really awful if I ever hear you say that about yourself again. Second, you're going to have a really super awesome teacher—me—so your odds of success are higher than normal. Third, you're so good with people. Maybe you don't notice it, but I do. I'm very envious of the way people are just naturally drawn to you like bugs to a fluorescent light."

"What a strange but nice compliment." She laughed.

"Okay, so maybe the bug zapper wasn't the best analogy, but the point is still valid. You have this amazing ability to connect with anyone and make them feel comfortable. I mean, look at me! I have an entire social group because of you, and we are very different people."

"You have friends because of who you are, Lennon. I didn't make people be friends with you."

I held up my hand. "This is your pep talk, lady. Don't try to change the topic. How about a compromise? You come with me to the shop for a couple weeks, just to try it out. If it goes badly, you don't have to do it."

She nodded her head, dragging her teeth over her lower lip.

"Okay, yeah, that sounds like a reasonable plan."

I clapped my hands together. "This is going to be so great, you'll see!"

She laughed, shaking her head at my obvious glee. "Did you really think I was going to be mad at you? Is that why you were doing that whole routine out in the hall?"

My mood took a drastic dive. I looked down at my hands.

"No. I mean yes, I was worried you might be a little upset with me, but that's not why I was nervous about talking to you."

"So...?" She dipped her head down trying to make eye contact with me.

I took a fortifying breath, bracing myself for her reaction.

"I like Sebastian."

There was a long pause before Paige spoke.

"You were nervous about telling me that you like Sebastian? You two are friends so that's not exactly breaking news, babe."

"Right, that's true. The thing is that I... I like Sebastian as more than a friend."

As soon as I released the words into the universe, it was like they became a living thing. They had weight and significance. They had the power to make me very happy or very sad. And they wound their way around us, filling the space with an almost tangible heaviness.

Then Paige let out a maniacal laugh.

"Finally! I thought you were literally never going to admit it."

And then, much to my horror and amazement, I started sobbing. At first, it was just a few tears, but once the dam broke, there was no turning back. Paige let out a startled noise and then launched herself at me in a move straight from the WWF.

"Lennon, what on earth is going on? Why are you so upset?" she asked, rubbing a soothing path up and down my back.

"How could I be so stupid?" I managed through sobs. "I like him so much, Paige."

She hugged me tighter and made some more of the incoherent hush noises until I was all cried out. She released me to grab a handful of tissues and shoved them into my hands. I wiped at my face furiously, mad at myself for the excessive display of emotion and for what I had just admitted.

"All right, sweetie, are you ready to talk this out?"

I would never be ready to talk this out, but I nodded my head anyway.

"I've been trying to convince myself that Sebastian is just a friend. Well, that's not exactly true—I struggled, I still *am* struggling, with why he even wanted to be my friend in the first place, but here we are. I thought if I adhered to a strict system of classification everything would be fine. But it's not working. He just keeps forcing himself into my life and doing really nice things and I don't mean to sound superficial but he's very attractive and I find all his muscles extremely appealing. And then there's the whole Patrick variable. He's exactly my type, but he doesn't make me light up like Sebastian does." I dropped my hands into my face and groaned. "That sounded ridiculous even to me."

Paige let out a soft laugh. "It doesn't sound ridiculous at all. The thing I'm over here struggling with is the whole 'classification system' you've got worked out."

I perked up. The classification system I had devised was territory I was much more comfortable with.

"Oh, that's easy. After collecting a significant amount of data on Sebastian, I was able to place him into the friend category, whereas the same exercise resulted in Patrick being placed in the potential boyfriend category. Categories are useful when thinking about relationships, because they allow you to create expectations that are manageable within the classification. Additionally, biologists and psychologists examine the process behind relationships differently, but they have largely reached the same conclusion: that emotional responsiveness is critical to a successful relationship. We're the most emotionally responsive when we are able to practice empathy with our partners. Empathy requires some shared basis of understanding. For example, I can sympathize with your distress over having to take a math class, but I can't empathize with it because I love math. However, if you said you were nervous about making friends at school, I could empathize with you, because I'm always nervous about entering new social environments. If you collected the data on two people and used it to create a Venn diagram, the space where those circles would overlap is where the two individuals shared similar data points. Patrick and I would have a huge portion of our circles overlapping, but Paige, I don't think Sebastian's circle would even be touching mine."

"I might not be an expert on biology or psychology, but I do watch a lot of Dr. Phil and your theory is absolute garbage. Being emotionally responsive doesn't require empathy; it requires you to acknowledge the other person's humanity and accept it. Good relationships are about validating each other's feelings and building each other up. You don't have to have tons of things in common to do that. I love you even though I can't always empathize with what you're going through." She paused, reaching over to take my hand. "I think, if you were to be honest with yourself, Sebastian is your own personal Everest and that scares the absolute shit of you."

I sniffled. "And you said you weren't smart."

"Do you want to know why I made that terrible, awful attempt to set you two up?"

Finally, an easy question that I had no problem answering.

"I would love to know the answer to that question."

"I grabbed a drink with Sebastian one night after our yoga class, and by 'drink,' I mean a smoothie, just so that imagination of yours isn't running wild. I think we really bonded over the horror of a seaweed-mango smoothie, and he confessed that he was having a hard time meeting people here. In England, people flock to him—especially women—because he's Sebastian Kincaid, and LA hasn't been much better. And while I definitely can't empathize with that problem, I can imagine how hard it would be to tell if someone was interested in you or your fame."

I waited for her to continue. When it became evident that she was waiting for me to respond, I couldn't keep the confusion out of my voice.

"And that made you think of me because...?"

"Because you're one of the realest people I know. You are one of the most genuine people I've ever met, Lennon. I know it can be hard for you, but you wear your heart on your sleeve and it's *such* a big heart. Sebastian struck me as someone who needed that big old heart in his life."

I fought back a fresh round of tears. "That might be the nicest thing anyone's ever said to me. I'm really lucky you're my friend."

"You sure are." She let out a laugh at the surprised expression on my face. "The question is, what are you going to do about this development? Are you going to stick to your Venn diagrams telling you to go with the safe choice, or are you going to light up your life?"

"I'm going to get lit!" I exclaimed. Paige and I looked at each other and burst into laughter.

"I mean, that's not a terrible idea either," she said through laughter.

By the time I left her apartment, I felt like a huge weight had been lifted off my shoulders. Paige was right. I was scared. I had big feelings for someone who was so far outside my comfort zone that it was terrifying. It didn't help that this person also had to be an international soccer star who could probably have any woman he wanted. But talking to Paige made me feel like no matter what happened with Sebastian, I would be okay—because I had friends who would make sure of it.

32.

Kay: You know what's been super fun this week?

Kay: Listening to Aaron talk non-stop about his new pals Sebastian Kincaid and Tom Harris.

Kay: OMFG! He got the picture of the three of them framed and is currently trying to get Harrison to let him hang it in the waiting area.

Paige: LOL that's kind of precious.

Kay: We'll see how precious you think it is Friday.

Harrison: Lennon, I forbid you from ever speaking to any of my employees again.

A few days later, some of my initial enthusiasm for operation "Get Lit" had faded and the rest was quickly being murdered by an exploding engine. My appearance was starting to rival Boomer's for most frazzled. Today, I was sporting a black pencil skirt and a white button-up blouse that I had spilled latte all over when I tripped walking down the stairs. Not going *upstairs*—nope, I literally fell down the stairs. When I rushed to the bathroom, I noticed that I had missed a button somewhere, and was one button off all the way down my blouse. To complete the look, I was rocking one navy shoe and one black shoe.

So, Wednesday was going great, thank you for asking.

Janie had texted me that I was on my own for lunch, so I was perusing the contents of the cafeteria solo.

"Hey, Lennon."

I turned toward the voice of the one person I absolutely did not want to see today.

Holy HAL, could this day possibly get any worse? I tried to muster up a smile and turned to answer.

"Hi, Theo."

"It's been a while. How have you been?" he asked, sounding

sincere because he was a perfect human being who of course would care about his fellow humans.

"Good, I've been good. And you?"

I took the opportunity to study his face. It was the same face that had starred in all my daydreams for years, but I was surprised to find that it didn't hurt as much to know that those daydreams would never come true.

"Things are good. Did you want to join us?"

Such a nice guy. I followed his thumb to a table where Sam was seated. It might have hurt less to know that Theo and I were never going to happen, but I would still rather go swimming with piranhas than have lunch with him and Sam.

"Thanks, but I'm super busy right now, so I think I'm going to work through lunch today."

"Sure, maybe next time."

We said our goodbyes and I proceeded to load my tray up with pasta salad, French fries, and chicken nuggets before heading back to my office. I had planned on working through lunch, but I found myself on the internet searching for "How to break up with someone you're not actually sure you're dating." After scanning the results, I decided to refine my search and entered "How to tell if you are dating someone."

I clicked on the first link that sounded even remotely useful. My eyes darted to the top of the page, where a shirtless Sebastian was trying to sell me a razor. *Are you freaking kidding me?* My life had to be some sort of cosmic joke to whoever was running this show. I set my head down next to my plate of food and contemplated just going home.

"Oh shorts," I cursed, "is that ketchup?"

From this angle, I was eyelevel with what appeared to be a blob of ketchup on my blouse. I sighed. There were some problems even a Tide-To-Go pen couldn't fix.

Maybe the position I was in cut off the air supply to my lungs, subsequently depriving my brain of oxygen, but it suddenly felt like I was having an out-of-body experience. I could see the problem with the first-stage engines clearly, and I knew how to fix it. I shoved my tray away from the keyboard and got to work.

Three hours and two meetings later, I was a hero. Statues would be erected in my honor and little children would sing songs about me. I could already see the parade Spatium would throw for me on what I was sure would be a national holiday. I shut the door to my office and pulled out my phone.

Four rings later, Sebastian's voice sounded in my ear.

"Lennon, what's wrong?" His voice was hushed but the worry was loud and clear.

"Nothing! Are you busy?"

"No, we're just reviewing some game footage for Friday," he said, sounding less concerned.

"I'm sorry! You didn't need to step out of your meeting. We can talk later. It's not important," I said on a rush, suddenly feeling silly for even calling him in the first place. I was just so excited and relieved to have the engine issue fixed, and he was the first person I wanted to share the good news with.

"You never call me, and it's the middle of the day. Out with it. You're making me worried."

"You know the problems we've been having with the engines? Well, I figured it out this afternoon and all the tests we ran in the CAD are very encouraging. I think I did it!"

A tiny squeal may have escaped at the end.

"That's fantastic, love. I'm happy for you." He sounded so genuinely happy that it made my smile widen to the point that my cheeks hurt. "I knew you would figure it out."

"I was just so excited that I couldn't wait to tell you. I really didn't mean to interrupt your meeting."

"I'm glad you did. We'll celebrate later, okay?" I could hear the smile in his voice and could imagine the crinkles that were probably accompanying it.

"Yeah, I'd like that." I dug deep to find the tiny well of courage that lived somewhere in me. "Hey, um, do you have any plans on Saturday?"

"I have a massage in the morning, but nothing after that."

"Would you want to go to a party with me at a friend's house? It might be lame and it's kind of a drive, but it would be more fun if you were there, I think."

Silence stretched for a second that felt more like a century, in which I planned how I would change my name and move to Siberia.

"Are you inviting me to go to a party with you?"

I wrinkled my brows in confusion. "Yes. Or I'm trying to, but I completely understand if you'd rather do something else or have other plans."

"I'd love to. Hey, I've got to run but we're on for Saturday."

I was half-dead but still managed an "okay have a good day." Then I hung up faster than I thought was possible, just in case he changed his mind in the millisecond it normally took to hit the end-call button.

The door to my office flew open, slamming into the wall so hard that I dropped to the floor out of pure instinct. I did not want to die before Saturday. Did tornados happen inside buildings?

"Lennon, you did it, you glorious nerd!" Janie's booming voice filled my office.

I peeked over my desk to see her holding a familiar white bag in her hand and smiling like the maniac she truly was.

"Is that a bag from Lola's?" I asked, my desire for baked goods overriding my survival instinct. I stood and reached for the bag, peering inside.

"Oatmeal raisin cookies for the human responsible for saving this multimillion-dollar project. You deserved a reward."

"Thank you! I ended up working through lunch, so these cookies look extra delicious right now." I ripped off a huge chunk of cookie and shoved it into my mouth. "So good."

Janie's eyes travelled from the unwashed mass of hair piled haphazardly on top of my head, down my stained blouse, and finally to my mismatched shoes.

"What the actual hell happened to you?"

I gazed down at myself even though I knew exactly what she

was talking about.

"Yeah." I swept some of the crumbs off my blouse. "It's been a day. It started very badly, obviously, but it's really turned around and now I have the world's best cookies in my mouth. Oh! And I invited Sebastian to go Will's party and he said yes. Can you believe it?"

Janie shook her head, smiling at me. "Yeah, you doofus, I can totally believe it. Look at you, solving problems and making moves. My baby is growing up!"

I shrugged, polishing off the last pieces of cookie stranded at the bottom of the bag. The strange thing was that it kind of did feel like I was growing—not up, but maybe growing into myself? And then I remembered that I had misbuttoned my shirt that morning and was rocking two different colored shoes.

Oh well, you can't win 'em all.

33.

I was feeling much more human by the time Friday rolled around. All the tests we'd been running on the first-stage engines were very promising, which meant that I was finally sleeping and feeling less like stepping into traffic with my eyes closed.

I left work a little early to pick Paige up for her first official day of training. I was much more excited about the whole thing than she was, but I was determined to make this work and Paige was a firm believer that a person's energy was contagious. I was going to be the flu of excitement, dang it!

I texted Paige when I was outside our building and had to fight a grin when she came out of the door. She was wearing a pair of high-waisted, cropped tweed dress pants with a white puff-sleeved dress shirt. Her blonde hair was out of its signature high ponytail and loosely curled. She basically looked like she was ready to take Wall Street by storm, not headed for a night at a tattoo shop—not that I would ever mention that fact. I wondered if I should text Harrison and warn him not to mention Paige's outfit or I would tell Mom he was having unprotected sex.

"Hey," she said, opening the car door and hopping in. She adjusted the pleats on her pants as she got settled in my not-so spacious car—a signature nervous move of my own.

"Hey! You look so nice! Did you have time to eat or do you want to stop on the way?" I sounded way too cheerful for the question.

She gave me a confused look and pressed a hand to her abdomen. "No thanks, I'm too nervous to eat."

"Huh. I've heard that is a thing some people experience. Fascinating." I hit play on the "Get Pumped" playlist Janie and I had made for Paige this afternoon.

Janie and I had very different ideas of what songs should be included on this playlist, so the whole thing was honestly kind of a mess. Lizzo turned into Beyoncé and Beyoncé turned into Linkin Park.

Paige picked up my phone and scrolled through the songs. "Did you make this playlist?" she asked, looking up from my phone.

I squirmed in my seat under her questioning stare, unable to tell if she was upset by the expression on her face.

"Janie and I made it this afternoon to help you get pumped. Research has shown a strong correlation between music and our emotions. When we listen to music, we experience a form of emotional mimicry, where our emotions mimic the emotions in the songs which can cause a release of dopamine that actually makes us feel happier. Also, there are tons of super interesting studies about how music affects consumer behaviors and how companies use that to their advantage. So Janie and I thought it would be a good way to get you pumped for your first day. We obviously did not agree on the song choices."

Paige laughed at the obvious look of frustration on my face as I thought about the hour we'd spent arguing over what should be included in the playlist.

"It is kind of a hot mess, but it's also amazing. Thank you for this. It really does mean a lot that you guys made it for me."

We spent the rest of the car ride laughing at the mismatched songs, so while our playlist may not have gotten Paige pumped up, it did take her mind off her nerves until we parked. I heard her take a deep breath as she opened the car door and knew she was reciting one of the mantras she'd taught me to use when I was feeling anxious. I gave her a reassuring hug before we walked through the door.

Lou swiveled around when he heard the front door open, his eyes opening comically wide when he took in Paige walking next to me.

"Lennon!" he greeted me, shoving away from the desk and coming to stand in front of us. "And who is this lovely female specimen?"

"Uh, this is my friend Paige. I'm going to train her to do all the office stuff, so Harrison isn't such a grouch all the time." I motioned toward Lou. "Paige, this is Lou."

Lou grabbed Paige's hand and pressed a kiss on her knuckles. "Enchanted."

"What is happening?" Paige asked out of the corner of her mouth.

"That's Lou being Lou, just roll with it."

"Louis! No giving the new girl one of your diseases!" Kay yelled, poking her head out of her station. "Hey Paige! We keep pepper spray in the desk drawer especially for Lou. Just take it out and he'll run away."

Lou shook his head back and forth and sighed.

"Don't listen to her, sweet Paige. I've been turning down her advances for years. She's just a bitter old woman."

Kay barked out a laugh from her station without even a pause in the hum of her tattoo gun.

"Jesus fuck. You all are lucky I'm the HR department." Harrison's booming voice had us all jumping around to face him. I watched the color drain from Paige's face. Lou was still wearing his signature grin, highlighting his acquired immunity to Harrison's bark. "Is there literally anything else you could be doing besides harassing my new employee?'

"Harassing? *Moi*?" Lou feigned horror, complete with hand covering his heart. "I would never. I think you'll find welcoming new employees is listed in my job description."

Harrison crossed his arms and glared at Lou, who was still grinning unrepentantly. Paige looked like she was praying a sinkhole would suddenly rip the earth out from under her feet. I reached over and slipped my arm through hers, steering us both around the desk.

"Okay, so I think I'll just take over the front desk. Lou, do you think you could find a second chair for us?"

"Anything for you, tater tot," he said, shooting a wink at Paige.

"Tater tot?" Paige whispered to me, keeping her eyes on Harrison.

"I eat a lot of tater tots." I shrugged. "Lou likes to give people nicknames that no one else uses or *wants* anyone else to use."

Lou reappeared with a chair that looked suspiciously like the chair from Harrison's office. Based on the growl Harrison emitted, it was in fact his chair, but thankfully, he just shook his head in disgust and walked to his station. Paige visibly relaxed.

Lou pulled out the chair for Paige with a flourish of his hand and a "Mademoiselle."

"Thanks." Paige smiled up at Lou, taking the seat. She was saved by the entrance of a large man who I recognized as one of Lou's clients. He was working on a large piece that would eventually cover his back and wrap around his left arm to spill onto his chest.

I groaned. "Lesson number one, don't do anything that Lou could in any way construe as encouragement."

I walked Paige through the check-in process for returning clients, then showed her how the appointment software worked. As I expected, she was a quick learner and had no trouble figuring out how it worked. Lou's client shot her a wink and a "thanks, darling" before following Lou to his station.

Harrison: Why is your friend dressed like she's about to teach first grade?

I glanced up to make sure Paige wasn't paying attention to me. She was busy being a good employee, messing around with the program.

Me: Her name is Paige and you know it. She is dressed professionally for her first day of work. You should be thankful your new employee is taking her job seriously.

Harrison: I don't want her scaring clients away.
Me: I am not even going to dignify that with a response.

Since I already had my phone out, I checked on the score of Sebastian's game. They were down by a goal, but there were still forty-five minutes left in the game. And then, because I was fully committed to going down the rabbit hole that was a crush on Sebastian Kincaid, I quickly reread the text message exchange from earlier in the day where we'd made plans for the party tomorrow. Of course, I was trying to decide if this counted as a date if the word 'date' was never actually used or implied in any fashion. *Baby steps, Lennon, baby steps.*

"Okay, Lennon will get you all taken care from here," Aaron said, leading a petite brunette to the front desk. "It was nice meeting you, Chloe. Give us a call if you're having any issues."

"Thank you so much. I absolutely love it." Chloe gave him one last wistful look and then turned her attention to us. I noticed Paige openly admiring Aaron. There was probably an entire group of women who met once a month to support each other after their encounters with him.

I got Chloe checked out while explaining the process to Paige. I watched in awe as Paige effortlessly made small talk with Chloe. It turned out that Chloe had a Svadhishthana symbol tattooed on the inside of her arm to help boost her creativity. They chatted about different chakras and what helped them unlock their full potential. By the time Paige was done, I knew Chloe was super into yoga and was in her third year of school at UCLA studying art, even though her parents really wanted her to focus her energy on something more practical like graphic design.

"And you thought you weren't going to be a good fit for this job." I swiveled in my seat to give Paige the old 'I told you so' look.

She just shrugged. "She was nice and easy to talk to. It's only the first night, but so far, it hasn't been anything too groundbreaking."

Aaron walked out of his station and came around the desk.

He leaned his delightfully sculpted arms on the counter and gave Paige a wink.

"You must be Paige."

What was happening with all the winking? Had everyone suddenly developed a tic in their orbicularis oculi muscles? Lou only winked at me when he knew he was about to do or say something that was going to make Harrison have a conniption.

"Yes, hi!" Paige gave him a wave that looked smooth and unruffled, unlike my limp-wristed, flail move. God, genetics really were so unfair.

"I'm Aaron," he greeted her with that panty-melting grin. "It's nice to meet you."

"You too! I've heard so much about you." She grunted when my bony, pterodactyl-like elbow connected with her rib. "Lennon said you guys really enjoyed the soccer game the other week."

"It was awesome!" He reached into his pocket and pulled out his cellphone. I got a glimpse of the screen. It was the picture I took of him, Sebastian, and Tom Harris. "Lemme show you some pictures."

I could hear Kay's groan from her station and barely managed to hold in the laugh that had threatened to escape earlier. But bless her heart, Paige oohed and ahhed over every photo, managing to look interested and more than likely earning Aaron's eternal friendship.

"Did you eat?" Harrison's voice boomed from behind us.

"Cheese and rice, Harrison, that was super creepy even for you," I answered, still trying to locate my heart after he'd scared it straight out of my chest. How did such a large guy manage to be so stealthy? "No, I didn't eat yet. I thought maybe we could order something here before it gets busy."

His gaze swung to Paige, who looked like she might be holding her breath. "Did you eat?"

"No," she squeaked out, hands gripping the arm rests on Harrison's chair like she was in danger of sliding to the floor.

"All right, use the card to order pizza for everyone," he said, turning to stalk back to his chair-less office.

I waved my hand in front of Paige.

"Earth to Paige, are you okay?"

She jerked her head around to face me, nodding it so hard I worried for her cervical vertebrae.

"Yes, yep, totally fine. Why do you ask?"

"No reason," I answered, turning to the serious business of collecting pizza orders from everyone.

The rest of the night went smoothly, largely because Harrison was fully booked and spent the rest of the time in his station. He made one brief appearance to grab a few slices of pizza, and that was the only time I saw Paige's smile falter. I felt like an evil scientist, thinking that watching Paige and Harrison navigate each other was going to be very interesting.

34.

I woke up the next morning feeling like a jumbled mess of nerves and excitement. The pot of coffee I consumed did nothing to help the slight shakiness in my limbs or the racing in my heart.

I glanced at the half-full cup resting on the sink counter. I promptly poured its contents down the drain.

"Today, you have betrayed my trust. I never thought I would see this day."

Boomer hissed from the other side of the door, indignant that he was once again banned from the bathroom while I was showering. I opened the door and he flew in, looking frantic.

"Geesh, calm down. You didn't miss anything exciting. And you could be in here all the time if you stopped knocking my toothbrush into the toilet."

He curled up on the bathmat and began systematically cleaning his paws, showing his complete lack of remorse for his crimes against my toothbrushes. I sighed and continued combing the tangles out of my hair.

I had considered wearing one of the cute, trendy outfits I had ordered online with Paige's help, but I felt like wearing them would be dishonest somehow. If Sebastian weren't going with me, I wouldn't even have thought twice about what I would wear: my new *That's What I'm Tolkien About* T-shirt with a pair of nicer leggings. So, somewhere between shaving my legs and washing the shampoo out of my hair, that was what I had decided to wear.

The truth was, I was just Lennon—a little quirky and a lot nerdy. I wanted Sebastian to like *me*, the me with all her strengths and all her weaknesses, not a glossed-up version. If he couldn't like me just as I was, it would completely suck and probably break my heart a little, but I would have to find a way to be okay with it. No one was worth being half of yourself.

I braided my hair across the crown of my head (thank you, YouTube), letting the rest hang down my back, and added a little makeup before slipping into my clothes. I shoveled down some Lucky Charms and an apple toaster strudel, because health, just in time. Sebastian texted me that he was here just as I was putting my dishes in the dishwasher. I made sure Boomer had enough water and then gave him a hug and kiss—against his strong opposition—before heading out the door with a little extra pep in my step.

I opened the door and stopped in my tracks. Sebastian was leaning against a car that made me believe in love at first sight. The man leaning against the car was not bad either, but that car...! *That. Car.* I walked over to him, taking in the sleek aerodynamic body, which had been painted a bold red.

Running my hand lovingly across the car, I turned an accusatory look toward Sebastian, who was holding the door open for me. I slid in, stink-eye still in full force, and watched him walk around the front of the car before turning an admiring eye to its interior.

"You didn't pick me up in this bad boy last time," I said before he even had the chance to buckle his seatbelt.

He gave me a confused look. "I did not. I have a few cars."

I chose to ignore the "a few cars" part of his response because the craziness of that statement would be obvious to a solid 98% of us mere mortals.

"Yes, but this isn't just any car." I turned in my seat to face him, a wide, wide smile stretching the muscles of my face. "This is the 2019 Audi TT RS, the only five-cylinder engine commercially available."

He shifted the car into gear and I almost moaned. Holy torque, Batman. He accelerated, shooting me a naughty grin that suggested he knew exactly what this car was doing for me. This time I let the gasp slip past my lips.

"Did you hear that firing sequence? 1-2-4-5-3. OMactualG."

"It's pretty brilliant, yeah?" There was a hint of laughter in his voice, along with something else I couldn't quite put my finger on, especially with half my brain literally melting over this car.

"Brilliant? Brilliant? That doesn't even... Sebastian, did you know that people have been modifying this bad boy and hitting 8 on the drag strip? We are sitting behind 354 pound-feet of torque."

Sebastian shifted in his seat and cleared his throat. "So you like my car?"

"I don't like it, I *love* it! Don't even get me started on the updates they made to the body kit to give this model an even more streamlined design." If this were a television show, those cartoon hearts would have been pouring from my eyes. I might have discovered the one thing I found more attractive than Sebastian.

"The 400 horsepower doesn't hurt either," he chimed in, lovingly caressing the dash.

"Yeah," I sighed dreamily. "My grandpa would love to get his hands on this engine. Hey! Do you think I could take a little peek under the hood sometime? I promise I won't touch anything. Okay, that's a lie. I promise I won't mess with anything."

I was prepared to beg, borrow, and steal to get my paws on that engine, which might be necessary since my request appeared to physically pain Sebastian. He adjusted his position again, making me wonder if the driver's seat was uncomfortable to sit in.

"Yeah, absolutely. Any time, love." His voice sounded gruff. Some people were super weird about their cars. Who was I to judge? And honestly, if this were my car, I didn't know if I'd be thrilled with the idea of someone poking around under the hood. "You mentioned your grandpa; is he into cars?'

"Yeah, he loves cars," I answered, half-distracted and covetously eyeballing the torque, boost, and power gages. My environmentally friendly car had none of those things, but the gas mileage totally made up for it. Yes, totally made up for it, because saving the Earth was sexy—or at least it had been until five minutes ago when I'd felt the rumble of this monster.

"Is that where you get your love of cars from?" His question forced me out of my lustful thoughts about his car.

"Definitely. My grandpa and uncle actually own a garage. Harrison and I spent a lot of weekends there as kids when my mom had to work. He always used to have a project in his garage at our house, too, and he let me help with them. He's probably the reason I became an engineer." Without my being aware of it, my hand had been absently tracing the scar bisecting my chest. I lowered it back to my lap. "Now he mostly tinkers with appliances that people bring him to fix."

We rode in silence for a while, me listening to the sounds of the engine being piped into the cab, and Sebastian thinking about who knows what. I was the one who ended up speaking first.

"What about you? You obviously have an appreciation for superior automobiles."

He glanced at me out of the corner of his eye.

"I'm not an aerospace engineer by any stretch, but I do have a healthy appreciation for a well-made car."

I looked over at him, trying to sort through the dozens of questions swimming around in my head, all vying for airtime.

"Where did your love of cars come from?" I paused, trying to think of the right way to phrase what I wanted to say next. "I guess I'm imagining most of your focus being on soccer. Er, football."

The corner of his mouth ticked up.

"You're not entirely wrong. There's a show on the BBC that was popular when I was growing up, *Top Gear*, that my dad loved. We only had one TV growing up, so we all watched whatever Mum or Dad wanted to watch in the evenings. I watched a lot of *Top Gear* when I was home."

"Before you went to the youth training camps?" I asked before my brain could catch up with my mouth. I felt the heat crawl up my neck and flood my face. If I had a time machine, I would have gone back ten seconds so Sebastian would never find out what a stalker I had turned into since meeting him.

He tore his eyes off the road to hit me with a cocky grin. "You looked me up."

I looked down at my hands, suddenly very interested in what was happening with the hem of my shirt.

"It was a purely academic endeavor. I had no idea who you were and that bothered me, so don't let it go to your head."

He huffed out a laugh. "Thanks for that. You know how to chop a bloke off at the knees."

I made a mental note to look up the expression 'to chop one off at the knees.' From the context clues, I assumed it had something to do with humility, a concept I wouldn't have thought Sebastian was familiar with until I'd gotten to know him.

We made it out of the hellish LA traffic onto an open stretch of highway. Sebastian effortlessly navigated around the few cars in front of us and then accelerated with an ease that made me feel lighthearted.

"You didn't learn how to drive like that from a TV show." My voice came out sounding breathless, with an unmistakable note of awe thrown in. I couldn't even be sorry about it. He had *earned* that awe.

He just smiled and rested his elbow on his knee in a pose I found inexplicably sexy. I leaned my head against the head rest, rolling my head slightly so I could take Sebastian in without being too obvious about it. He was dressed casually, in a dark blue Henley and a pair of jeans that gripped his thighs in a way that made me irrationally jealous. The dark blue of his shirt highlighted the ink that was visible on his forearms thanks to the haphazard way he had shoved up the sleeves. Everything about this man was so effortlessly handsome, from the way it looked like he had simply run his fingers through his hair to the light stubble that dusted his strong jawline. Even his cologne was just strong enough to make my ovaries sit up and take notice, but not so strong that it filled the small interior of the car. And I was alone with him in this powerhouse on wheels, making easy conversation and sneaking eyefuls.

I was suddenly very much looking forward to the car ride ahead of us.

35.

Thirty or so minutes later, we turned onto Will's street. I took in the driveway already filled with cars, and the line of cars that stretched down one side of the street. Shorts. I hadn't even thought about the parking situation—but in my defense, I hadn't expected Sebastian to pick me up in such an expensive car. Not that the Porsche Cayman he had picked me up in for our football game was small change either, but I was used to seeing Porsches cruising the streets of LA.

"Oh no—Sebastian, I'm so sorry. If you drop me off, I'll run in and ask Will if you can park in a neighbor's driveway."

"What are you on about? There's plenty of room on the street," he said, sounding genuinely confused by the panic evident in my voice.

"You cannot park this car on the street! What if someone tries to steal it? Or sideswipes it? What if a kid hits a baseball and it breaks a window? What if—"

"Lennon, relax, love. It's just a car. Nothing you listed is fatal." He expertly maneuvered the car between a Honda with patches of rust and an older model Ford.

These were my people, and I was afraid Sebastian was going to be as out of place amongst them as his car so clearly was. I hesitated a minute, trying to force myself to calm down, before exiting the vehicle.

"I love this car. Do you remember when we were little, how kids used to say 'If you love it why don't you marry it?' I would,

Sebastian. I would marry this car even though I'm positive that would be illegal in all fifty states and probably some territories," I told him as he joined me on the passenger's side. I meant every single word. I'd put a ring on it in a heartbeat.

He let loose an incredulous laugh that I felt all the way in the tips of my toes. He placed his hand on the small of my back and gently propelled me away from the real love of my life and toward the driveway.

"I tell you what, I'll let you drive home if you feel up to it."

If I was lucky, one day I would be telling our kids the story of how their parents met. I imagined they would ask me when I knew I loved their dad, and I would tell them it was this moment. The moment he offered to let me drive the car I couldn't afford in this lifetime or the next twelve. My poor heart never stood a chance.

We made our way up the driveway in silence. Sebastian was walking so close to me that I could feel the heat from his body being absorbed by my own. It was doing nothing for the horde of bats that were pinging around in my stomach. I suddenly couldn't remember why I'd thought inviting him was a good idea. I knew this was not Sebastian's idea of a good time, but I was a greedy, greedy Gus who wanted more time with him. And maybe—if I was being honest—I wanted to see if he would try to fit into my world like I was trying to do for him.

A huge cutout picture of Gandalf—the Grey, not the White—was taped to the door along with a sign that said "You Shall Not Pass (just kidding, come on in)." Will was always so fantastically nerdcore. I snuck a quick glance at Sebastian to see if he was completely horrified.

"Wow, he's really gone all out," Sebastian commented, opening the door for me and giving me a smile completely devoid of judgment. I released a small breath that might have sounded like a laugh.

"Yeah, Will's kind of famous for his themed movie and game nights. I've been to a Marvel Marathon and a *Game of Thrones* night that were pretty intense. I saw two Cerseis get into a fight with a Daenerys." Someone dressed as Frodo walked by, offering us a hello as he went. I watched Sebastian take in the Frodo impersonator and the other people scattered through the part of the house we could see, who were all sporting different costumes.

"Should I have dressed up? I feel like the one kid not wearing a costume at Halloween." He looked down at his normal clothing and then over at my Tolkien shirt. I could have sworn he looked a little nervous.

I blame what I did next on the deep understanding I have for the feeling of being the odd one out. I threw my arms around his abdomen and squeezed him to me. I felt those strong arms wrap around my back, pulling me even closer. I let myself linger there for one beat and then another, loving the way I was surrounded by the warmth of him. I leaned back just enough to unbury my face from that glorious chest.

"You look perfect. I'm not really into cosplay or LARPing. There's nothing wrong with it." I shrugged, feeling the need to defend my people. "It's just not my thing."

One hand left my back to straighten my glasses.

"That's good, because I'm not too keen on the idea of dressing up like a hobbit, if I'm honest."

"Lennon, you made it!" Will's voice burst my bubble.

I stepped out of Sebastian's arms to greet Will. It did not escape my notice that one of Sebastian's hands found its way to my hip. Will was dressed as Gimli, which was a fantastic choice for him. He was vertically challenged with unruly red hair and a matching beard. If I hadn't known better, I would have thought he had been preparing for this moment all his life.

"Hey, Will. Your costume is pretty amazing." I motioned to Sebastian. "This is my friend Sebastian. Sebastian, this is Will. He belongs to the same dojo as Janie."

Sebastian stuck out his hand. "Nice to meet you, mate."

"Great accent!" Will batted his ax out of the way to shake hands with Sebastian. "Where are you from?"

"Manchester," Sebastian replied matter-of-factly.

"Awesome. I studied abroad in England for a semester and it was amazing. I'd love to go back. Do you guys want a drink? Marley and I started brewing our own beer and we made a special miruvor brew for today." He waved us into the kitchen where half of the Fellowship were involved in a boardgame.

"I'd love to try it!" I leaned toward Sebastian to whisper, "Marley is Will's wife and miruvor was a special drink given to Gandalf by Elrond, Lord of Rivendell."

Judging by the expression on Sebastian's face, that speech did nothing to clear up his confusion.

"So should I drink it or not?" he whispered back to me.

"Definitely. In *Lord of the Rings*, miruvor had the power to grant renewed vigor and strength. I don't know what the version brewed in Will's garage is capable of, but I'm betting it will at least give you a mild buzz."

Sebastian chuckled, his breath setting my perpetual flyaways into motion. Will handed us each an unlabeled bottle.

"So, Sebastian, what brings you stateside?" Will asked before Sebastian had a chance to take a drink.

"I was traded to the Novas from United."

"Cool, you play soccer. I used to dabble myself," Will said, fake dusting off his shoulder. I have never wanted to throat punch someone more in my life, and I'd grown up with Harrison. My head swiveled from Will to Sebastian, desperately thinking of something to say to distract from Will's totally idiotic comment.

Sebastian looked momentarily taken aback, but recovered much more quickly than I did. He gave Will one of his half-grins that somehow managed to convey interest without a trace of the condescension he was entitled to, because clearly whatever the hot sauce Will had dabbled in, it was not even remotely equivalent to being a professional player.

"Yeah? Always happy to meet a fellow footballer. What'd you play?" Sebastian asked. I wondered if it was his years of interacting with fans that allowed him to continue this conversation with a smile on his face.

Will blinked at him. "Uh, I played soccer."

"It's actually called football, so…" I felt the need to correct Will, and my hackles were starting to rise. I took a sip of my ale and my esophagus promptly did a 'heck no' and rejected the pungent liquid. I sputtered into my elbow, tears welling in my eyes. Holy mackerel, this stuff was truly terrible. Sebastian was giving me a concerned look, and I motioned to the bottle in my hand with a discreet shake of my head.

"I meant, what position did you play?" Sebastian turned his attention back to Will, which gave me a chance to wipe at the tears in my eyes. This stuff was not giving anyone vigor or strength.

"Oh right," Will laughed. "I'm a few ales in already, if you know what I mean. I mostly played goalie."

"What up, my fellow uncostumed homies!" Janie appeared at the top of the basement stairs. She was wearing a hunter green tank top that said "Where the Halflings Are" that I was very jealous of. It had the picture of the Wild Things at the rumpus, but the Wild Things were hobbits. So fantastic.

I rolled my eyes but couldn't keep the smile off my face. "Your shirt is amazing! Sebastian, this is my friend Janie. She also works at Spatium, in accounting."

Sebastian shot her one of his signature grins. Based on the look on her face, Janie was not immune to its effects either.

"Nice to meet you, Janie." He stretched out his hand for a handshake, but Janie ignored his outstretched hand and reached over to squeeze one of his biceps.

"Wow, these are nice. Not used to this sort of musculature around here."

"Janie!" I exclaimed, smacking her hand away. Sebastian was watching her with a bemused expression, much to my relief.

"I want to apologize but I'd be lying, so how about I just get you both something non-toxic to drink."

"That is an acceptable peace offering," I said, taking the bottle from Sebastian's hand and placing them both in the garbage.

"I feel like I should have some say in this, since it was my biceps," Sebastian pointed out.

"Trust me, I just saved your life," Janie said, handing us both new drinks sporting a brand-name label. "It's an ale so it still goes with the theme, but it won't strip your insides like turpentine," she continued. "Greg and I saved you two a spot on a couch downstairs. Unless you want to join a twelve-hour board game?"

"That's going to be a hard pass for me," Sebastian answered very quickly. "Did you want to play?"

I couldn't help laughing at the hopeful expression on his face.

"No, I'm good. I would much rather watch the movies for the hundredth time."

We followed Janie into the basement and around the chairs filling the space. People had brought their own folding chairs or bean bags, and I saw a few of the more hardcore people had sleeping bags on inflatable mattresses.

I spotted Greg sprawled out on one of the L-shaped couches toward the back of the room. Will had created a large projection screen on one of the walls, so it was like being at a more comfortable, haphazard movie theater. He sat up when he saw us approaching. I said hello and made the obligatory introductions. Sebastian sat down on the opposite end of the couch, stretching his long legs out in front of him. I surveyed the available seating options trying to decide where I should sit. I felt Sebastian's long fingers encircle my wrist, and then he was tugging me down next to him. I sat awkwardly, as straight as possible, to avoid any of my body overlapping his.

Janie snorted. I shot her one of my finer side-eyes and sat very still. We must have missed *The Fellowship of the Ring*. I recognized the opening scenes of *The Two Towers*. I shifted carefully, my spine already aching from sitting so straight. I was a sloucher. I should have listened to my mother and worked on my posture.

"Are those two hobbits boyfriends?" Sebastian asked.

I looked at him, surprised by his question. "Have you never

seen these?"

He grimaced. "Not a single one. I hope that's not a deal-breaker for you. I literally have no idea what those little blokes are going on about.'

I scooted closer, so I could give him a brief explanation of the plot without disturbing the other viewers, and tried very hard not to go on too much of a *The Hobbit* tangent. He watched me, a soft smile on his face the entire time.

"Got it. They have to get the magic ring to Mordor before the evil eyeball finds them and destroys Middle Earth."

Why this moment felt right to tell him about my heart, I couldn't articulate. Snuggled up to his side in the dark gave me a false sense of safety, I suppose, and there was no way to really explain my deep love of these stories without also explaining my heart defect. His arm wound its way around my back, forcing me closer.

My hand traced the familiar path on my chest. I felt Sebastian's eyes following the movement.

"I love these stories. I do. I read them over and over again when I was growing up. Nobody builds an entire universe quite like Tolkien, but I read anything with elaborate world-building." I paused, taking a breath for courage. "I was born with a hole in my heart. It's not necessarily a big deal. Most holes close as the child grows older, but for whatever reason, my hole got bigger instead. I had to see a ton of pediatric cardiologists and other specialists, so I was home-schooled until I was sixteen. I couldn't run around with Harrison or the other kids because too much physical exertion usually triggered an arrythmia and I passed out a lot. Reading was such a great escape for me, especially as I got older."

Sebastian's eyes bounced from the hand still tracing my scar to meet my gaze. Worry was broadcast on every feature of that handsome face. Even the hand on my hip had tightened, digging into the sensitive flesh there.

"But your heart is okay now?"

"It is. I had open-heart surgery to close the hole when I was fifteen," I rushed to reassure him, because he looked absolutely devastated. "I check in with a cardiologist annually and the patch is in great shape."

"Why didn't you say something when I took you to play soccer? Lennon, I could have hurt you."

He scrubbed his free hand down his face, the sound rough like sandpaper. I pulled his hand down, placing it over my heart, hoping he could feel the steady thump that beat so much harder with his hand touching me. I lifted my head so our eyes met.

"Sebastian, I'm fine. If it wasn't safe for me to do something, I would tell you. I've been seeing a cardiologist forever. My heart is fine. I'm fine."

His eyes searched my face and then lowered to look at my small hand covering his larger one, pressing it into my chest.

"That's why you said you ate healthy as a kid. Why didn't you tell me sooner?" His voice had an accusatory edge that made me feel terrible for ever doubting the sincerity of his friendship.

"I don't really have a good answer for that one. It's hard for me to talk about it. People never know how to react, and it makes me feel even more different than I already do most of the time."

He flipped his hand around so that he was holding mine now, lowering our clasped hands to his lap. His thumb stoked along the curve of my hand sending aftershocks through my body with each pass.

"I love every single thing about you that makes you different."

Without warning, he leaned down and pressed a kiss to my temple. He tucked me closer into his side, turning his attention back to the movie.

"I don't care what anyone says, the chubby one is into that froyo guy."

36.

As promised, Sebastian let me drive his car home, but my time behind the wheel did not last long. A few jarring starts and stops after we got out of the neighborhood had me pulling into the first gas station I spotted. The engine had a whole lot more power than I was used to in my hybrid—not that I would ever admit it. I told Sebastian that I was just super tired and it was clearly affecting my driving skills. I solidified that version of the truth by promptly falling asleep for the rest of the ride home. Waking up to Sebastian's face was like waking up from a good dream to find yourself in an even better dream.

Two days later, I was still fantasizing about the kiss he'd placed on each of my cheeks, so close to my mouth that I would have had to turn my head only the slightest movement to have his lips where I really wanted them. We had been serenaded by the romantic sounds of Boomer moaning and body-slamming the door.

This was the first Monday in a while that I hadn't dreaded going to work. The tests we had run in the simulator had all gone well, so our first prototype was officially in construction. We were announcing a contest to name the rocket later in the week and I was actually pretty excited to hear what people would come up with. I was temporarily reassigned to a team performing routine maintenance with a few necessary updates on some of the commercial satellites we currently had in orbit.

It wasn't as sexy as building a spaceship, but it was still one of my favorite tasks.

"Ready for lunch?" Janie waltzed into my office, interrupting my daydream—erm, work.

"Very." I shoved away from my desk, grabbing my phone. "Word on the street is that it's pizza day."

We made our way to the cafeteria discussing very important topics like whether there would just be pizza or calzones too, and whether there would also be breadsticks. My heated fantasies had really worked up an appetite.

Trays filled to capacity, we slid into a booth and dug in.

"So, you and Sebastian looked pretty cozy Saturday," Janie said, dipping a breadstick in some marinara sauce.

"There wasn't a lot of room on the couch. We didn't have much of a choice."

I had known it was only a matter of time before Janie brought up Saturday. I could feel her eyes on us the whole night. She'd also taken Sebastian's side of the argument over Sam and Frodo's relationship, and then wowed him with her Gollum impression.

"You're welcome. Man, I am such a good wing-woman." She sounded way too impressed with herself. "I fully expect you to name your first-born girl child after me."

"I'm sorry?" I paused, putting my stromboli back on the plate. "What exactly did you do to 'wing-woman' me?"

Janie gasped dramatically. "How dare you? Do you know how many people I had to scare away from that couch so you two could cuddle instead of sitting in very uncomfortable folding chairs? I told Sara that Greg had gas."

"It sounds like I should be thanking Greg."

She pointed a breadstick at me. "I know what you're doing. Don't deflect. What happened after you guys left?"

"Sebastian drove me home. Well, I drove a little too, but he drove most of the way."

"Cool." Janie dragged out the word, the tone of her voice making it clear that she could not care less about who drove home. "Thanks for the play-by-play. But I meant what *happened* happened?"

"I don't understand." She groaned, throwing her hands up in frustration. My eyes widened. "Janie, are you talking about sexual relations?"

"Please, and I cannot stress this enough, *never* say the phrase 'sexual relations' again. It literally makes me die a little bit on the inside. But to answer your question, yes."

"No! Of course not. Why would you think we would be doing that?" I lowered my voice so the last words were barely audible over the noise of the cafeteria.

"Uh, because you're not dead?" She sounded incredulous. "If Sebastian Kincaid had been rubbing up on me all night, I would have had my panties off before the car even stopped."

"I honestly feel like I just stepped inside the Twilight Zone. What are you even talking about? Sebastian and I aren't dating. We're just friends."

"Oh, really? Because your body language was telling a very different story. And don't even get me started on the way you looked at him all dreamy." She sighed, making googly eyes. "He's clearly into you. Jump his bones! And then tell me everything. I need very specific details. Like how many packs do his abs have? Does he have one of those sexy-as-hell V things pointing to his —"

I leaned forward and shoved a piece of stromboli into her open mouth.

"I don't know what you think you're talking about. Sebastian is not into me like that, I don't think."

Janie wiped off a spot of sauce from just above her lip while managing to look like she was physically restraining herself from reaching across the table to strangle me.

"How are you not picking up on any of the clues that he is *super* into you? When was the last time you had a friend of the male persuasion who cuddled with you while watching a movie? Also, I'm going to go out on a limb here and say that Sebastian's idea of a great Saturday isn't a LOTR marathon, which should tell you everything you need to know."

"This is a clear case of confirmation bias. You know that I have more-than-friendly feelings for Sebastian, and you think that Sebastian returns those feelings. Therefore, you are interpreting ambiguous data in a manner that supports your hypothesis that Sebastian likes me."

"Oh my fucking God, Lennon, this isn't rocket science. He held your hand, he pulled you practically onto his lap, he kissed your freaking forehead, and found a way to basically be touching you the entire night. Please tell me how any of that is ambiguous." Her face was actually starting to turn an alarming shade of red. "I repeat, this isn't fucking rocket science!"

I looked down at my plate, taking a few seconds to order my thoughts before responding.

"I'm scared, okay?" I watched her face soften as she absorbed my confession, transforming her expression from frustrated to understanding mixed with sympathy. "I like him a lot. Way more than is smart. I get that the idea of leagues is completely arbitrary, but it doesn't change the reality that he is way out of my league. We exist in two totally different worlds. I don't know how to reconcile that with the signs that he may have feelings for me too. I don't want to get my hopes up."

"I get that, Lennon, I really do. We're humans, which means we love us some categories. Even when you understand that those categories are dumb and arbitrary, it's still easy to get wrapped up in them. But I also think you need to give Sebastian a little credit. Trust that he isn't just some hotshot professional athlete, because we both know you wouldn't be into him if he fit that stereotype," Janie said, managing to infuse the perfect amount of softness and firmness into her voice.

"You're right. I know everything you're saying is valid, but that doesn't make it easier or less scary."

"Yeah, but sometimes you have to be brave to get what you want. I mean, look at Marie Curie. Madame Curie was a woman, so she wasn't supposed to be intelligent and driven. She was supposed to be meek and subservient. Everyone was like 'but you are a woman,'" Janie said in a horrible French accent, "'you cannot do zee science,' and Marie was like 'hold my pipette, bitches.' And now we have X-rays!"

I laughed, but she held up a finger to stop me from responding.

"Don't interrupt me, I'm on a roll. I have one more point to make and that will conclude my speech. You and Patrick were perfect together on paper, same category and everything. And look what happened with him. He ghosted you."

I let out a strangled gasp. "He did not ghost me!"

She arched an eyebrow. "How many days ago did you last message him?"

"Three," I admitted. "But maybe he hasn't checked his email lately."

"Or his text messages? Time to face it, girlie, you got ghosted." She smiled smugly, ripping a breadstick in half with her teeth.

"Ugh, I know I should be thankful that it appears Patrick has lost interest, but I still feel kind of annoyed. I thought our date went really well, and he indicated that he was very interested in a second date. Plus, I spent a lot of time coming up with a breakup speech that didn't actually utilize the words 'break up' since our relationship status was undefined."

"Men are dogs. Accept it and move on," she said, like she hadn't just spent a solid thirty minutes trying to convince me to have sex with a man. "Listen, you need to decide whether you're going to be a Marie who goes after her dream and gives humanity the gift of polonium and radium, or if you're going to be a coward who splits frozen dinners with her cat. Your choice."

"Geez Louise, when you put it like that…" My phone dinged, making me forget what I was going to say. Both our eyes darted to the screen.

Sebastian: We never got to have that celebration dinner. Wednesday?

Janie's face said it all. Time to be brave. I picked up the phone and sent my response.

Me: I'm free Wednesday.

I looked at Janie, nodding my head firmly. Hoping like crazy that this newfound bravery lasted another two days.

37.

My bravery had deserted me. It was completely, totally AWOL. I paced the sidewalk outside Sebastian's gorgeous building and read his last message for at least the tenth time.

Sebastian: I'm so sorry. Practice ran long. I'm running about 20 minutes late. I'll be there as soon as I can.

Sebastian: I can call security and have them let you into the building if you'd like.

He'd sent that message over thirty-five minutes ago. I wasn't mad. LA traffic made the very best-intentioned estimates spectacularly wrong. I had driven straight here from work and gotten stuck multiple times myself. But every second that ticked by made me more and more nervous.

I stopped pacing, craning my head up to take in the building. His building had security. Security and a well-manicured lawn with plants and flowers. My building had a door that was supposed to lock but had been broken since approximately the beginning of time. Our landscaping was the occasional dandelion that managed to break through a crack in the cement. A warm breeze ruffled the flowing pink blouse I'd borrowed from Paige, sending one of the thin straps sliding down my shoulder. I slid it back into place, turning to walk to my car. This was a bad idea. I wasn't prepared to be brave on Sebastian's home turf. Splitting frozen dinners with Boomer didn't sound that bad.

Too late. Sebastian was jogging toward me with a duffel

bag slung across one shoulder. I gulped. His sleeveless shirt put his arms on full display, and the muscles of his legs were highlighted with each step. Biceps, and triceps, and deltoids; oh my! Time slowed down and I heard each thump of my heart pounding in my ears. My ovaries promptly told my head to shut the frick up right now and then did a happy dance in celebration. I felt slightly lightheaded by the time he came to a stop in front of me, and I said a silent prayer that I wasn't actually drooling.

He gave me a chagrined smile, leaning forward to place a quick kiss on my cheek. He smelled like dried sweat and fresh sunshine. Fresh sunshine? My brain had clearly shut off.

"I'm so unbelievably sorry."

It took a few seconds for his words to break through the hormone fog that had flooded my brain.

"It's okay," I sighed, my cheek tingling from his lips. "LA traffic is the worst."

He chuckled, sliding his hand down my arm to take my hand. He led me toward his building, sneaking glances at me from the corner of his eye. I didn't call him on it, because I was sneaking too many glances of my own.

"Are you sure you're not mad?" he asked, holding up a toggle to the fancy security box.

The door beeped, followed by a click. He leaned forward and tugged the door open. I kept my eyes on those biceps the whole time. Watching them flex while performing a simple task made that lightheaded feeling return in full force. Even the blast of air conditioning that hit me when I walked in did nothing to cool me down.

"Of course not," I finally answered, not bothering to look at him because I was too busy taking in the gorgeous lobby, complete with an actual security desk. "Things happen."

"You're amazing, do you know that?" he asked, waving to the two men behind the desk and heading to the elevator.

"For not being mad at you over something that's not your fault?" I scrunched up my nose in confusion. I stepped into the elevator and watched as he held his toggle up to an electronic pad above the normal elevator buttons.

He didn't answer my question, just gave me one of those wide smiles that made those crinkles I was so fond of appear. My stomach chose that moment to let out a very loud grumble that seemed to echo in the empty space. I could feel the heat flooding my cheeks, but I just shrugged and forced myself to maintain eye contact. Hunger was a normal part of the human experience, and I couldn't help it that my stomach got a little dramatic about it.

"I feel like such an ass for keeping you waiting."

I didn't hear the words that followed as the elevator doors opened, revealing an absolute dream of an apartment. I supposed the actual term for this space was 'penthouse,' but whatever you called it, it was unreal. Windows made up one entire wall, revealing the lights of LA leading to the hills in the distance. The open-concept space allowed my eyes to roam from the kitchen, equipped with gorgeous stainless-steel appliances, to the living room with its one wall of paving stones surrounding the fireplace. The living room had a huge wrap-around leather couch that faced the windows, and a gigantic flat screen TV mounted over the fireplace. My eyes immediately found the enormous bookcase, which was filled with books and other knick-knacks. It was the only sign that the apartment was actually lived in. I turned to face Sebastian.

"This is really amazing. The view is incredible, and that bookcase is a dream." I set my purse down on a table by the door, where he had set his keys, and made a beeline for the bookcase. My hand trailed over the spines as I read them. "Where did all these come from?"

"I like to read." Sebastian's voice was so close it startled me and I turned around to face him. "I know I should switch to an e-reader, but there's just something about being able to hold a book in your hands. They're one of the only things I brought with me, actually."

I wanted to pinch myself, or him. I couldn't accept that this man was even real.

"Do you ever bend the corner of the page to save your spot? You know, instead of using a bookmark," I asked, one hand gripping the edge of a shelf waiting to hear his answer.

His eyebrows, dipped forming a deep V. "No. I can't say I've ever done that."

I nodded my head, simultaneously trying to keep myself from tackling him. Just when I thought I couldn't possibly be more attracted to this man...

I was in so much trouble. So, so much trouble.

"Are you okay?" He took a step closer, visually inspecting me for signs of distress.

"Yes," I squeaked out. "So fine."

He gave me a questioning look. "Okay, dinner is in the oven already, but the fridge is full of stuff if you want to grab something real quick. I'm going to hop in the shower, so make yourself at home. I'll be right out."

More aggressive head-nodding because I honestly didn't even care about food anymore. That's how far gone I was. I watched as his hands grabbed the hem of his shirt and lifted the edge up slowly, revealing a swath of skin as he took a step back toward the hallway. He stopped, giving me a questioning look, before turning his gaze downward to where both of my hands were tugging the hem of his shirt downward. I swallowed, refusing to loosen my grip.

"Lennon, what are you doing love?" His voice held that mix of slight confusion and more than a little amusement—a tone I was getting more and more familiar with every time we talked.

"Umm, I'm... it's just that... I thought you were going to take off your shirt," I explained, pausing when he still wore the same confused expression. "Right here. Where I could see your chest. Naked."

I wanted to shrivel up into nothingness. I closed my eyes, momentarily horrified by the ridiculous explanation I'd offered. When I opened my eyes, I kept them on the hardwood floor visible in the gap between our feet.

"And that would be bad?" he asked, one hand resting under

my chin, forcing my head up so our eyes met.

I searched his gaze, wishing I could read minds. *Be brave, be brave, be brave* played on repeat in my head. I closed my eyes and took a deep breath, fortifying myself for whatever came next.

"I don't think there would be any going back for me if I saw you without a shirt on, Sebastian. I'm already having such a hard time convincing myself that we're just friends, and that your friendship is enough."

The confession was little more than a whisper. Both his hands covered mine as he gently pried my fingers off his shirt, ignoring the sound of protest I made. In one fluid movement, he pulled his shirt over his head. There was a real possibility that I momentarily lost consciousness. My eyes greedily ate up the expanse of skin now on display, trying to memorize every dip, every crevice. Then, his hands were back on mine, slowly moving them to rest on the bare skin of his chest. His flesh felt like fire under my palms. My gaze traveled up all the intricately inked flesh to meet his eyes, filled with an intensity that made my heart pound impossibly faster.

"What—"

His lips crashed to mine before I could finish my question. Not slow or gentle like the kisses he had pressed to my cheeks and forehead—his mouth moved over mine with a hunger that silenced all the questions in my head. I groaned into his mouth, his tongue sweeping past my open lips. His fingers pressed into my hips so hard that I knew they would leave bruises. I felt my back hit the bookshelf as his lips traveled across my jaw to a spot just below my ear. I leaned my head back, granting him easier access to that previously uncharted territory. He nibbled the spot again, his tongue soothing the slight sting his teeth left behind. A moan escaped from me—or him, it was impossible to tell.

His mouth traveled back the way it came until it found mine again. This time his mouth moved over mine slowly like he was savoring the taste with every pass of his lips. My hands suddenly remembered they existed and traveled up his chest to wind around his neck, the ends of my fingers gently tangling in the soft hair at the nape of his neck. This time I was sure the growl that I felt in my chest, rather than heard, came from him. He gently pressed his mouth to mine once, twice, before he pulled away. I kept my eyes closed for a few heartbeats, trying to calm down. When I opened them, they took in that so-handsome face, which was wearing an expression that was almost more devastating to my heart than his kisses.

He smiled, easing the tension in my chest.

"You've no idea how long I've wanted to do that."

"You did?" I searched his face, trying to judge his sincerity.

He nodded, his hands moving to straighten my glasses before cradling my face between them, his thumb outlining the curve of my jaw.

"Yeah. How could you not know?"

I chewed on my lip, my eyes moving between each of his. "I thought… I don't know what I thought. I'm honestly still trying to wrap my head around the idea that you want to be my friend."

He leaned forward, pressing a kiss to my forehead.

"I still want to be your friend… and so much more."

I nodded my head, because my mind was so busy trying to process this new information that words didn't seem possible. I glanced down and grimaced. All that glorious skin was still on display and my hands were still exploring it as if the secret to world peace were written in Braille on his chest and abdomen—but judging from the bulge in his athletic shorts, he wasn't too upset about my roaming fingers. He turned his head toward the kitchen before stepping back, finally severing the contact. My poor hands stayed in the same position, hoping beyond hope they would be reunited with the wall of muscle they were just getting to know.

"I'm going to go take that shower." His gaze swept over my face. "Are you going to be here when I get back?"

My ovaries screamed, *"Yes! I'll come with you so you don't have to worry and I'll even wash your back! And your front! I will wash all the things!"*

I nodded mechanically, blushing furiously at the directions my thoughts had gone. Sebastian chuckled like he knew exactly what I was blushing about and walked away. I stood very still, listening for the sound of a door closing. When I finally heard the soft click of the door, I let out a gust of air and finally lowered my hands, then proceeded to do a happy dance, bouncing around in a tight circle while squealing softly (I hoped). What in the world, Carmen San Diego? Sebastian kissed me and I kissed him back! Even I had to admit that this was pretty conclusive evidence that he had feelings for me that went beyond friendship, and although my brain was still furiously trying to catch up with my libido, I was pretty sure he had even confessed to as much.

I did one more bouncing circle move before I pulled myself together. With my luck, Sebastian would bust me dancing around his room like I was possessed.

I took in some more of the books lining his shelves, impressed by the variety and more than a little ashamed that I had labeled Sebastian as nothing more than a professional athlete. I found the full collection of *The Watchmen* and smiled. He appeared to be a big fan of biographies, which I hated, but the discovery made me smile instead of panic at finding yet another difference between us.

I moved to look out the huge windows. The sun was setting, casting an orange glow over the city. It looked like the entire city was laid out below me.

"The view is what sold me on this place."

I whipped around, startled by Sebastian's voice. He was standing right behind me in a pair of grey sweatpants and a black V-neck T-shirt that showed a few of the tattoos on his chest. His damp hair had been casually brushed back with his fingers, the path they'd traveled still visible. I turned back to face the window solely out of self-preservation.

"It would be impossible to pass up this view." Then I gave voice to my thought from moments earlier. "It looks like the whole city is laid out below us."

A beep from the kitchen drew our attention away from the view. Well, half of my attention. The other half was appreciating the beauty of a pair of grey sweatpants. Sebastian took my hand and led me into the kitchen. He hit a button to turn off the timer, slipping on a pair of oven mitts. *Sweet Baby Yoda, have mercy on me. I might not survive this dinner.*

He bent slightly at the waist, opening the door to pull one dish after another out of the oven, setting them on the stove as he went.

"I feel like I should confess that I'm not responsible for actually making any of this food. I have a meal service, and I called this one in. I will take full credit for the menu, though. That was all me."

The smell of the food combined with my current view had my mouth watering so much that I had to swallow before I could respond.

"I promise not to hold that against you. Everything smells delicious."

Cue obnoxious noises coming from my abdomen. Sebastian looked over his shoulder and smiled.

"Why don't you go sit at the table? I'll bring everything over."

I shook my head. It felt wrong to sit and wait to be served while Sebastian did all the work, especially since he had rushed home from practice.

"Let me help. You've already gone to enough trouble. I'm feeling a little useless, especially since you wouldn't let me bring anything."

He nodded to the table.

"Go. Sit. I'm wooing you.'

My first reaction was to chuckle, because Sebastian Kincaid had used the word 'woo,' but the meaning of his words set my feet in motion. There was absolutely no way I was going to stand in the way of a good wooing. Also, I was absolutely starving and slightly concerned that arguing would slow down the getting-to-eat part.

I walked to the large dining table, remembering our first meal together when Sebastian had told me he hadn't actually eaten at his table yet. Now it was set with fancy place settings and candles. I ran my fingers over the silverware, amazed at how much thought he'd put into this evening. I took him to a movie marathon and he planned a romantic dinner. Same thing.

I slid into one of the chairs and tried to figure out what to do with my hands. I folded them in front of me, placing them on the table. It looked like I was praying. I slipped my hands onto my lap, tapping my fingers on my thigh.

Sebastian placed a plate in front of me and I actually moaned. Steak in finishing sauce with mashed potatoes and a cheesy pasta that looked like mac and cheese on steroids, and not a vegetable in sight! My stomach did its own happy dance. If it had a vote, Sebastian's woo game was a winner. My eyes darted to his face.

"I feel like I've used this phrase at least a dozen times tonight, but Sebastian this looks amazing. I can't believe you did all of this."

He dropped a kiss on my head and mumbled something, heading back into the kitchen. He reappeared, carrying a bottle of champagne. When he was close enough that I could read the label, I held up my hand to stop him from pouring the liquid gold into my flute.

"That is a very expensive bottle of champagne." My hand moved to grip his forearm. "I don't think you should open it."

Sebastian looked momentarily startled, his face the picture of confusion. "Why not? This is a celebration dinner. Celebrations call for champagne."

I released his forearm to throw my hands up in exasperation, almost whacking him in the process.

"I figured out a problem at work, not won the Nobel Prize!" A very large part of me was screaming at me to shut up and let the man woo me with his delicious food and expensive champagne. "This is too much."

"It's not too much," he said. There was an emotion in his voice that I didn't understand, but it almost sounded like gratitude. He poured me a glass and then filled his own. I stared at the golden liquid, trying to convince myself that the bottle didn't actually cost more than my rent. "Lennon, I can hear you thinking from over here. Talk to me."

The hint of nervousness in his voice was enough to snap me out of it.

"I think you're doing a great job. With the wooing," I clarified. "Everything is perfect. Thank you."

"You're welcome." His smile was as soft as his voice, and I thought that particular combination might be more dangerous than the sleeveless shirt that showcased his biceps. My eyes drifted down and widened when they saw his plate.

"You forgot to put any of the good stuff on there. It's all meat and vegetables." I couldn't keep the frown off my face. "Is that quinoa?"

What kind of person passed up garlic-and-chive mashed potatoes for broccoli and squash? I don't know if I could be in a relationship with that kind of person. They probably stole candy from babies and replaced it with carrot sticks. Wait, were we *in* a relationship? I was so lost in my head that I almost missed his answer.

"I try to cut out carbs and simple sugars during the season. Most of my diet is high protein and vegetables with some healthy grains. Occasionally I indulge with some Chinese takeaway." He winked at me. "But I'm generally pretty strict about it. I'm getting too old to bounce back from a bender."

This poor, poor man. While I couldn't argue with the results of this diet from Hades, I couldn't imagine having a job that required me to cut out every food group that brings people joy.

"Did you know that many evolutionary biologists believe that our ancestors' protein-heavy diet is responsible for our brain growing? Our big brains gave us a huge advantage over predators and the environment, because our temporal cortex was one of the areas that grew, allowing us to gather and interpret more information. So your diet might actually be making you a better player in more ways than one."

"I did not know that. Does that mean you want some of my vegetables?"

"Nope. Nice try, though. I'm very comfortable with my brain size."

We ate, sipping champagne and talking about our days. I was finding Sebastian's schedule kind of fascinating. It was a whole new world that I had so much to learn about and I loved how patient he was answering all my questions.

I heard my phone ding with an incoming text from my bag. I sighed, setting down my fork.

"I'm sorry. I need to check my phone really fast. Paige was going to stop by to feed Boomer. I just want to make sure he hasn't escaped or burned down our building or something."

Sebastian's laughter hit my back as I hurried to grab my phone. It was a message from Paige. I said a silent prayer that everything was fine, and let out the breath I was holding when I saw the picture Paige had sent. It was a selfie of her and Boomer. She was wearing a huge smile, Boomer smashed up against the side of her face looking furious. One arm was sticking straight out at the camera, claws fully unsheathed. Everything about his body announced he was already plotting his revenge.

Paige: Fed your demon cat. Look how much he loves his Auntie Paige!

I laughed, walking back to the table with the phone in my hand. I passed it to Sebastian, sliding back into my chair, and smiled when I heard his chuckle.

"You couldn't have gotten one of those perfectly nice-looking cats on the website?" His smile took the sting out of his words. "He looks like he's one hug away from snapping."

"Don't let his face fool you. He's really a snuggly ball of love wrapped up in a demon. He actually loves hugs."

"If you say so." He didn't sound at all convinced. "But I'm still going to watch my shins around him."

"That's fair." Boomer was still regularly trying to use Sebastian as a human jungle gym. "Destruction is his love language."

I took another sip of the champagne, letting the bubbles play across my tongue. I was never going to be happy with my grocery-store-sale booze again. This man was going to ruin everything for me.

"I wanted to ask you something," Sebastian said, one hand twirling the stem of his champagne flute. "But I don't want you to feel any pressure to say yes."

I leaned back in my chair, patting my stomach contentedly.

"This would be a really great time to ask me for anything. Literally anything. I would give you a kidney right now. Or part of my liver. It'll grow back."

"I'm good on organs." He took a breath, his shoulders unusually tense. "We don't have a game this weekend, so the team is having a picnic. It's at a teammate's house. Nothing fancy. He has a pool, so there'll be swimming and probably a dozen kids hopped up on sugar. There will also be hot dogs."

A wave of emotions threatened to overwhelm me. Shame and guilt that he was clearly so nervous about asking me to go to something so normal. Panic and fear because the idea of meeting all those people at once was my worst nightmare. Happiness and excitement because he had invited me. *Brave, brave, brave.* My big-girl panties were going to be worn out from all this pulling up.

"I would love to go with you. That sounds fun."

Fun like my annual exam or walking on rusty nails. If he heard the tiny quaver in my voice, he didn't call me on it. Instead, he steered the conversation to less anxiety-producing topics.

We made plans for Saturday while we cleaned up from dinner, which consisted of placing everything in the dishwasher, because of course he had a housekeeper. I wanted to stay longer but the yawns kept escaping. By the fourth yawn, Sebastian was leading me down the elevator to my car against weak protests from me. I wanted to stay where there was the possibility of more kisses and maybe the chance to get my hands on those abs again, even if it meant I would probably roll into the office looking like a zombie tomorrow.

"You didn't have to go through all this trouble, but I'm glad you did," I told him, fidgeting with my keys, trying to stall.

"Me too." He took one step closer and then another, never breaking eye contact. "Have I ever told you how hard it was to get you to go out with me?"

I nodded, my heart pounding. The look in his eyes made me take an involuntary step back. My glasses were dangerously close to fogging up. "You've mentioned that before, yes."

"Mmmm, have I?" His hands came up to cup my face. "In that case, have I ever told you how glad I am it worked?"

I shook my head as much as his hands would allow, his heated gaze warming my insides.

"So, so glad." He punctuated each word with a kiss. He leaned back, just an inch. "Goodn—"

I leaned forward, hands fisted in his shirt, and slammed my mouth to his. This new brave attitude was going to be good for something besides giving me an ulcer. It took him a second to respond, but then his lips were moving with mine. I sighed into his mouth as his tongue swept between my lips, meeting mine again and again until I felt weightless. He nibbled on my lower lip and then soothed it with his tongue, causing me to press myself closer. I was relatively confident public indecency was only a minor misdemeanor. This was worth the fine. Sebastian finally broke the kiss on a groan. He opened my door and gently guided me down into the seat.

"Goodnight, Lennon. Text me when you make it home." His voice sounded rough and delicious.

"Goodnight to you too," I finally managed, helping pull my door closed. My shaking hands took a couple of tries to get the key in the ignition. I waved, pulling away. I watched him in the rearview mirror, standing on the sidewalk with his hands in his pockets, until I was too far away to see him clearly.

"Sweet velociraptors on Mars, I kissed Sebastian," I said into the quiet, sounding as astonished as I felt. I still couldn't say that I appreciated the unpredictable nature of human interaction, but at least for tonight, I could say that being surprised wasn't always bad.

38.

Thursday was a blur of meetings that helped distract me from worrying about the cookout. But, by the time I pulled up to the curb outside our building to pick Paige up Friday evening, I was seriously considering telling Sebastian that I had food poisoning and couldn't go to the cookout. Paige hopped into the car, immediately turning to face me with her hand extended.

"Let me see it! I can't believe he broke up with you over the phone."

"It was technically over email." I punched in the passcode and handed her my phone.

Lennon,

I know I shouldn't have waited so long to respond to your message. I honestly just didn't know the right way to do this. I met someone at the bachelor party the weekend after our date. I didn't set out to meet anyone that weekend, obviously. It just happened. I really enjoyed getting to know you, and I think you are an amazing woman. I truly hope you meet someone who deserves you.

Patrick

"What a dick! Well, Patrick, you don't break up with someone over the phone—or email or whatever this was—I can tell you that much. Did you check his social media to see who this new girl is?" Paige asked, glancing up from the screen.

"No." I shrugged. "I was trying to break things off with him. It all worked out for the best."

"I still think he deserves a swift kick to the nu—"

I cut her off mid-threat. "You work one night in a tattoo parlor and you're already threatening violence. Janie would be so proud. Speaking of Janie, we should just pretend like I never heard from him. It's safer for everyone."

Paige nodded in agreement. "She told me that she couldn't fit a body bigger than five-foot-six in her trunk. How does she know that?"

"I have no idea, but I'm very confident that I don't want to find out." I glanced at her. "You seem less nervous than you were last week."

She chewed on her lip thoughtfully for a moment.

"Yeah, I'm really starting to feel like I might be able to make this whole thing work."

"You're totally going to make this work!" I smiled at her. "Harrison even thought you did a good job last week."

That was what my mom called a 'Glinda the Good Witch lie.' It was a variety of lie designed with good intentions to help its recipient.

Paige sat up straighter in her seat.

"He did?"

"Yep, he was definitely impressed with your first night," I lied.

It really was just the teeniest of white lies. I had pointed out what a great job Paige had done the following Sunday, and he just grunted in response. I chose to interpret the grunt as agreement. See? It barely even counted as a lie. I hoped whatever corner of hell I'd just reserved for my eternal resting place had a coffee shop, but it was worth it to watch Paige breeze through the doors of Bad Wolf with the confidence I was used to seeing in her.

Kay's head popped up from behind the counter. She smiled and waved at us, looking relieved.

"Hey ladies! Not that I'm not usually happy to see you anyway, but Lou somehow deleted the appointments for the next month and I have no idea how to fix it. Harrison is about three minutes from murdering someone, and we're back to putting everything on sticky notes."

Her words had me picking up my pace, and I hurried around the corner with Paige following close behind. I sat in the seat and started troubleshooting.

"I installed a back-up for the scheduling software after the last time Lou deleted the schedules," I explained, as I searched for the right link. "It's like the Cloud for this particular software. It automatically saves everything twice a day, so we should be able to restore everything that happened before the last upload. In theory, you shouldn't have lost many appointments."

"Where is everyone else?" Paige asked Kay. The shop was eerily silent except for the music playing overhead and the buzz of a tattoo gun.

"Lou is hiding from Harrison. The last time I saw him, he was locked in the bathroom." She grinned. "Harrison put himself in time out with his sketch pad, and Teddy has a client. Aaron isn't scheduled to be here for another half hour."

"On a scale of firecracker to Chernobyl, how mad is Harrison?" I looked up from the screen just in time to see Kay wince, cutting a quick glance in Paige's direction. Not good.

"Three Mile Island," she responded. "He was not in a great mood even before Lou messed up the software, though, and to be fair to Lou, it's honestly our fault at this point because we keep letting him work the front desk."

"Lennon!" an angry voice called out from behind us.

Paige and I jumped like synchronized swimmers, spinning around to watch Harrison round the desk looking like he was still on the verge of going full nuclear meltdown.

I pasted a big old smile on my face.

"Hi, Harrison. I'm almost done getting the appointments back on the schedule. We'll be back up and running in no time! Hey, I heard that taco truck you like so much is parked a couple blocks away tonight."

He just grunted, crossing his arms without breaking his

glare. If his eyes had lasers, we would all be dead.

"Why haven't you called your cardiologist back?"

Shorts! I had totally forgotten to call my cardiologist to schedule my follow-up appointment after my yearly exam.

I held up my hands. "I just forgot. I was so busy with work and things. It slipped my mind. I'll call first thing Monday. Did they call Mom?"

"After they tried to contact you multiple times." He placed extra emphasis on 'multiple,' just in case I wasn't already feeling bad enough. "Mom panicked and called me right before you got here. You need to call her back."

This didn't feel like the right time to point out that she could have called *me* if she wanted an explanation. I reminded myself that these very annoying people loved me very much and were worried. I was the one who'd had the failing heart, but they were the ones who had to watch me get sicker. I stretched my smile even wider, aware that it probably looked as fake as it felt.

"I'll call her as soon as I get this fixed."

"Now," he barked, then turned his death rays on Paige. Kay and I both tensed, ready to defend her from him if needed. "Paige, come to my office."

He turned, stalking back to his office without even waiting for a response. The Neanderthal just expected to be obeyed. Paige stood, took a deep breath, and then started walking down the hall like she was preparing to face the firing squad. I started thinking of ways to punish Harrison if he said even one small thing to upset Paige—but it hadn't escaped my notice that a new chair had mysteriously appeared behind the front desk. That was the only thing keeping me planted in my chair instead of running down the hall to press my ear against the door.

"Tater tot!" Lou appeared out of nowhere, plopping down in Paige's chair. "Where's your beautiful sidekick?"

"She's in Harrison's office." I couldn't help smiling back at him. He was just so dang hard to be mad at. I suspected that was how he was still breathing.

It was his turn to grimace, but it quickly turned into his signature grin.

"She's too pretty to kill." Kay and I both swatted him. "Ladies, hands off the goods. I know I'm hard to resist, but please try to be a little professional. This is a workplace."

Kay groaned, walking back to her station and leaving me alone with Lou.

"Are you sure you don't want me to show you how to use the scheduling program?" I asked him for the hundredth time. "It wouldn't take long, and you wouldn't have to hide from Harrison in the bathroom anymore."

"Okay, first of all, I was not hiding in the bathroom. Nature calls when nature calls. And I don't *want* to learn how to use the program." He wiggled his eyebrows. "The last time I fucked it up, I didn't have to work the front desk for like a solid two months. Plus, it's hilarious watching Harrison try to keep his shit together."

I gave him a playful punch to the shoulder and my best imitation of a Harrison scowl. "I am going to hold you personally responsible if Harrison upsets Paige."

Lou was saved from further threats by the appearance of two walk-ins. Both he and Kay had free time for an initial meeting, according to the newly resuscitated schedule, so I directed the clients to the artists' books and got Kay from her station. Paige was sitting in her chair by the time I was done, twirling the end of her ponytail and looking thoughtful.

I approached her cautiously, not knowing what to expect. I had never known Harrison to be intentionally cruel or to take his frustrations out on the innocent, but his gruffness could come off the wrong way if you weren't used to him.

"Hey, everything okay?"

"Do I dress weird?" she asked me, looking down at her high-waisted pencil skirt that tied in the front with a bow. Oh my everloving ninja turtles, I was going to murder Harrison.

"What? No, why would you think that?" I responded dutifully, even though I was very confident that I already knew the answer.

She shook her head. "Never mind. Your brother wants to know when I can start officially working."

I expected her to sound more enthusiastic about that news. I should have crashed that meeting. Dang it.

"That's good, right?" I asked, when the expression on her face didn't change. I was going to murder Lou first, for practice, and then I was going to murder Harrison. I could text Janie for backup. Harrison definitely wouldn't fit in her trunk.

She finally turned to look at me, nodding her head firmly.

"Yes, it's good. Great, actually. I told him I would need to put in my notice at the studio and that I'm not sure yet what my class schedule is going to be, but he wants me to come in when I can."

I searched her face. "Are you sure you're okay? Do I need to go yell at Harrison? You know I won't be mad at you if you don't want to work here, right?'

This time when she smiled at me it was genuine. She leaned forward, giving me a quick hug.

"I'm fine. You don't need to yell at Harrison, and I do want to work here. Everyone is really nice, even your brother in his own way. It's hard to explain. I guess... going back to school didn't seem real, you know? It feels real now." She sighed. "Change is part of growth. I'm growing new roots for a new journey."

I really hoped she hadn't mentioned the 'new roots' part to Harrison. He probably needed to learn meditation practices more than any other human on Earth, but he definitely did not respond well to what he called "hipster shit."

"And growing can be fun and exciting," I added. "With amazing abdominal muscles and a chest that belongs on a statue."

She blinked at me, then threw her head back and let loose a laugh that drained the last bit of tension from her shoulders.

"The kiss was that good, huh?"

I couldn't keep the goofy smile off my face. "Yeah, it really, really was. I'm so glad I listened to you and Janie."

"You forgot to mention my amazing matchmaking skills,"

she pointed out, laughing when I rolled my eyes. "Admit it! I'm awesome."

"You're awesome, but I'm still not sold on your matchmaking skills."

"I already admitted that I need to work on the actual setup, but I'd say you and Sebastian are solid proof of my skills. Have you decided what you're going to wear tomorrow?"

I organized the pens on the desk. Nerves were bubbling up from the pit of my stomach just thinking about the cookout.

"I decided on the jean shorts with the flowing cream cami. I liked that option the best. It felt the most comfortable. How serious do you think Sebastian was when he told me to bring a swimsuit? It's probably optional, right?"

"No, I think he meant for you to bring a swimsuit, because it's a cookout with a pool. And he's probably dying to see you in a swimsuit."

I groaned, lowering my head to the desk. I rolled it sideways to look at her. "Do you think he'll believe I have a terrible chlorine allergy?"

She shoved me gently, making my chair roll in the opposite direction of my head. I didn't bother scooting it back.

"Stop being ridiculous. Wear the red suit. You radiated confidence as soon as you put that one on. And confidence is half the battle."

"I keep imagining all these perfect people lounging around the pool looking fabulous. No one has cellulite or thighs that touch. Paige, my thighs have a very close relationship with each other."

She wheeled me closer and dragged me into an upright position.

"Listen, everyone has something about their body they're not crazy about. I can't say that the idea of going to a pool party with WAGs would thrill me either. But you have to remember what's most important here: You're going to get to see all those professional athletes in their swimsuits."

I couldn't resist laughing. She had a point. I did not hate the idea of seeing Sebastian in a swimsuit. Not at all.

"I can't argue with that logic. I'm nervous about meeting all those new people at once. I don't want to embarrass Sebastian. I like who I am, out of a swimsuit, I really do, but I also know that I'm not my best when my anxiety takes over. I just wish there was a way I could prepare for this cookout, but there are too many unknown variables." I straightened my spine. "I'm going to try, though. I trust Sebastian. I trust that he meant what he said the other night. I also need to be more open-minded."

Paige hit me with that blinding smile of hers. "It's like I'm watching my baby bird grow enough confidence to spread her wings and fly from the nest. In a very hot red swimsuit."

The door opened and Aaron walked into the shop, followed by a small group of girls. I watched as Paige chatted with the group, easily getting them all checked in, and then effortlessly switched her attention to Aaron, who was doing his best to charm her. I smiled, thinking that I might not be the only baby bird ready to make the jump.

39.

I stood outside my building hoping from foot to foot, bright yellow tote slung over my shoulder. I was sweating more from fighting the anxiety clawing to get out than from the California sun beating down on me. Sebastian had texted me a few minutes earlier to let me know he was only a few minutes away. His text brought an instant surge of nausea and the need to move, like I could outrun the anxiety. I said goodbye to Boomer and headed down the stairs. I paced, fighting the increasing anxiety by reciting all the reasons I knew there was nothing to be anxious about.

I stopped when I heard the unmistakable sound of the engine I knew belonged to Sebastian's car. Sure enough, I saw a bright flash of red turn the corner and stop in front of where I stood. I opened the door, getting in the cool interior before he even had the chance to get out.

"Hi," I breathed out, the sight of him in sunglasses and another one of those V-neck T-shirts that gave you a peek of the tattoos that crawled across his left shoulder and onto his chest momentarily making me forget my anxiety. Even my nerves appreciated the sight.

He turned in his seat, reaching across the console to gently draw me closer with one of those big hands curled around the back of my head. His lips brushed across mine gently. I felt his smile against my lips. I opened my eyes slowly, wanting to stay in the calm of that kiss for a few seconds more.

"Hi," he said, the low timber of his voice causing me to involuntarily shiver. I would never, ever, ever get tired of listening to the way his accent made every word seem somehow *more*. He pressed one more kiss to my lips, this one a little hungrier. I huffed a small sound of protest when he drew back, eased the car away from the curb, and then reached for my hand.

I focused my attention on the gentle glide of his thumb over my hand.

"How did it go with Paige last night?" Sebastian asked, glancing at me.

"Really good. I showed her how to order supplies and load new pictures on their social media, so there's not a lot left I can show her. She does so well with the customers, too. I hope Harrison appreciates what an amazing sister I am." I scrunched up my nose, remembering how much barking he had done last night. "But I'll settle for him just being nice to Paige."

"I think I need to meet your brother."

I was vigorously shaking my head before he even finished that thought.

"You're not going to meet him for a long, long time. What did you end up doing last night?"

"Grabbed dinner with Tom after practice, then fell asleep on the couch icing my knee like the old man I am. I used to think it was a sin to stay in on a Friday; now I'm falling asleep on the couch watching old football games."

I smiled at him. "You can always borrow Boomer if—"

He cut me off. "Absolutely not. I'm not cuddling with a bloody cat. Especially that cat."

I could feel my anxiety trying to work its way into the conversation, waiting to pounce and drag me under. It was like a physical thing with enough weight to smother me. My heart rate accelerated in the silence that had settled over the car. It felt like my body was starting to crawl with nervous energy, my breath coming in soft pants. I started tapping a rhythm on my leg with my free hand, counting by sixes to focus my mind. I glanced over at him. He looked so relaxed and casual, so confident in his own skin. I sighed.

"I have to tell you something." My gaze drifted to my hand wrapped up in his. "Do you remember how I told you about my heart? About how I couldn't run around with the other kids and was home-schooled?"

He nodded, his face still soft, contradicting the muscle twitching in his jaw. I would wonder about that later.

"I spent a lot of time alone or with my family. I didn't have a ton of friends. Most of my friendships were over the internet. I wanted to go to public school so badly. After my surgery, I enrolled in the same school as Harrison. I was so excited for my first day. I had all these ideas of how it would go—all the friends I would make, having a locker. My first day was so overwhelming. Our school was pretty big so there were a lot of people and I was —well, still am—super shy. Anyway, the cafeteria at lunch was... not fun. I didn't have anyone to sit with and the first table I asked wouldn't let me sit with them." I saw Sebastian flinch out of the corner of my eye, his hands gripping the steering wheel like he was trying to choke the life out of it. I squeezed his hand. "It was a long time ago and I made plenty of friends. I just felt like I needed to explain why I'm the way I am."

"There's nothing wrong with you." Sebastian's voice was hard.

I rushed to reassure him. "You're right. I'm not doing a good job explaining. What I should have said is that I have really bad social anxiety. Sometimes being in large crowds of people gives me a panic attack. I'm feeling really anxious about the cookout, and I'm afraid that I might embarrass you."

He swung his head to look at me. I could almost feel the anger radiating off of him, but even worse was the trace of disappointment I heard in his voice.

"You could never embarrass me. I fucking hate that you think that you could ever do anything to embarrass me."

"Thank you for saying that, but what if I start rambling about supernovas or the size of primates' brains?" I wanted to believe him, I really did, but I had embarrassed myself enough times to know it was possible.

He lifted our joined hands and pressed a kiss to the back of my hand.

"Then people will learn about supernovas and the large brains of primates and be amazed that my girl is so smart." The genuineness behind his words slowed the frantic pace of my heart. "Thank you for telling me. I'm going to need you to let me know when you're feeling anxious and how I can help."

This man. How did I get so lucky? It seemed impossible that we had gone from that night at the club to holding hands in the car with Sebastian offering words of encouragement.

"I will, I promise."

"The first time I played at Old Trafford I puked in the locker room. I was so nervous when I finally made it onto the pitch, I had to do laps just to keep from puking again," he offered.

I proceeded to ask him so many questions about his life in Manchester that I barely noticed we had arrived until Sebastian put the car in park. I looked out the window, taking in the gorgeous two-story house. Balancing out the Richie-Rich vibe of the house was a man chasing two screaming kids around the front yard. It was difficult to tell if it was a game or if he was actually trying to round them up.

"Ready?" Sebastian asked, hand already on the handle.

"Ready," I confirmed with what I hoped was a smile. We both exited the car, and the man chasing the kids gave up and jogged over to us.

"Kincaid, you made it." His gaze shifted to me. "You must be Lennon?"

I nodded, offering a wave and a hello.

"Lennon, this is Roger." Sebastian turned, pointing to the two kids who were now chasing each other. "One of those is his."

Roger laughed, placing his hands on his hips. "The girl-child is ours, unless you want her."

"Roger!" a small brunette called, swinging open the gate to the fence and closing it behind her. A smile swept the frown off her face when she saw us. "Oh my goodness, you must be Lennon! I'm so excited to finally meet you!"

My eyes widened in surprise. I waved while also trying to think of something to say to this person, who knew a lot more about me than I knew about her. Roger saved me.

"This is my wife, Brooke." He wrapped an arm—which rivaled Sebastian's in the muscle category—around her shoulders. "Her genes are responsible for the demon child."

She elbowed him in the ribs, making him wince.

"Hush your mouth. Our baby girl is an angel," she said—just as the girl finally caught the slightly larger boy, throwing him to the ground by the back of his shirt. Sebastian and I both choked down laughter, our eyes meeting briefly. "Let me introduce you to everyone." Brooke lunged forward and wrapped her arm around mine, leading me away from Sebastian.

He tensed, his eyes finding mine. I shrugged with my free shoulder and gave him what I knew was a sad excuse for a smile. I didn't want him to feel like he needed to babysit me after my confession in the car.

"Don't eat her pie," Roger whispered in my ear as I passed. When my eyebrows drew down in obvious confusion, he just mouthed "trust me."

"Roger said you were an aerospace engineer?" Brooke's statement sounded more like a question. My brain was busy working on overdrive. Half of it was processing the knowledge that Sebastian must have been telling his teammates about me, and the other half was trying to understand the dire pie warning. The thought that Sebastian had told people about me sent a warm feeling rushing through me, which helped tamp down the flare of anxiety I felt walking away from my lifeline.

"I am, at Spatium."

"Girl, that's amazing! You are officially the smartest person I know." She looked over her shoulder and shouted, "Roslyn Wells, you get off James right now!"

The slight twang I had noticed earlier became more pronounced when she was yelling. I made a mental note to ask her where she was from. I followed her through the gate and took in all the activity. Men and women were scattered around the well-manicured yard in small groups: Three men stood around a large grill with drinks in their hand, a group of women fussed over a picnic table filled with food, and a few kids splashed in the large pool in the sunny part of the yard. Brooke waved at one group of women and led me further into the yard. She inclined her head toward two women wearing very small leather skirts and midriff shirts that didn't cover as much as my bathing suit.

"Over there you have Julie and Charity. Stay far away from them. Charity has slept with half the single men on this team. The girl gets passed around more than a soccer ball and she's meaner than a snake to boot. She's currently sleeping with Pete Garrison. Just in case you ever need proof that men think with the wrong head." I nodded, trying to keep up. "Julie is just a bitch. There's not really a nicer way to say it. She's dating Sully. He came over from Norway, bless his heart. He doesn't know any better."

I followed her around the yard as she pointed people out to me, introducing me as we went. She seemed to accept me into the fold without question, which did a lot to decrease my anxiety. We made our way over to a group of four women huddled around a stroller.

"And these will be your new best friends." She waved her hand around the small circle of women, all holding glasses of wine except for a tall blonde who was taking large drinks from a beer. "Ladies, this is Lennon!"

All four heads swiveled to look me over at once. Normally, that type of concentrated attention would have made me throw up in my mouth, but all these women wore such openly friendly expressions that it only made my stomach do a tiny trapeze act. The tall blonde was the first one to break the silence and then everyone started speaking at once. Brooke finally held up her hand.

"Y'all are going to scare her off! One at a time."

"Hey, Lennon, we're all just so excited to meet you," said a brunette with intricately braided hair that hung down her back in a thick rope. "Oh, I'm Lindsey Malone. I'm married to Trevor. I'd point him out but I lost track of him about twenty minutes ago." She did not seem at all concerned about that fact.

The tall blonde with the beer introduced herself next. "I'm Gretchen Stewart—why are we doing last names? It feels like I'm in school and now I have to say three fun facts about myself. Anyway, the redhead at the grill is mine. No one will give him the tongs because he'll burn everything, but he's still going to make a play for them every five minutes. I made it into a drinking game."

I laughed. The woman with hair so blonde it was almost white chimed in.

"It's true. It's our favorite team cookout day drinking game. I'm Maggie. Are we doing last names or not? Collins." She shrugged. "It felt weird not to say it. My husband Chris is the other one trying to keep the tongs away from Gretch's husband. I teach third-grade math."

"Are we doing jobs too?" Gretchen asked. "I'm a physical therapist, for the Novas actually. I spend a lot of time with your boyfriend. Holy shit, that sounded terrible! I meant with his knee. Is that worse? It sounded worse, right?"

"Ignore her. She pre-gamed before the cookout," the fourth woman said. "I'm Tony Franklin. And this sweet boy is August. It's his first Novas cookout too."

I looked down at the baby snuggled into the stroller with a blanket and big floppy hat keeping the sun from touching any part of his body. He was so chubby it looked like his cheeks had eaten his eyes.

"He's adorable. How old is he?" I asked, glad to have an easy follow-up question on hand.

"He'll be six months on Tuesday. Longest six months of my life." Everyone chuckled, and she gazed at the sleeping baby affectionately. "But the best six months too."

"So, Lennon," Lindsey said, "tell us everything!"

I hesitated, not sure what she meant by 'everything.'

"I'm an aerospace engineer at Spatium," I repeated, trying to come up with more interesting facts about myself. You never realize how incredibly uninteresting you are until someone asks you to talk about yourself. "I have a cat and a mild addiction to teen romantic comedies on Netflix."

"Same," Brooke said. "Teen romcoms and terrible Hallmark movies are my jam."

"How did you two meet?" Lindsey asked. "We have to get all our information from the husbands and they never ask the right questions."

"Our friend Paige kind of set us up."

"Kind of?" Gretchen asked, one blonde eyebrow quirked up.

"Neither one of us actually knew it was a setup. It didn't go well and Sebastian showed up a couple days later to apologize."

A group of three women exited the house carrying martini glasses. They were all wearing form-fitting sundresses and wedge sandals that showcased their manicured toes. All three women had perfectly styled hair and flawless makeup. They seemed overdressed for a cookout, or at least the cookouts I had attended. Though to be fair, a large portion of those had taken place in the parking lot behind Bad Wolf.

Tony leaned in and said in hushed tones, "We call them the Real Housewives of the Novas. They're all really terrible human beings who spend their time doing Pilates and bathing in the blood of virgins. For reasons none of us understand, they think they're better than the rest of us WAGs."

"Whatever you do, don't look them directly in the eyes or you'll turn to stone," Maggie whispered.

"Well, who do we have here?" The woman who appeared to be the leader of the group stopped in front of us, her gaze sweeping from my Converse-covered feet up to my wind-blown hair. Unlike the five women standing beside me, her gaze was critical and assessing, as if she was sizing me up.

"Kimberly, this is Lennon, Sebastian's girlfriend," Brooke answered, with an edge to her voice.

"Aren't you just the cutest little thing? And such an interesting name." Kimberly's voice was sugary sweet, enough to give you a toothache. I felt all five women move in closer to me. Kimberly made a motion with the hand holding her drink, the sun catching the huge diamond ring on her hand and almost blinding me.

"You're not at all what I would expect for Sebastian, but I love this journey for him," added the tall, willowy woman standing next to Kimberly, her martini glass dangling from fingernails that had been sharpened into points. She could have been Janie's evil twin. "You're totally adorable."

"I love the all-American girl look. Not everyone could pull that off." The third woman's thinly veiled insult had Gretchen inching forward.

"I was just saying the same thing about your extensions, *Beatrice*." She placed extra emphasis on her name.

"I go by Trixie. I think I've mentioned that to you before, and it would be great if you could remember it this time. I'm sure you have baby-brain, so I understand. I can give you the name of our nanny service if you want."

Trixie was thinner than thin, but looked like she was three seconds away from throwing her martini in Gretchen's face. I was basically a spectator at this point, head swiveling back and forth between contenders.

Tony pulled the stroller closer. "The baby is mine, and we're all set for childcare. Thanks, though."

Kimberly gave her a sympathetic look, placing one hand over an unnaturally perky breast. "I just think it is so brave of you to keep working. It must be so hard to find the time to work and be a good mom."

My head pivoted toward Tony. Even I knew those were fighting words. As if the ripples of tension could be felt throughout the backyard, husbands and boyfriends suddenly descended on our group. I felt a hand slide around my waist and I looked up, smiling at Sebastian. The grooves in his forehead relaxed and he returned my smile, tucking me into his side.

"Are you making friends?" he whispered in my ear, making me shiver despite the afternoon heat.

"I think so," I answered honestly.

"Sebastian, we were just getting to know Lennon. We're just so happy you finally brought her around for one of the team events. I was starting to think we were never going to get to meet her." Kimberly batted her lashes at Sebastian using that same voice, oozing with fake sweetness.

I felt Sebastian stiffen. I rubbed small circles on his back, trying to silently communicate to him that her words didn't bother me. Gretchen's husband looked like he was physically restraining her.

"And now you've met her." Sebastian's voice was dripping with disdain. It sort of reminded me of the night we met. I liked it much more when he was using his snob tone for good. He smiled down at me. "Let's get you something to eat and drink, love."

I didn't think it was just my imagination that the last word was said a lot louder than the ones that came before it.

"Sounds good." I smiled wide, knowing my happiness was written all over my face and not caring one bit. I waved at the group and let Sebastian lead me to the grill. The smell of barbecue made my mouth water and temporarily banished thoughts of the blood bath I had almost witnessed.

Sebastian greeted the only man left standing at the grill after the other two had abandoned him, presumably to prevent World War Wives.

"I'm going to grab us plates and drinks. What do you want to drink? It looks like they have a bit of everything."

"I'll have a beer. Something light and not too hoppy, please."

I wasn't a huge beer drinker, but I didn't think wine was going to complement barbecued meat on smashed buns. I watched as Sebastian walked to a table littered with plates and forks, then bent to dig around in a cooler. I angled my head to take in the way his dark blue linen shorts highlighted a very round butt.

"Your hot dogs are almost done."

"My hot dogs?" I blushed, hoping he hadn't noticed me blatantly checking out Sebastian's butt, but also confused as to why I was given the honor of claiming the hot dogs that looked grilled to perfection.

"The ones Sebastian insisted we have for you. He said they were the same brand they sell at the stadium or something. I'm Tyler, by the way." He extended his free hand and I slid my hand forward into his, giving it a firm shake.

"I'm Lennon." He probably already knew my name, but I felt like I should introduce myself anyway. "Everything smells so good."

He smiled at me, turning his attention back to rotating various meats. "That's because we've managed to keep Henry away from the grill."

I stood awkwardly for a second trying to come up with small talk, even though all I wanted to do was find Sebastian and thank him for the hot dogs. Thank him long and hard, with lips and hands. How did I ever think he was self-absorbed?

The man himself appeared with paper plates and two beer bottles in his hand. As soon as he got in range, I wrapped my arms around his middle, squeezing, and stood on my tiptoes to place a kiss on that spot under his jaw that was made for kisses.

"What was that for?" His husky voice and those little crinkles at the corner of his eyes had me leaning in for one more hug.

"Nothing, just felt like it."

He pressed a quick kiss to my head. "Thank you. What do you want to eat?"

I hmmed, pretending to think about it. "The hot dogs look really good."

I could feel his eyes on me as I placed two buns on my plate. I attempted to ignore him as Tyler placed the hot dogs in them.

"Did he tell you about the stadium dogs?" Sebastian finally asked, shooting a look at Tyler, who was suddenly super interested in something happening in the yard.

"What?" I tried to sound confused. "Stadium dogs?"

He sighed, shaking his head. "You're a terrible actress."

"I don't know what you're talking about." I tried and failed to keep the smile off my face. "Do you want some of this pasta salad?"

I dumped a huge spoonful on my plate. It was the good kind, with big chunks of cheese.

"I'll have a bite of yours," he answered, loading his plate with vegetables and fruit salad. I looked down at my plate, filled with chips, pasta salad, and an unidentified substance that might be taco dip. Sometimes the sedentary life really was the good life. I would choose pasta over muscles every time.

I followed Sebastian to two open chairs at a folding table. We ate our meals, chatting with the people at our table—okay, Sebastian chatting with the people at the table. The best part of lunch wasn't the specially requested hot dogs or the delicious pasta salad, but the way Sebastian found an excuse to touch me the entire time, a hand resting on my thigh or sweeping a strand of hair away from my face, and the way he stole small bites off my plate giving me a secret smile each time.

40.

I stood in front of the mirror in the white-tiled bathroom looking myself in the eyes.

"You can do this." I tried to be firm and authoritative like my mom during every pep talk she'd ever given me. "It's just a swimsuit."

My stomach gurgled loudly. I clenched my hands into fists, rolling my eyes at my reflection. I was more nervous about leaving the bathroom in a modest red swimsuit than I had been about defending my senior thesis to a room full of my professors and peers. I turned one way and then the other, looking at my body encased in the red nylon from different angles.

"You're being ridiculous. You look good in this suit. Everything is staying in place; all your wobble is contained. And hey! If you ever stop being ridiculous and leave this bathroom, you will get to see Sebastian in a bathing suit. He might even be one of the Europeans who wears a speedo. But you'll never know unless you leave this room."

Great, I'd resorted to bribing myself. I growled in frustration.

Three hard knocks caused me to jump, accidently knocking the soap off the counter Boomer-style.

"Lennon, are you all right in there?" Sebastian's concerned voice sounded from the other side of the door.

"Yep, just... uh..." My eyes landed on the bottle of sunscreen in my bag. "Looking for my sunscreen!"

I whipped the floral sarong around my waist, haphazardly tying it, and grabbed the bottle of sunscreen. I counted to three and then opened the door, hand clasping the sunscreen held out in front of me.

"Here it is," I laughed woodenly. "I thought I forgot it, and that would have been terrible because this skin burns. Approximately 9,500 people are diagnosed with skin cancer every day, making it the most common form of cancer worldwide, and people with less pigment in their skin can be more susceptible to getting it. And this skin clearly has no pigment." I held out my arms like chicken wings. "I mean, just look at it."

Sebastian's eyes were glazed over and laser-focused on my chest. I glanced down, worried one of my tiny tots had popped out when I opened the door, but both girls were still covered.

"Sebastian?"

He cleared his throat, adjusting his stance so that his hips were pointed away from me.

"Christ... you look... fuck it."

His hands were on my waist shoving me backward. My mouth started to form a question but the words died on my tongue as his mouth descended on mine. This wasn't a kiss—no, he was devouring me. I forgot about the swimsuit and my nerves as his tongue clashed with mine.

I was vaguely aware of the door slamming shut and the cool granite of the counter against the exposed skin of my back. My hands moved up his back and across the muscles of his tense shoulders to tangle in his hair. His hands glided up my rib cage, stroking the underside of my breasts. I was panting as his mouth traced the curve of my jaw to plant open-mouthed kisses on my neck, his light beard scratching the tender skin there and causing my hips to jerk forward, searching for the same friction. He responded with a growl, one hand moving down my body to hook behind my knee. He lifted my leg up, placing it around his hip so I could feel his hardness where I wanted it the most. I could hear incoherent words tumbling out my mouth, trying to urge him on. His hand left my leg to part the gauzy material of my sarong and then travel up my thigh.

"Please. Please. Please," I begged, not knowing what I wanted, just knowing that I needed something.

"Everything okay in there, mate?" The crisp accent on the other side of the door was like a bucket of cold water being poured over me. I whimpered in frustration.

Sebastian cursed under his breath, dropping his forehead to mine. I reached up to adjust my glasses, bringing his face into focus. He was visibly trying to catch his breath, fingers biting into the flesh of my thigh.

"Do you think he'll go away if we ignore him?" I asked hopefully, my leg sliding down his leg, a sure sign of defeat and no orgasms.

He only sighed, lifting his forehead from mine.

"No, he's a persistent little shit."

"He's right, and I've got to piss," Tom Harris added from the other side of the door. This was one immigrant I was suddenly fine with deporting. "Quite badly, actually."

"Sod off!" Sebastian yelled, his voice like gravel.

My hips jerked reflexively in response, connecting with the very large bulge in his swim trunks, causing him to bite back a groan.

"Sorry," I whispered, trying to put some distance between us. I watched as he adjusted himself and turned away from me.

"I'm going to have to piss in one of these plants if you two lovebirds don't open the door soon."

Sebastian took several deep breaths and then opened the door. Tom was leaning against the doorframe, arms crossed, with what Harrison would call a shit-eating grin on his face.

"A little afternoon debauchery in the bathroom, Kincaid? Well done, mate."

My face was the exact same shade as my swimsuit. I kept my eyes locked on Sebastian's back.

"Go to hell, Harris," Sebastian barked. He turned back to take my hand, his grip at odds with the harshness in his tone.

I let him lead me out of the bathroom, avoiding eye contact. I could hear Tom's laugh echoing through the space as we walked away. There was a very real chance that I would never be able to look him in the eye again. I hurried to keep up with Sebastian, suddenly less concerned about appearing in a physically gifted group in my swimsuit than about staying in the same spot with Tom heckling us.

"You don't think he'll tell anyone about that, do you?" I asked, trying to tighten the knot keeping my sarong up with my free hand.

"Not bloody likely. He'll be telling anyone who'll listen."

And he wasn't wrong. Tom was soon regaling people with a much sexier, very imaginative version of interrupting our bathroom make-out session. It wasn't long before everyone at the cookout knew. Sebastian didn't help anything. He basically spent the rest of the cookout fondling me in the pool, and then managed to make toweling me dry one of the most erotic experiences of my life. An R-rated performance that did not belong anywhere near a general audience. I exchanged numbers with Brooke and the "new best friends," my cheeks still tinted red.

Sebastian spent the entire car ride home stroking my leg, venturing above the hem of my shorts and then back down my thigh to rest on my knee. Each pass of his hand sent ripples of awareness through me. I squirmed in my seat so much I was worried the leather of the seats would be worn by the time we reached my building.

"Did you want to come up? To my apartment? Where I live?" The words tumbled out of my mouth in the single boldest moment of my life as soon as Sebastian put the car in park.

Sebastian's 'yes' overlapped with the end of 'live,' and then we were both tumbling out of the car. For the first time in my tenancy, I was glad my apartment building's lock was chronically broken. Sebastian made a beeline for the stairs. I was hot on his trail enjoying what the movement did to his butt in those shorts. Was I a butt girl? I was so focused on his butt that I missed one of the stairs and fell forward, one knee hitting a stair, arm frantically grabbing the rail. But I was up and moving before Sebastian even realized what had happened.

My hands were shaking so much it took me three tries and help from Sebastian to get my door unlocked. It felt like my body was vibrating with more energy than an electron cloud.

"Did you know the Rutherford model of the construction of atoms comes from Manchester?" I said, pushing the door open. "The Bohr model is more accurate since we know stable atoms exist. All atoms would have to collapse under the Rutherford model, but it's still used more widely."

Sebastian shut the door, caging me in with his forearms. "I had no idea."

He was clearly done talking about atom models. His mouth kissed a gentle path down my neck while his hands found the hem of my shirt and lifted it over my head. I felt his eyes sweep over my chest like it was a physical caress, lingering a little on my scar.

"It actually healed really well." My fingers traced the groove. "I know it looks terrible, but being so young meant that my skin was able to heal a lot better than most people who need open-heart surgery."

Sebastian placed his hand over mine, moving it down to my side. His head dipped, placing a line of kisses down the scar. Hot tears filled my eyes. I tried to force my eyes to absorb them. He was just too much, made me feel too much. As if he could sense the shift in my mood, he straightened to place kisses on my closed eyes, thumb swiping at the tears that had escaped.

"Talk to me, Lennon."

I shook my head, like I could shake the unwelcome thoughts from my head.

"I'm sorry," I sniffled. "You're just being so nice about it. I don't hate my scar, I really don't, but not everyone reacts well to it. I know it's objectively ugly."

Sebastian once again reached for my hand, this time leading me to my bedroom. He scooped a sleeping Boomer off the bed and deposited him in the hall, shutting the door against his angry yowls. His attention back on me, Sebastian placed his hands on my shoulders, guiding me down to the bed. I watched, fascinated, as he pulled off his shirt. He turned so his left hip was eye level and pointed to a discolored patch of skin.

"A cleat. Took ten stitches to close it." He rotated his knee toward me next, showing a scar slashed across it. "Meniscus, ACL, scar tissue. Three surgeries later and it still hurts every time I play."

His hand moved to the scar dissecting his left eyebrow. "And this beauty was a tennis racket wielded by an angry sister. It only needed five stitches, but my eyebrow never grew back."

Finally, he stroked down the bump in his nose, moving closer to me with every pass until my hands reached out to rest on his hips. "I don't even know how many times it's been broken at this point. Headers, elbows, too many blows to count."

I shifted to kneel on the bed so I could press a kiss to the scar on his eyebrow and the disjointed bump on his nose.

"All your scars just make you more handsome. I thought that the night you came to Spout." I punctuated my sentence with a soft kiss to his lips.

His hands hooked around my back, unclasping my bra then moving the straps down my arms slowly. I swallowed as the cool air hit the sensitive skin on my exposed breasts. The fingers of his right hand traced the entire length of my scar, now that the path was unobstructed.

"This scar made you the brave, amazing woman you are, and I am so fucking crazy about that woman." The reverence in his voice almost made my tears reappear.

His hands moved to cup my breasts and then he was moving over me, pressing me back on the bed. Despite his words, I couldn't help sending out a silent plea of "please be enough" as he unbuttoned my shorts and ripped them down my legs. He placed a kiss just above my underwear, making my hips rise off the bed. He ignored my silent plea, his lips burning a path up my abdomen before lavishing each breast with attention. He flattened his tongue over my nipple, making me frantic. My fingernails bit into his shoulders, looking for purchase and trying to pull him closer at the same time. I felt his hardness press into me right where I wanted it, and I was done waiting. I pushed him up enough that my hands could reach the button on his pants and then I was shoving them down his legs. He grabbed a condom out of the pocket before helping me remove them the rest of the way.

My eyes immediately darted to the erection straining the material of his boxer briefs, and I silently gave thanks to whatever force had decided that I got to see this man naked. Before I could look my fill, he was moving over me again, one hand stroking up my thigh while the other moved my head to expose my neck for more of those open-mouthed kisses that made me crazy. His fingers reached the spot that ached for him the most, leisurely rubbing me over the damp material. I moved faster, needing more. He nipped at my earlobe and I thought this was how I would die. I would die if he didn't touch me.

"Please, Sebastian, please," I begged, moving my hips faster and reaching for the bulge in his underwear. He moaned, jerking into my hand as I stroked him over the material. Those wonderful fingers gripped my panties and ripped them down my legs so fast that the movement barely even registered. He spread my legs, opening me for him, and then one of those long fingers was filling me.

I arched off the bed, whimpering in relief. I made noises I didn't even know I was capable of making as he pumped his finger into me.

"You're so tight, baby," he growled in my ear, adding a second finger and stretching me. He slowed his pace, then withdrew them completely.

"No, no, no." I grabbed his wrist, trying to pull his hand back to me. He chuckled, tugging off his briefs with his free hand. "Oh. Yes please."

"So polite," he teased, tearing open the condom and rolling it down his length.

His hands were on my thighs, opening them wide enough

for his hips, the tip of his erection rubbing against my opening. He bent down, kissing me, and then thrust forward, filling me completely. We both moaned. He was motionless for a minute, letting me adjust, only the strained muscles of his neck giving away how hard it was for him to hold back. My hands squeezed his butt, trying to urge him on. His hips started moving, setting a slow, steady pace. It was too much and not enough at the same time. Every cell in my body felt like it was on fire.

"So good," he whispered in my ear. I nodded my head, too far gone for words. He brought one of my legs up, draping it over his hip to deepen the angle. The new angle caused each thrust to hit just the right spot.

"Sebastian," I gasped, when his head dipped down to take one of my nipples into his mouth. The light scrape of his teeth pushed me over the edge. "Oh God!"

I squeezed my eyes closed as waves of pleasure moved through me. He slowed down, letting me ride out my orgasm while he whispered rough words of encouragement.

When I had some control over my body again, I opened my eyes and took in the man hovering over me. I rolled my head to the side to take in the veins on his forearm where it rested next to my head. I moved my hips in a gentle circle.

"Lennon." He bit the word out, my name sounding like a curse and a prayer.

I made the same eager little circle and his control snapped. He set a punishing pace this time, each movement pushing me a little farther back on the bed. Sebastian lowered himself until it felt like there was no space between us, his hips pounding into me. My sensitive flesh tightened around him and I heard him grunt, hands tightening in my hair as he came.

I stroked up and down his back while he caught his breath, marveling at the muscles and naming them as I went. He propped himself up on his elbows, taking some of the weight off me, and looked down at me with a soft, satisfied smile. One hand moved to push the hair off my forehead.

"Good?" he asked, and somehow I knew he was asking about

my well-being and not the sex.

"Very," I responded enthusiastically, smiling up at him. My stomach chose this minute to let out a very unsexy rumble. "A little hungry."

He laughed, kissing me long and hard. I sat up when he broke the kiss and watched him hop off the bed, removing the condom and tossing it in the trashcan. So much glorious naked man on display.

"Let's get you fed."

Food truly was my love language—food and that naked backside.

41.

We snuggled on the couch watching Netflix waiting for our food to arrive, me in an oversized shirt and him in his underwear, over strong opposition from me. That man should never wear clothes. His nakedness was a public service to all heterosexual females. Boomer crouched under the coffee table, his tail twitching in irritation, pouting and occasionally taking a swipe at one of our feet. My phone dinged, alerting me that my order from Chang's Kitchen was approaching. Sebastian got up, heading for the bedroom while I darted into the kitchen to stay out of view. I wasn't sure how much of a tip would be required to heal the emotional trauma for Jason if he saw me without pants, but I had to believe it would be a hefty sum. Sebastian reappeared in shorts just as there was a knock at the door.

"I got it," he told me, eyes dropping to my bare legs.

"Hey Len—who are you?" Jason accused, sounding surprised. "Where's Lennon?"

"Who are *you*?" Sebastian fired back, seeming more amused by the scrawny teenager than upset.

"I'm Jason Chang, Mr. Chang's grandson. Where's Lennon?" he demanded.

Sebastian glanced at me, sporting a smirk that screamed trouble. I shot him wide, panicked eyes and shook my head. He turned his attention back to Jason, placing a hand on the door.

"She's just in the bedroom. Do you always ask this many

questions when you're delivering food, mate?"

Jason snorted.

"Yeah, right. I don't know who you are, buddy, but I've been delivering food to Lennon for almost two years and I've never seen a guy before. She's got a cat. Screw it, I'm calling the police."

I raced to the door, lack of pants forgotten, and ducked under Sebastian's arm.

"Jason! I'm fine! This is my friend—"

"Boyfriend," Sebastian interrupted, letting the arm that was still holding the door drop to my shoulders.

I rolled my eyes. "This is my boyfriend, Sebastian."

"No shit? Good for you. I honestly never thought I'd see the day." Jason handed me the bag. "You crazy kids have a good night. Oh, and make good decisions!"

He wiggled his eyebrows dramatically and then sauntered down the hall, apparently mollified now that he was sure I wasn't in the clutches of a serial killer. Sebastian chuckled and closed the door.

"I know I should be offended, but I'm honestly kind of touched," I said, getting two plates down while Sebastian unloaded the contents from the bag. "He was actually going to call the cops on you."

Sebastian just chuckled. "I'm mostly concerned about the amount of takeaway you're eating."

We loaded up our plates with food and returned to the couch. We ate in silence for a while. I watched him over a pile of lo mein, a question I'd been dying to ask him for a while on my mind now that my stomach was full.

"Can I ask you something?"

Sebastian turned to face me, one eyebrow winging up.

"That doesn't sound promising, but all right."

"What happened the night we met at the club?" I glanced down at my plate, dreading his answer but needing to know all the same.

He sighed. "Lennon, I don't know that you want to hear about it after we just had sex for the first time."

That had my eyes lifting back to his. He looked so serious it made my heart ache a little.

"I do want to know. I need to understand. I hate not understanding things and whatever I'm imagining is probably worse than the truth anyway."

"I thought Paige had asked me to the club. As a date."

Or not. That was actually a lot worse than I had been imagining. Sebastian had liked beautiful, bubbly, outgoing Paige. She was my opposite in every way.

"Oh. I understand," I said, trying to play it cool but fully able to hear how dejected I sounded despite my effort.

"No, you don't." Sebastian set his plate down and then took mine out of my hands, setting it next to his and drawing me into his arms. He nestled me into his lap, my head resting on his chest while his fingers ran through my hair.

"I agreed to the trade because I was tired. I'm getting old." He hushed my protest. "I'm getting old in professional athlete terms. I don't know how many years I have left. My knee kills me after every game and practice isn't much better. The reality is that my body doesn't bounce back like it used to."

He was quiet for a moment, working his fingers through a tangle. I stayed silent, content to give him the space he needed.

"When I first started, I lived the hype on and off the field. I'm not proud of a lot of it, if I'm honest. Most of the women I was with were using me for the status or to be able to say they were with a footballer—which was fine, since I was using them too. It got old, though, not knowing when someone was genuinely into you. I was tired of it all. I love the game but everything else was weighing me down. So I took the trade. I needed a change and the space to get sorted." He paused again, shifting me in his arms. "You already know I met Paige during her classes. She didn't know who I was when we met, and she didn't seem to care when I told her. It was so refreshing. I admit that I didn't handle it well when I found out she was just trying to set me up. It felt like another person using me for something. You'll never know how sorry I am for it."

I listened to the steady beating of his heart, drawing comfort from the sound.

"Just one more question, and you don't have to answer it. I know it's not really any of my business. Did you go home with one of the girls from the club that night?"

"No." He answered without hesitation. "I felt like an absolute ass when I saw you leaving. I finished my drink and left alone. I kept seeing your face. I couldn't get you out of my head. There was just something about you."

I smiled, tunneling closer to him. "I'm sorry too. For doubting you."

He placed a kiss on my head. "You have nothing to be sorry for, love."

"I couldn't understand how you could be interested in me. We seemed so different. I don't know if you've noticed, but you're incredibly hot. I still wonder how you could possibly want to be with me sometimes, but I'm in too deep to care anymore."

He laughed. "It isn't exactly rocket science, Lennon. You're so beautiful and you walk around having no idea. You're so smart and kind, and you're always finding new ways to amaze me. You are one of the most genuine people I've ever met and you own me for it. I don't deserve you but I'm still a selfish bastard, after all."

I swallowed, trying to get my emotions under control before I spoke.

"You're like my own personal gamma ray burst." I looked up, seeing the question on his face. I tried to explain. "They're one of my favorite phenomena in space. They're the brightest electromagnetic burst events in the universe—that we know about, anyway. Gamma ray bursts result from the most cataclysmic and spectacular events in the cosmos, like two neutron stars colliding. The event results in high radiation energy being released in a huge burst, which appears as a flash of really beautiful, colorful light."

Sebastian curled one of those long fingers under my chin,

lifting my head enough to kiss me. Later that night, tucked under the covers, Boomer sneaking onto the pillow next to Sebastian, I fought sleep. I wanted to take in this feeling. My last thought as I drifted off to sleep was that my heart felt so full.

42.

It was strange how quickly something that seemed so unbelievable such a short time ago could become such an important, almost necessary, part of your life. Sebastian and I settled into an easy routine. We spent most nights at my apartment, even though it was much more cramped than his penthouse. His belongings were scattered all over the small space. His biographies were mixed with my science fiction books, and I finally broke down and cleared out a drawer for him. Most nights we spent curled up on the couch reading or watching TV. When he was traveling for away games, we made good use of video calls. It was still mind-boggling how things had gone from 'mine' to 'ours'—and how much I loved it.

I had attended most of his home games, sitting in the WAGs box, proudly sporting my Kincaid jersey. Brooke had been right about my new best friends. She, Lindsey, Maggie, Gretchen, and Tony had quickly become my guides to the foreign land of the WAGs—and my friends. I even managed to plan a girls' night that included Janie, Paige, and Kay.

I hadn't been lying when I told Sebastian he had come into my life like a gamma ray burst—but instead of creating a new element, he had created this beautiful life with me that I couldn't have imagined before him.

I turned the key in the lock pushing open the door to my apartment. Sebastian was staying at my place again. I had worked late because I was leaving early in the morning for a two-day conference in Phoenix. I smiled when I saw him asleep on the couch, ice pack on his knee and Boomer passed out cradled in one of his arms. Lucky cat. Boomer cracked open an eye when I set my purse on the floor, leisurely stretching out a leg and letting out a yawn. I made my way to the couch, careful not to step on the open book laying on the floor. I bent down to pick up the book and set it on the coffee table. I took a minute to admire Sebastian while he slept before placing a kiss on his forehead. He opened those not quite green eyes and smiled sleepily at me.

"Hey baby, what time is it?"

"A little after seven," I answered, squeezing into the space between him and the edge of the couch.

He kicked the ice pack to the ground and shifted to accommodate me and Boomer, who was busy stretching out all four of his legs to keep me from being able to lie down. My cat was also more than a little in love with Sebastian. One arm slung over my waist, he dragged me in closer until my body was completely pressed against the length of his, Boomer's tail wrapped around my neck. I pretended like he was affectionately tightening it around my throat in his own version of a hug.

"Are you all ready for tomorrow?" Sebastian asked, his thumb making small, soothing circles on my back.

I sighed. "I'm as ready as I'll ever be to present to a room full of people, but I am excited to show off the modifications we made to the first-stage engine designs."

"Are you sure you don't want me to come with you?"

Sweet baby Yoda, I loved this man. I needed to tell him soon. Clearly, the whole bravery thing was still a work in progress, but it was getting harder and harder to keep my feelings in.

"I'm sure. You can't miss two days of practice just because I'm nervous. You have a game Saturday."

"It's just one game. I'll live if I don't play." He placed gentle kisses along the curve of my neck, lifting Boomer's tail as he went.

"Thank you for offering, but I'll be fine. It's just nerves. I can always call you for a pep talk. Plus, we can't have phone sex if we're both in the same place."

I laughed as he flipped me over without warning, shifting on top of me and sending Boomer flying off the couch.

"You little deviant." His hand slid up my shirt, cupping my breast with a gentle squeeze.

"I thought you were completely knackered," I said in my best British accent—which sounded a lot like the old man in Monty Python.

"I got my second wind when you started talking about phone sex." He rolled his hips to prove his point.

I groaned. "Okay, you talked me into it. Orgasms, then food."

Three orgasms later, my limbs were limp noodles and I didn't care about food for quite possibly the first time in my life.

I shot up when my alarm blared right next to my ear, frantically hitting the snooze button on my phone. I rubbed my eyes, completely disoriented. My body might have been awake but my brain was still struggling to come to terms with it. It felt like I had just fallen asleep. I decided that it had to be the middle of the night and my alarm had just malfunctioned. I lay back down, snuggling up to the warm body occupying the other half of the bed. Sebastian rolled over and groaned.

"Did they have to book a seven thirty flight?" His voice was still rough with sleep.

I just whimpered in response, sitting back up and throwing my legs over the side of the bed. We both moved like zombies, brushing our teeth and pulling on clothes. I'd hated Sebastian for forcing me out of bed and into shower last night, but this morning I silently conceded he was right. He pointed out my mismatched shoes at the door and I dragged myself back to the bedroom to change. Through an unspoken agreement, we moved down the hall toward the elevator, Sebastian dragging my suitcase behind him.

We didn't speak more than three words the entire ride to the airport. Sebastian parked in the drop-off lane outside LAX, expertly navigating through the traffic to find an open spot. He moved around the car, grabbing my suitcase out of the trunk as he went. I stood on the curb, actively reminding myself to continue breathing.

"Do you have your computer?" Sebastian asked, setting my suitcase down.

I nodded, patting my carry-on. "Yep, and the flash drive. I left my will to live in bed though."

He chuckled, pulling me into a hug. We said goodbye to each other all the time. He had away games that meant he sometimes spent half the week away from home. But I found my heart squeezing tight anyway, not wanting to step out of the strong arms banded around me. I rested my head on his chest and closed my eyes, wanting to savor this last minute. I felt him shaking me lightly by the shoulders.

"Lennon, did you just fall asleep?"

"Hmmm? I don't know. Maybe?" I responded sleepily.

He chuckled, giving me a kiss and then physically turning me around to face the door of the airport.

"Text me when you land. Don't forget to eat something before you get on the plane."

"I will. I love you," I tossed over my shoulder, too tired to realize what I had just said. I took a step toward the door but a hand on my arm stopped my slow progress. I turned around to find Sebastian looking at me, the tired expression he'd wore moments earlier long gone.

"I love you too." He closed the remaining inches between us, kissing me again and placing my hand on the handle of the suitcase I had left sitting by him. "And you forgot your suitcase."

I gave him one last smile and headed into the airport with a sudden burst of energy that sustained me until I found coffee. Mornings were wild.

43.

Our presentation went off without a hitch. I felt like the engineering version of a superstar. People were coming up to me to introduce themselves and ask questions. I couldn't even make it through lunch without an interruption. I silently mused that this must be what it was like for Sebastian all the time. The rest of the team looked like they were also enjoying the attention. I had opted for an earlier flight than everyone else, because I had no desire to mingle at the mixer that night. One mixer a week was my max.

I changed out of the suit I had worn for the presentation and slipped into comfortable clothes for the journey home. The concierge called a cab for me and I was back at the airport in under an hour waiting for my flight home. Because I always insisted on being at least two hours early, I had plenty of time to kill. From a semi quiet bar I found near my gate, I called my mom to let her know that the presentation had gone well. Since the cardiologist incident, I had been making more of an effort to call her during the week. It was nothing; I already knew the tests were fine, but I had forgotten to make the appointment to go over my care plan for the next year. I knew I had scared her, though.

I talked to her while I ate dinner and sipped a glass of wine. One glass of wine turned into two as I finished eating while half-listening to the local news. *Entertainment News Tonight* started just as I heard them announce that the boarding process was starting for my flight. I still had time, so I sipped my wine and scrolled through my emails while I waited for the bartender to bring me the check. My eyes shot to the television when I heard Sebastian's name.

"It looks like Sebastian Kincaid is back to his old ways," one of the anchors said. "And ladies on two continents are breathing a sigh of relief."

"That's right, Gwen. He had been rumored to have settled down with an astrophysicist he met through a mutual friend. I mean, can you imagine?"

Both women laughed, making my stomach turn sour. I wasn't even a freaking astrophysicist! I mechanically dug my debit card out of my wallet and handed it to the bartender, not even bothering to look at the check. My eyes were glued to the television.

"But last night, Mr. Kincaid was spotted with a new woman outside Scene Six," Gwen reported with pursed lips.

The screen flashed to a picture of him with his arm wrapped around a tall blond woman. I recognized her by the small tattoo visible on her shoulder—it was the same woman he'd been pictured with in that sleazy tabloid in the grocery store. The next picture was of him helping her into his car. Time slowed. I couldn't stop watching even as I signed the check.

The other anchor chimed in. "The very same woman was spotted outside Kincaid's house this morning, wearing what appears to be the same outfit she left Scene Six in last night."

Sure enough, a slide show of pictures flashed across the screen showing Sebastian in sweatpants and a T-shirt hugging the same woman from the night before. Then he was kissing her cheek and putting her into a cab. It looked like nearly identical to the scene from the pictures in the magazine.

I had told myself so many times that the tabloid pictures didn't matter, because whatever had happened, it was before we were together. And if it niggled at the back of my mind sometimes, I ignored it—I was too happy to care about what had probably been just a made-up story anyway. Hadn't the same magazine claimed to find Elvis' long-lost twin? But, I couldn't ignore it this time.

Oh God. I thought I was going to throw my cheeseburger back up. I couldn't believe what I was seeing. My mind screamed at me to stop watching, to get up and walk away, but my body refused to move.

"Rumor has it this mystery woman is from Kincaid's hometown and has made numerous trips to LA to visit him."

I shoved out of my seat, completely numb, and made my way to the gate to board. I woodenly handed my ticket to the gate agent and walked down the ramp. I was suddenly happy to have the window seat. I shoved my carry-on under the seat in front of me and turned to face out the window. The tears were falling down my cheeks faster than I could wipe them away. I swiped at them furiously.

How did this happen? He told me he loved me yesterday. The tears fell faster when I remembered the sweet text he'd sent me this morning—this morning, when he was with her. Had he sent me that message while he was still in bed with her? My phone vibrated in my hands. I switched it to airplane mode without even bothering to look at the messages. My vision was too blurred by tears to read anyway.

The man who took the aisle seat kept sneaking worried glances at me. I closed my eyes and took a few deep breaths, trying to calm down. The last thing I needed was to be kicked off this flight.

I replayed the pictures from that trashy program over and over again in my mind as we taxied and took off. The pictures were proof—solid evidence that he had been with someone else last night. But somehow it still didn't make sense. Doubt kept warring with the hurt until I wasn't sure what I was feeling.

"Do you want something to drink?" the flight attendant asked, turning my attention away from my thoughts.

"A ginger ale, please." My voice sounded strained and I knew my tear-stained cheeks told a sad, sad story.

She handed me the whole can of ginger ale with a compassionate smile. "Bad day?"

I nodded, a tear escaping out of the corner of my eye.

"The worst," I answered, allowing myself to be a little dramatic. It wasn't every day you found out from national television that your boyfriend might be cheating on you.

It wasn't the worst day of my life. Not by a long shot. My mind understood that I was being dramatic but my heart didn't seem to care. I remembered those days I had lain in the hospital bed that had been brought to the house, scared to close my eyes at night because I was secretly afraid I might not wake up. I knew I'd had worse days, but my heart hurt. It was a physical pain that reminded me of the days right after surgery.

"Hang in there, sweetie." She offered the words of encouragement with a sympathetic smile, then steered the cart down the aisle.

I ran my fingers up and down the scar on my chest, sipping on my ginger ale and trying to keep the tears at bay. No matter how objective I tried to be, I couldn't shake the doubt that kept creeping in. Sebastian had never given me a reason not to trust him. His words and actions had always proven true. I thought back to all our evenings together—even when he was at an away game, he spent most of his evenings on the phone with me. Something wasn't adding up. Until that show, I hadn't once doubted that Sebastian loved me; even long before he'd said the words, I knew it was true.

I loved him—and more importantly right now, I trusted him. I needed to stop reacting and be reasonable. By the time the plane landed, I was firmly convinced that the show hadn't told the whole truth. I needed to hear Sebastian explain what had happened. Somehow, I knew his explanation would make things okay, because in my heart of hearts, I knew him. Maybe it wasn't rational, but it felt right.

I wheeled my suitcase into the hot evening air and scanned the curb lane looking for Sebastian. My heart lurched in my chest when I saw him. He looked terrible, worse than I did. His hair was sticking out in every direction like he had repeatedly pulled at the ends with his fingers, and there were dark circles under his eyes. He looked more unsure than I had ever seen him. I walked toward him and he rushed to me, reaching out to touch me but dropping his hand at the last minute. That broke my heart more than anything else.

"Hi." I threw the word out into the void.

"You saw them." His face was grim. "Lennon, I can explain. I tried to call you but you weren't answering."

"I was on a plane. My phone was on airplane mode. I must have forgotten to take it off when we landed," I explained, trying to sound calm.

"Right, of course." He sounded so deflated that I fought against the urge to comfort him. I wanted to put him out of his misery. I just didn't know how to yet.

"Move it along, folks," a security guard yelled from the street.

Sebastian took my suitcase and walked to the car, tension radiating off his body. I got in and buckled my seat belt. I watched him walk around the car, bracing himself before he opened the door and got in.

He steered the car away from the curb, merging into traffic. His hand was on the wheel, gripping it so hard that his knuckles were white. I couldn't take it anymore. I reached over and took his free hand in mine.

"Just tell me what happened, please?"

He glanced at me briefly, his surprise written clearly on his face.

"Her name is Anna, and I swear to you, Lennon, I have never been with her, even before we were together. She's a friend of my sister Lucy. They went to university together, and Anna's a model or something. She occasionally comes to LA for photoshoots." He glanced at me again, clearly trying to judge the impact of his words. The tightness in my chest had already started to ease. I rubbed my thumb across his knuckles. "Lucy called me last night because she got a phone call from Anna, and she sounded really messed up. Lucy was really worried about her so

I said I would go to the club and check on her. But when I got there Anna was so drunk I couldn't just leave her. I got her out of the club and into my car, but she passed out before I could figure out where she was staying. I didn't want to leave her alone in that shape anyway, so I took her back to my apartment. Nothing happened. She slept it off and I put her in a cab the next morning. I had to do the same fucking thing a month or so ago and the media made a big deal out of it. I should have called or texted you, but it was so late and I didn't want to wake you up. I knew you had to be up early for your presentation. I'm so, so fucking sorry, Lennon. But I swear to God, I would never do that to you. You can call Lucy right now if you want."

I burst into tears, relieved and embarrassed and even a little ashamed. It was like my body couldn't house all of those emotions at once and needed to purge them.

"Fuck."

I heard his rough curse through my sobs. He steered the car off the highway at the first exit we passed and pulled the car into a parking lot. He reached across my lap to unbuckle my seat belt, then pulled me awkwardly onto his lap as much as the tight space would allow. He whispered words of apology and love until I stopped crying.

"I'm so sorry." I let out a watery sigh. "I didn't mean to cry. I don't really even know why I'm crying. I'm sorry."

"What are you sorry for?" he asked, tilting me back so our eyes met.

"Because there was a solid forty-five minutes where I doubted you, and I shouldn't have. It was totally unfair." His eyes widened in disbelief. "I should have waited to hear your explanation first. You've never given me any reason not to trust you."

He was shaking his head, and one hand came up to cup my cheek.

"I love you so much, Lennon. I can't believe you're mine. I am such a lucky bastard."

I gave him a watery smile.

"You really are."

He leaned forward, kissing one corner of my mouth and then the other. He looked at me, eyes so full of love, and kissed me again. I tried to pour all my love into the kiss just in case my words had left any doubt about how I felt. My elbow hit the horn, making us both jump apart guiltily. We looked at each other and laughed, easing the last bits of hurt.

"Let's go home," I said, crawling off his lap. "I want to see our fur baby."

"I stopped by this morning to feed him. He was a little salty about being left alone last night so don't expect a warm welcome." Sebastian started the car and pulled out of the parking lot. My eyes landed on an ice cream shop a few buildings down.

"Hold on. I can wait just a few more minutes." I pointed to the ice cream shop. "I need some ice cream after all those feelings."

He smiled at me. "Anything you want."

He reached for my hand, cradling it in his lap as he drove. My free hand reached for my scar, to trace the same familiar route it had on the plane—only this time with more gratitude than I could have expressed in words. My heart was a pretty tough organ, after all.

EPILOGUE

6 Months Later

"What do you think they're doing in there?" I asked Aunt Jen.

"I don't know but I'm more concerned about what you're doing to those tomatoes right now."

I looked down at the smashed pile of tomatoes I was supposed to be dicing for the taco bar. My mom tsked from my other side, where she was stirring her famous crock pot pulled pork. This wasn't the first time Sebastian had come home with me for Sunday dinner, but it was the first time Grandpa had invited him to the garage. Making matters worse, Harrison had gotten up to follow them and had banished me to the kitchen when I tried to join them.

"I'm sure they're just getting to know each other," Mom said, sneaking a sly glance at Aunt Jen.

"I don't feel good about this at all." I set down the knife and then picked it back up. "I should go check on them."

"No you shouldn't," Aunt Jen said, reaching out to stop me. "Leave them alone."

I sighed. "Fine, but if Sebastian is murdered, it's going to ruin my dinner and I'm not going to be happy about it."

"No one's getting murdered," Paige chimed in, carrying a covered dish with tortilla shells to the table. "Harrison's been doing a lot better with Sebastian lately. I think he almost smiled earlier."

I liked to think of Harrison and Sebastian's relationship as a work in progress. They'd spent the first couple of months glaring at each other and speaking in single-word exchanges. Recently, they had graduated to full sentences. Grandpa wasn't that much better. The first time I'd brought Sebastian to dinner, he was casually sitting in his recliner holding a baseball bat.

"At least let me turn down the music so we can eavesdrop," I said.

I reached for the remote to turn down the music my mom had insisted on playing at a volume that made conversation difficult—and made it impossible to hear what was happening in the garage.

Aunt Jen swatted my hand away, moving the remote out of my reach.

"You don't need to eavesdrop," Mom scolded. "You need to focus on what you're doing before you lose a finger. Stop worrying about them."

The men walked into the kitchen, drying their hands off on a rag. Uncle Frank must have joined them at some point. I quickly scanned them for visible injuries. No one appeared to be bleeding or sporting a black eye, so that was a good sign. The only noticeable injuries were the small scratches on Harrison's arms, which he had arrived with. I had asked him about them earlier, but he had answered with only a grunt and scowl.

They grabbed plates and made themselves tacos. I smiled to see all the food on Sebastian's plate. He was definitely enjoying the off season. They sat down at the table, which had been expanded to include two more seats, and attempted to sneak bites off their plates without my mom noticing.

I followed the women down the line of food, content to savor the moment. I had managed to get two weeks off work, so Sebastian and I would be leaving Saturday to visit his family. I was incredibly nervous to meet them, but looking forward to the trip. I had talked to his parents and sisters a few times on video chats, and they seemed pretty excited to meet me and see Sebastian.

"Everything okay?" I asked Sebastian, taking the seat next to him.

"Fine."

"What happened out there?" I asked, trying to pry more information out of him since he had gone monosyllabic on me all of a sudden.

"We were just talking," he shrugged, all nonchalant as if they all hung out on the regular.

Okay, well I wasn't about to let this weirdo ruin a perfectly good taco night. I looked up to find everyone's attention focused on the two of us. The three women were all wearing matching goofy smiles. Paige even shot me a thumbs-up before Harrison dragged her hands down. I swallowed nervously.

"Lennon." Sebastian's voice had my head slowing turning back in his direction. "I have a question to ask you too."

I nodded my head, heart pounding out of my chest. I watched as Harrison got up and opened the basement door. Boomer shot up the stairs and into the room, making a beeline for the table, something shiny dangling from his collar. The scratches covering Harrison's arms suddenly made much more sense.

"What the cheese whiz are you doing here?" I asked, scooping him up as he darted by my legs. I gasped as my eyes landed on the beautiful ring tied loosely to his collar.

"We've been talking so much about what my future looks like lately." My gaze locked with Sebastian's. He took Boomer out of my arms, his face serious as he turned his attention to the small knot. It came free with a few gentle tugs on the string. I watched as he took the ring in his hand, holding my breath the entire time. For once in his life, Boomer sat quietly, as if even he understood the significance of the moment.

"Football used to be the most important thing in my life, but now when I think about what the future holds, the only thing that matters is that you're there with me. You've taught me so much—about supernovas and gamma ray bursts and about the kind of man I want to be. So, Lennon June Walker, will you spend the rest of your life teaching me things?"

"Yes," I managed through my tears, launching myself on him and smashing Boomer between us. "I love you so much."

I heard the cheers from the people I loved most around us,

but all my focus was on the man whose face I held in my hands and whose hands held my entire patched-up heart.

This surprisingly sweet, fierce man had taught me more than I could ever have imagined that first night at the club. And like the good student I've always been, I loved every minute of learning.

ACKNOWLEDGEMENT

A huge thank you to all of you for reading Lennon and Sebastian's story. Dreaming up their story gave me so much joy, and I hope you felt some of that joy reading it. I never imagined I would be sharing these stories with readers, and I am so thankful for each and every one of you. To all my STEM gals, you freaking rock! I am in awe of you. Seriously. As an astronomy camp dropout, I am amazed by your knowledge. To all my anxious gals, I hope you keep being brave. I know how hard it is, and I'm cheering for you! And to all my fellow, LOTR loving nerds, you keep being awesome!

A special thank you to my wonderful, amazingly patient husband. I could go on and on, but he truly makes this whole thing work. Not only is he a constant source of encouragement, he is also an excellent source of wine and snacks. He basically does everything but write the books, and I know writing would still be just a dream without him.

I feel that it's only right to thank my faithful assistant, Batman Tupac. He's old and grouchy but is always available to discuss the plot when I am thinking things through. He's got some pretty strong opinions when he's not napping. He really is a very good dog.

ABOUT THE AUTHOR

Emily Mayer

Emily Mayer is a part-time lawyer, full time storyteller, and wannabe writer. She lives in Central Ohio with the two loves of her life; her husband and her dog. If she isn't working, you can usually find her somewhere with a book in her hand.

Printed in Great Britain
by Amazon